TRUE GOLD

KATHRYN BARRETT

OMNIFIC PUBLISHING
LOS ANGELES

Omnific Publishing
1901 Avenue of the Stars, 2nd floor
Los Angeles, CA 90067
www.omnificpublishing.com

First Omnific eBook edition, September 2015
First Omnific trade paperback edition, September 2015

The characters and events in this book are fictitious.
Any similarity to real persons, living or dead,
is coincidental and not intended by the author.

Library of Congress Cataloguing-in-Publication Data

Barrett, Kathryn.
    True Gold / Kathryn Barrett – 1st ed.
    ISBN: 978-1-623422-14-1
    1. Romance — Fiction. 2. San Francisco — Fiction.
    3. Grief — Fiction. 4. Twins — Fiction. I. Title

10 9 8 7 6 5 4 3 2 1

Cover Design by Micha Stone and Amy Brokaw
Interior Book Design by Coreen Montagna

Printed in the United States of America

A little madness in the Spring is wholesome
Even for the king.
~Emily Dickinson~

CHAPTER ONE

Connor Forrest wasn't in the habit of picking up girls in the park—not literally, anyway. Of course, had he read his horoscope for the day he would have known the "outdoors offered opportunity for uplifting beginnings," but Connor would no more have read his horoscope than he would traipse through Golden Gate Park barefoot.

In fact, none of his regular reading material—*The Wall Street Journal*, *Barron's*, *Financial Times*—even featured a horoscope section, although some, including Connor, had compared their stock predictions to fortune telling.

Despite the fact he was only one generation removed from the emerald turf of his mother's Ireland, Connor was a man who had forgotten he liked poetry. He was a man who had little time for introspection, a man who denied the existence of fairies, leprechauns, and true love. A piece of perfectly thought out logic, on the other hand, could make him weak in the knees.

So, as the early morning mist spread like a lambswool blanket over Golden Gate Park, Connor had no clue what Fate had in store. His life, including the vision of himself he'd carefully groomed for almost forty years, was about to change.

At this hour, the park was filled with the smells of wet eucalyptus and well-trimmed grass, as well as the more pungent scents of the

San Francisco Bay and the unruly Pacific—a strange convergence of wild and tame, whimsy and convention.

The damp clung to Connor's skin, mingling with the sweat that dripped from his coal black hair, highlighted by a single strand of gray. By the time he finished his run, the sun would have chased away the mist, basting the thousand-acre park in preparation for the hordes of visitors perfect March Sundays always attracted.

His custom-made running shoes pounded the asphalt in precise rhythm to his breathing. As in everything else, Connor Forrest expected perfection from his own body, and usually found it. The seven-point-five-mile run would be accomplished in exactly one hour, and he would be back in his apartment, showered, and dressed in time to meet the Japanese investors he had invited for brunch.

This section of the park was nearly deserted at this time of the morning. It had occurred to him to have a member of security along on his jog, but he hated the presence of even the most unobtrusive personnel. Even more, he hated the thought that he was becoming increasingly paranoid as rumors regarding his wealth increased at a rate rivaling last year's Forrest Funds performance.

The path curved around a knot of eucalyptus trees and entered a clearing. Connor's gaze caught a flash of red ahead. A lone woman occupied the trail, jogging at a relaxed pace. She seemed more intent on examining the surrounding scenery than in getting a good workout. Her ponytail swished as she strained to catch a glimpse of something up ahead—the roof of the Japanese Tea Garden, Connor guessed.

His mind registered the fact that she was an attractive addition to the scenery herself—tanned, blond, great legs, obviously in good shape. He couldn't see her face from this distance, but on closer inspection it would no doubt turn out to be quite ordinary. The odds, he had found, were usually against a total run on beauty.

Either way, it made little difference to him—trawling for women in the park wasn't at all his style. Therefore, the thought that he would inevitably pass her up brought only mild disappointment. Watching her attractive figure had been a pleasant diversion, but one he didn't intend to prolong.

Just then, her ponytail turned in the opposite direction, toward a squirrel scampering up a gnarled oak. As her chin tilted upward to follow its progress, her foot slammed into a patch of water left over from last night's rain. The sudden splash brought her head down in surprise, just as her other foot landed on a smattering of acorns strewn across the path, another remnant from last night's storm. In the next instant, another squirrel risked a mad dash across the path in pursuit of its mate. In a hopeless effort at avoiding the squirrel, the acorns, and the water, she lost her footing. She gave a helpless cry as her ankle twisted; then she crumpled to the ground like an awkward ballerina.

Connor's feet reacted on cue, pushing him forward. The woman, meanwhile, struggled to sit up. With her knees pulled to her chest, she rocked to and fro, her face pleated with pain. He slowed his steps as he neared her.

She peered up at him and attempted a smile. "You can be the first to congratulate me. I just clinched the award for Most Talented Klutz." Her voice held an airy huskiness, an odd mixture of laughter and pain. Moisture threatened to overflow from eyes that should have been blue, with hair that color, but were instead a warm golden shade of brown.

Connor knelt in front of her. "You're certainly still in the running, but I'll reserve judgment until we've determined the extent of the squirrel's involvement. I think you may have been set up."

"Really?" She managed to grin up at him. "I didn't know squirrels were capable of malice of forethought."

"Of course they are. They're just rats with bushy tails, aren't they?"

She appeared to ponder that while he examined the ankle she held suspended above the sidewalk.

"Is this where it hurts?" he asked, gently clasping the cuff of her sport sock.

"Oww!" She sucked in a breath. "Y-Yes, that's it. My ankle. I must have twisted it when I fell."

His hand slipped to the back of her leg, the other still lightly supporting her foot. "Can you bend it?" He glanced again at her face. It was curiously trusting despite the pain he was no doubt inflicting. Up close he could see that, regardless of the odds, it was a very attractive face, though too lacking in age and experience for him to pay more than passing homage.

"Do I have to?" She winced, but obligingly attempted to rotate her foot from side to side. "I can move it. Barely."

"That's a good sign. Let's get this shoe off." He unlaced her running shoe and slowly eased it from her foot, careful not to bend her ankle any more than necessary. Then he gently peeled the sock around her heel and over her toes. With one hand supporting her calf, he explored the lower half of her leg and foot with a firm, yet gentle, touch.

She shivered when his hand slid over her foot. No protruding bones marred her skin, only a thin white line where an ankle bracelet must have prevented a perfect tan. "I don't think anything's broken," he told her. "Can you stand up?"

She gave him a hopeful nod. "I think so." He grasped her outstretched hands and pulled her slowly to her feet. The top of her head barely reached the apex of his breastbone. She looked down. Still clutching his hands, she attempted to put her weight on her injured foot. "Oww!" Feeling her weight give, Connor brought his arms up to support her.

"I don't think this is going to work," he said. "How far do you have to go?"

"I'm staying at the Towers." She nodded in the direction of the hotel nearly a half mile away.

"Good." He reached down and stuffed her discarded sock into her shoe, then handed it to her. "You hold this. I'll hold you."

Before she could muster a protest, he lifted her against his chest.

"You really don't have to—" she began, even as she automatically stretched her arms around his neck.

He raised an eyebrow. "You don't expect me to leave you here, do you?"

"No, but you—this—"

He simply shot her a look of calm authority, one that had settled many a convoluted deal in the past, and she immediately quit protesting and relaxed against him in resignation. "I bet you didn't know you'd be rescuing damsels in distress when you started out this morning, did you?" She peered up at him with gold-washed eyes, at this range startlingly potent.

"No, that definitely wasn't on my agenda today." He glanced down curiously at the appealing bundle in his arms. "But then, most damsels I know have better sense than to be alone in the park at this time of the morning."

"I usually run earlier than this at home—in Chicago," she told him.

"Aren't there rapists and muggers in Chicago?"

She gazed at him skeptically. "Are you trying to tell me there are evil villains running around this beautiful park waiting to snatch up helpless maidens?"

"Of course. In addition to the homicidal rodents."

She laughed. "It really wasn't the squirrel's fault," she admitted. "I was solving equations instead of paying attention."

"Equations?"

She nodded. "In my head. It's a habit. Some people listen to their iPod while they run. I solve for x."

Connor blinked. Another stereotype had just bitten the dust. Dumb blonde jokes would never be the same. She relaxed against him, her head tilted toward the sky. "But I guess I'm lucky Prince Charming came along and plucked me out of danger. By the way, my name is Rebecca Evans." She paused expectantly, but for some reason he hesitated to reciprocate with his own name.

"I'm pleased to make your acquaintance, Ms. Evans. But you're mistaken as to my identity. I'm not Prince Charming." Then in an unaccustomed fit of whimsy, he added, "I'm the Good Samaritan."

Her eyes widened. "You're kidding! I didn't realize you guys worked this park!"

"You really should keep track of things like that," he admonished lightly. "Especially if you're serious about winning the Klutz Award."

She giggled. Then her tawny eyes turned serious. "Thank you for stopping. I might have managed to crawl back to the hotel—" She glanced toward the ground. "But this is much nicer."

Above the damp tank top she wore, he could see the pulse at her throat, still racing from her exertion. She obligingly tightened her arms around his neck to ease the awkwardness of carrying her. He thought he felt her fingers touch the hair at the base of his neck, but it could have been warmth from the sun peeping out from behind the clouds.

Although she didn't weigh that much, the stamina he'd developed on the tennis court came in good stead. Despite the awkward load, he made quick progress to the entrance of the hotel.

A gray-haired doorman, wearing a starched maroon suit with gold epaulets, jerked to attention at their approach. "Can I help you, sir?"

"No, I've got it."

"Is there something I can get for you?" The doorman trailed behind, his expression determinedly eager.

Connor paused, looking down at the girl in his arms. "Which room are you in?"

"Six twenty-three."

He instructed him to send an ice pack up to her room, then continued across the burgundy-carpeted lobby to the gleaming brass elevator doors. A group of hotel guests, dressed for sightseeing, spilled into the lobby, mouths agape at the sight of him clutching a barefoot blonde against his chest, as if she were a bride he'd just nabbed out on the jogging trail. Another maroon-jacketed attendant rushed toward them to hold open the doors.

Inside the elevator, Connor eased her down, retaining his hold until she gained the support of the teak-paneled wall, then punched the button for the sixth floor. Rebecca tilted her head and smiled indulgently toward the closing doors. "They've obviously never seen the Good Samaritan, at least not in person."

"I try to maintain anonymity."

She gave him a conspiratorial look. "Your secret's safe with me."

She was one of those rare individuals who had the ability to laugh in the face of adversity, Connor decided. A sprained ankle seemed a lark in the park to her. Although he knew it must be painful, there wasn't a trace of it on her face.

He had to look twice to be sure there were no dimples denting her cheeks when she smiled. Not that dimples were something he normally looked for in a woman, he reminded himself. She couldn't be more than a year or two out of college. Not his type at all. His taste leaned more toward sophisticated women who knew the score and were willing to play the game on his terms.

And he always played on his terms. In tennis, he was a brutal competitor, quashing opponents without a trace of remorse, and in the boardroom, he was equally determined. Though his reputation wasn't quite as well known in the bedroom, there he was equally driven.

He knew without a doubt that this smiling young woman wasn't a skilled opponent, and she didn't possess the sophistication to compete in his world. That realization caused him an instant's regret before the elevator doors slid open at the sixth floor.

"The room's just down the hall. I think I can hobble that far," she told him. Nevertheless, Connor held her arm and helped her down the hallway.

At the door to her room, she let go of his arm, then reached down into her shirt and dug out a key card. She'd apparently placed it in her bra for safekeeping. It was still warm from its contact with her flesh when she handed it to him with a little embarrassed grin. "I've always wondered why they don't put pockets on jogging shorts."

He slid the key in the card reader. "How long are you planning to be here in San Francisco?"

"That depends on how well my job interview goes tomorrow. Oh no," she groaned, glancing down at her ankle. "Can you imagine what kind of impression I'm going to make when I hobble into that office tomorrow?"

But before he could comment, she looked up again and said with a shrug, "Oh well. At least I'll make an impression. Isn't that what counts? They're sure to remember the Girl Who Limped into the Room!"

"I'm sure you would have made an impression regardless," Connor assured her, helping her inside. "This will only serve to jog their memory."

She grimaced. "That wasn't supposed to be a pun, was it?"

He looked down at the shoe she still held in her hands. "Well, if the shoe fits…"

She laughed in that way people had when confronted with unexpected silliness, and Connor decided he liked the role he'd taken on: knight errant in gym shorts, picking up fallen women and slaying them with corny humor. He hadn't felt this lighthearted since he'd made the *Fortune* list.

Connor left the door ajar. It occurred to him that she was extremely willing to trust a man she had only just met in the park, a man she knew by no other name than "The Good Samaritan." He should probably give her a stern lecture on the dangers of allowing strange men into her hotel room, but for now he was willing to take advantage of that trust long enough to see that her ankle was attended to.

Housekeeping hadn't made it to her room yet, he noticed as he led her to the unmade bed. A single suitcase lay open on the luggage rack, and the business suit hanging in the closet was definitely female. Rebecca Evans appeared to be the sole occupant of the room.

Spying the empty ice bucket on the bureau, he said to Rebecca, who sat at the end of the bed examining her rapidly swelling ankle, "I'll get some ice while we're waiting for the staff to show up with an ice pack." But just then there was a knock on the door. He opened it to find a room service attendant, holding a plastic ice pack and one of the small first aid kits the hotel kept for emergencies.

"Is there anything else you'll need, Mister—"

Connor dismissed him before he could finish. "This will do for now. I'll call down if we require anything more." He went back into the bedroom. Rebecca was perched in the center of the rumpled bed, one hand gingerly poking the flesh of the injured ankle.

She looked up. "I think you were right. It's probably just a sprain. It happened once before, when I was nine. I was practicing tightrope walking on the clothesline." She laughed ruefully. "Needless to say I decided against a career in the circus."

"I'm sure there's an injury attorney somewhere who regrets that," he said, wondering briefly if there was a lawsuit in his future—his attorney had warned him that buying the hotel could expose him to such a risk. But the accident happened on the grounds of the city park, and this young woman didn't seem the litigious type.

He opened the ice pack, then approached the edge of the king-sized bed. He reached behind her, pulled a pillow away from the headboard and propped it under her foot. "Keep your leg elevated above your heart to reduce the swelling." He sat next to her, lowering the ice pack as he spoke. "And keep this—"

"Hey! That's cold!" She leaned forward, pushing his hands away.

Ignoring her protest, he resettled the bag on her swollen ankle. "This is necessary to keep the swelling down, I'm afraid. You'll get used to it."

She removed her hands reluctantly and leaned back on her elbows. "All right, Doc, if you say so."

He glanced up and met her trusting gaze, startled again by the golden caramel shade of her eyes. "I do say so."

Near the foot of the bed, her discarded nightshirt lay crumpled. Amidst the folds, he could just make out Pooh Bear's nose. Hardly the stuff of male fantasies, he reminded himself. Most of the women he dated wore silk to bed, when they wore anything at all.

He was becoming much too aware of the intimacy of the situation, sitting next to her on the unmade bed, both of them clothed in more sweat than fabric. She seemed unaware of any impropriety, however, perched on the pillows with a look that might be called cheerful, flexing her lavender-tipped toes. Perhaps having a strange man in her hotel room didn't faze her any more than it would many women he knew. But then he remembered how she had shivered the first time he touched the smooth skin on her leg, a response not caused by the ice. He suspected Rebecca Evans wasn't used to being touched by men she'd only known a few minutes.

He should have had the concierge send help up to her room immediately. He stood abruptly. "I think a doctor should have a look at this. There's one on call for the hotel." He crossed the room to the telephone on the desk. "It would probably be a good idea to have it X-rayed just in case."

"You mean you're not a doctor? I was convinced this was my lucky day and I'd timed my fall perfectly."

Connor glanced sharply back at her, but the soft smile that lit her eyes held no trace of guile. For an instant, it had occurred to him that her fall could have been a perfectly timed ruse. But there was nothing in that smile to suggest she thought he was anyone other than a considerate jogger who had come to her rescue. "No, I'm not a doctor, but I am employed full time rescuing damsels in distress," he replied. "Next time you're in trouble, just dial one-eight-hundred-DAMSELS."

He phoned the front desk and within minutes had arranged for medical staff to arrive as soon as possible. Then he turned to the woman on the bed.

She was gazing at him inquiringly. "Do you work here? At the hotel?" she asked. "You sound like…like you know how to get results."

Connor hesitated before answering. "Yes. They're sending a nurse up to take a look at you. If necessary, someone will drive you to the hospital for X-rays."

"I don't think that will be—" she began, but he ignored her protest.

"You'll want to stay off your feet as much as possible. If there's anything you need, just call down to the front desk. They can probably manage to find you some crutches or something to help you walk. You'd be surprised how many requests they're equipped to handle." He turned toward the door.

"Thank you for everything you've done, Mister—?"

Connor didn't want to answer the question in her voice. He wasn't prepared to have the look of guileless interest on her lovely face replaced by one of calculating avarice he had seen so often. Perhaps it was conceit on his part, but these days innocence was a rare commodity, and he didn't want to risk destroying the perception that she was as innocent as she appeared.

So, instead he said lightly, "No need for thanks. That's covered in the Good Samaritan Code of Ethics. Section III, 'Reimbursement.'"

She laughed, a throaty sound that almost made him forget he wasn't meant to be seduced. His gaze slid to her ankle. "Keep the ice on that until someone gets here. That should be soon." Then he leveled a warning look in her direction. "And in the future, Miss Evans, don't allow any strange men into your hotel room. You may find they're not all as harmless as I am."

He nodded in curt farewell and left the room, stifling the urge to stay and personally see to her well-being. The staff here would attend to that. Just in case, he intended to call again and instruct the management to make her as comfortable as possible. Mentally he assigned the task to the list of details he constantly juggled.

He ignored the tiny voice in his brain reminding him that Rebecca Evans was not just another detail involved in owning one of the most prestigious hotels in the Bay area. His success, after all, was partly due to the total control he exercised over his emotions. He never allowed sentiment of any kind to hinder his decision making.

This fanciful Sunday interlude he had shared with the guest in room 623 would soon be nothing but a pleasant memory.

After he left, Rebecca stared at the closed door. "Who *was* that man?" she murmured to herself. He had appeared out of nowhere, picked her up, whisked her into the nearest ivory tower, then disappeared without a clue to his identity. Maybe he really was some sort of fairy-tale prince, or at least a knight, misplaced by a millennium or so.

She smiled at the thought. He certainly fit the bill. Tall, dark, and handsome. In good shape, too. She had felt the steel of his muscles contract when he lifted her up. Knights nowadays probably had their own personal trainers to keep them in shape for the daring exploits involved in rescuing the wayward ladies of the keep.

The thought of herself as a helpless babe-in-the-woods caused her to chuckle as she lay back against the walnut-grained headboard. When not laid out on the ground, felled by a sprained ankle, she was as capable as the next person. She'd never been carried in a man's arms before — and he'd carried her across the park to the hotel as if she were nothing more than a bulky laptop. None of the men she knew would have the endurance, much less the nerve to impersonate a mythical humanitarian, in gym shorts no less. He looked more like a cover model for *Men's Fitness* than any Good Samaritan.

Too bad he had left so abruptly. She would have liked to thank him again, even though he seemed to consider it part of his job to come to the aid of injured tourists.

She remembered the quiet authority in his voice, a tiny hint of loneliness in his eyes…or was that just boredom? She unlaced her other shoe, shushing her fanciful imagination. Her sister Kim had always said she should be a romance novelist, rather than the computer programmer she'd turned out to be. But she'd always had better luck with hard drives than with her too-tender heart.

The man was probably someone from hotel management, maybe even someone from the headquarters of the Forrest Group, the new owner of the hotel. Now that she thought about it, he did seem more like a businessman than the doctor she had assumed him to be.

Maybe she would get another chance to thank him, after all. That is, if her interview with FGI tomorrow went as well as she hoped. She groaned. In her current condition, she would in all likelihood come across as a clumsy as well as a ditzy blonde, the very impression she tried so hard to dispel. Dyeing her hair was a possibility, but her personality would be a little harder to subdue. She was by nature gregarious, interested in other people, and often that came across as flighty. It was her luck to be born with brains, but did she have to be cursed with blond hair and a bubbly personality to go with them?

A polite knock interrupted her thoughts. Remembering her rescuer's parting instructions, she asked who was there before she invited the maid to come in.

CHAPTER TWO

By the next morning, Rebecca had almost gotten the hang of the crutches under her arms. With only a little practice, she'd managed to make a somewhat dignified entrance into the elegant headquarters of the Forrest Group, and then ruined the impression when the rubber-tipped end of her crutch jammed in the elevator opening. A business-suited stranger managed to free it, and as she got off on the third floor, she thanked him with a wide smile and a jab in the ankle.

So far, clumsy was ahead of ditzy by one point, she told herself as she headed down the hall in search of the employment office.

Fortunately, the rest of her interview went much more smoothly. After meeting briefly with the director of personnel, Martin Grainger, she was introduced to Bob Steele, who managed the computer network that enabled a corporation this size to function efficiently. Rebecca knew how important his job was, even if others only realized it when the network was down.

The state-of-the-art equipment he showed her was impressive. This was a company that was as dependent on the actual technical innovations they frequently gambled on as it was on the stock prices that rose and fell with each new twist in technology.

It was the computer models developed by the Forrest Group, she'd been told, that had enabled the investment firm to outperform most other mutual fund companies on Wall Street, despite being located on the West Coast.

Though she had spent the last year working as a computer programmer for the Chicago Board of Trade, Rebecca knew she didn't possess the killer instincts necessary for survival in the piranha-infested waters of Wall Street itself. Besides, it was the technical side of the finance industry that fascinated her. Her real love was traipsing through a maze of sophisticated hardware and intricate software. Delving into eloquent programming languages delighted her the way some people were touched by poetry, and harnessing the unimaginable power of the most advanced co-processors gave her a thrill she imagined was equal to sex.

The idea of helping to develop and maintain those financial modeling programs had intrigued her, but as she completed her tour of FGI headquarters, she realized the working environment was proving to be a plus as well. Bob had pointed out the daycare facility on the first floor, which she hoped to one day have a need for; the employee deli, where she had noticed a tempting selection of reasonably priced and healthy meals; and the indoor gym, which contained a top-rated collection of exercise equipment.

She was impressed by the company as well as the facilities. She'd heard nothing but praise; plus, they had recently been named by *Fortune* magazine as one of the Top Ten Employers.

All in all, moving to California held appeal. A good climate, a progressive work environment, and the only killer fish here lived far out in the Pacific Ocean.

Rebecca had all but decided to take the job — if they offered it to her, she cautioned herself now, as she and Bob stood aside in the main hallway while the doors to a nearby conference room opened and a dozen people surged out.

A familiar figure in a charcoal gray suit caught her eye. It was him! Her Good Samaritan, Prince Charming, and Dr. Ross all rolled into one. She'd been right; he *was* an employee with the Forrest Group. Her lips curved into a smug little smile. His game was over now. She would find out his name and thank him properly for his help and intervention, which no doubt had been responsible for the excellent treatment she had received at the hotel yesterday.

As he turned to head down the corridor toward them, she saw he was deep in conversation with the man on his right. When it seemed as if he would pass by without recognizing her, she clutched the rubber grip in her left hand and brought the metal crutch upward in a wide arc, blocking his path.

"Hey! Just the man I wanted to see. I thought I was going to have to track you down."

His head snapped toward her. His gaze briefly lit on her companion, then raked over her, taking in her "dress for success" suit and satisfied smile.

When he spoke, his voice was distantly polite. "Excuse me?"

"You didn't think you were going to get away so easily, did you?"

Instead of the friendly half-smile of recognition she expected, his face froze into a look bordering on disgust. In a flat, world-weary voice, he replied, "Miss Evans, wasn't it? Should I even ask what you're doing here?"

Rebecca gaped at him, wondering if she had misheard. But his ice blue eyes held the same harsh edge as his voice. "I—I'm here about…about—"

Before she could finish, he injected, "Never mind the explanation. I assume you're here looking for more 'help.'"

She blinked. Could this cold figure, looking at her as if she were the carrier of the Black Plague, possibly be the same helpful stranger she had encountered in the park yesterday?

"I—you—it's—I'm here about—about the job," she stammered, glancing helplessly at Bob, but he was staring at his phone in classic avoidance mode. "What other reason could I have for being here?"

"What other reason indeed." His voice was heavy with sarcasm. "Well, I have to hand it to you, Miss Evans, you certainly did find a novel way to make a first impression. No one's ever fallen at my feet before." He glanced down contemptuously at her bandaged ankle.

"Fallen at your feet! What on earth are you talking about, Mister—?" Then her wits belatedly resurfaced. "I told you I was here for a job interview—or maybe that was Dr. Jekyll I was talking to yesterday."

The frown on his face deepened, and when she saw the distrust in his eyes, the eyes that had looked at her with kindness yesterday, she swallowed the last of her graciousness and led with her pride. "And as for asking you for help, I'd sooner take my chances with the piranhas!"

She turned her back on him with the most dignified maneuver she could manage while hobbled by crutches. Bob's face had blanched, but she wasn't sure if his shock was caused by her words or the totally obnoxious behavior of the man formerly known as the Good Samaritan.

Overnight, it seemed, her Prince Charming had turned into the Prince of Darkness. She fervently hoped the man had nothing to do with the hiring and firing around here. In fact, she was beginning to wish he didn't even work for the Forrest Group. She still didn't know his name, and now she didn't care if she ever found out.

"Whoa! You mind telling me what that was about?" Bob said as soon as they were out of earshot.

She glanced at him, humiliation eating a hole in her gut. "I—it's a long story."

"I don't recall ever seeing the boss that upset," he said, a speculative look on his face.

"The boss?" A lump of dread forced its way down her esophagus, toward her stomach.

"That's right. That was Connor Forrest. How'd you piss him off?"

"Connor Forrest? That—that rude, thoroughly obnoxious man was Connor Forrest? *The* Connor Forrest?" Rebecca swallowed. Pissing off the head of the company was undoubtedly a bad career move, but she couldn't figure out what she had done. Not that it mattered anymore whether or not she had made a good first impression, or how good the lasagna was at the in-house deli. There was no way she would work for the Forrest Group, not if they won a thousand awards for "Most Congenial Work Environment." The brains behind the business, the world's "brightest billionaire," had turned out to be a first class bastard.

Bob gave her a look that told her "ditzy" was clearly in the lead now. She was probably the only single woman west of the Mississippi who couldn't recognize Connor Forrest, World's Most Eligible Bachelor, at twenty paces. She'd assumed the Wall Street legend was approximately the age of Warren Buffett, not Mr. Tall, Dark, and Droolworthy.

She gave Bob a tight smile of farewell then hobbled down the hall, silently cursing her gullibility. She should have paid attention to "StarGuide," an astrological forecast she'd heard on the radio before she left Chicago: *A first impression will trip you up.*

"Adrian, have Peggy make arrangements for us to go to Tokyo next week. I think we'll have the assurances they need by then," Connor said to his assistant, who nodded and left the office, taking an iPad full of notes with him.

The Japanese investors Connor had met with yesterday were demanding his people jump through flaming hoops. Today's account meeting had been filled with grumbling complaints from the staff members he'd assigned to hoop jumping. The same employees who once would have walked across live coals to clinch a deal were becoming complacent, especially since their portfolios were booming despite a somewhat bearish market.

It was time to inject new blood into their ranks. That thought brought him back to the subject that hadn't been far from his mind the last hour. Was it possible that Rebecca Evans was really here for a job interview with FGI? That seemed too much of a coincidence. What was the probability of a prospective employee falling and twisting her ankle in the park at the exact moment he came up behind her? People had tried dumber stunts to gain employment with his company. If it *was* a stunt to get his attention, that would certainly explain why she hadn't seemed the least bit nervous about him entering her hotel room. Then he remembered the look of pain on her face as he had touched her ankle.

Who in their right mind would fake an injury like that? She had genuinely been in pain yesterday; he had seen the swollen ankle himself. The fall in the park had to have been an accident. Had she then somehow discovered his true identity and decided to force her way in here to get better acquainted? Her eagerness in the hallway—why else would she have been so glad to see him, if not for some hope of financial gain?

He thumped his pen on the desk in disgust. He was becoming entirely too cynical. First that damned magazine article had thrust him into the limelight, then his photo accompanied the lead story in a supermarket tabloid. He frowned, remembering. If his stock purchases were guided by aliens, why hadn't they told him to cut his losses on TransPort Inc.? Next thing he knew, people would be calling on him to predict the future as well as extend a loan.

After some of the proposals that had recently come his way, a request like that would seem tame.

There was one way to settle the question. Martin Grainger would know if Rebecca Evans had a legitimate excuse for her presence in the building today. The fact that he had seen her with Bob Steele didn't make that possibility likely; Bob wasn't involved with hiring and firing.

He pushed a button on the telephone console. "Peggy, get Martin Grainger on the phone."

Ten minutes later, he hung up the phone, totally uninterested in the London stock closings that flashed across his computer screen. His rash behavior this morning had just cost the company a top draft pick. Rebecca Evans was a top graduate from MIT, with a Masters in Computer Science. She was a computer wiz, had co-authored several papers published in respected academic journals, and came complete with glowing recommendations from her colleagues at MIT as well as her most recent supervisor at the Chicago Board of Trade. She wouldn't have needed a faked injury to get her past the employment office. His meeting her in the park had obviously been a coincidence, until now a lucky one for her.

After Martin had filled Connor in — including the fact that she'd mentioned hoping to find her "tall, dark Good Samaritan" in order to thank him again — he had tactfully expressed doubt as to her "suitability" with the company. With office gossip as efficient as it was, Martin had no doubt heard of their exchange in the hallway. "Besides," he'd told Connor, "I really don't think she was as interested in working here as she first appeared. She *is* from the Midwest. Perhaps she's not eager to transfer to the Bay area."

"Nonsense. Get her on the phone before she checks out of the Towers. Tell her the job is hers. She's obviously qualified, and I don't intend to let a top MIT grad slip through our fingers." With a grimace of self-disgust, he had punched the button ending the call.

He stared distractedly at the symbols scrolling across the screen, realizing that he couldn't leave it up to Martin to convince Rebecca Evans to become part of the Forrest Group. He was the one who had jumped to conclusions and consequently insulted her. He would have to be the one to apologize to her.

Now he knew there was an excellent reason why he never let personal feelings interfere with business. With a few thoughtless words, he had probably just cost his company the savviest computer programmer not already hired by Silicon Valley.

Thirty minutes later, Connor knocked on the door to Rebecca Evans' room. He had already been assured by hotel staff that she was still in residence and wasn't scheduled to leave until later this evening, when they'd booked an airport shuttle for her.

His company had paid for her trip out here, put her up in his hotel, and now was in danger of losing any chance of employing her. Granted, there were other top graduates with her skills and training. No one was irreplaceable, Connor was well aware. But this time, it was his error in judgment that had allowed a potentially top-notch employee to slip away, and he refused to allow his own mistake to cost the company.

More importantly, his conscience bothered him. The look on her face when he had snapped at her had haunted him all afternoon. He didn't go around kicking puppies or knocking down old ladies. Insulting innocent young women wasn't on his list of preferred activities either.

The door opened only halfway, revealing the object of his thoughts. He realized she no longer resembled a kicked puppy. With amber eyes glaring at him in contempt, she looked more like an enraged cat.

"What are you doing here?" Her mouth tightened in distaste as she repeated the words he had spoken earlier.

"May I come in? I'd like to talk to you." He met her glare steadily.

"No, you may not." Her voice was bitter, no trace of the swallowed grins of yesterday. "You're the one who warned me not to go around inviting strange men into my hotel room, remember?"

"I'm aware you found my behavior this morning somewhat odd, Miss Evans, but if you let me in, I can explain."

"No explanation needed, Mr. Forrest." She emphasized his name. "You were rude, obnoxious, arrogant, overbearing—" She seemed to be casting about for more adjectives.

He helped her out. "Peremptory. Boorish. Abrasive. And churlish, I suspect."

Her gaze narrowed. "I don't know what kind of game you're playing, but I'm not interested. Yesterday you were obviously impersonating a nice guy, but today you seem to have developed a split personality." She paused for a breath, then added the coup de grace: "You could probably give Darth Vader a few lessons on Behaving Badly!"

He listened politely to her diatribe, arms folded across his chest. Then he said calmly, "I realize you must no doubt be thinking I'm some kind of sadistic psychopath." Her expression confirmed his words: He knew he was just below a psycho killer on her list of approved visitors. In fact, she would probably welcome Darth with a big bear hug before she let him past her door.

He adjusted his tactics. "My error in judgment was responsible for your embarrassment this morning. I'd like to apologize — and offer an explanation; however, if you'd prefer my head on a platter…"

She appeared to be thinking about it.

"I could check with room service. I'm sure they could fix something up. Perhaps an apple for my mouth instead of the foot that seems to be wedged in there now."

For a split second, the severe stare she had fixed on him wavered. Connor didn't blink.

Her mouth twisted in regret as she conceded. "All right, I suppose you do owe me an explanation." She opened the door wider and stepped back to allow him to enter. "But I'll scream if you turn back into Dr. Jekyll," she warned, closing the door behind him.

"I believe it was Mr. Hyde who tended toward the offensive, but I'm not going to turn into either one, I assure you." As he entered the spacious room, he saw the closed suitcase on the neatly made up bed. She had obviously been preparing to leave.

He paused near the small table beside the window. The employment materials she must have received during her interview were stuffed in the wastebasket. He turned back to face her, noticing again the crutches propped under her arms for support. "How's the ankle?"

She glanced up, suspicion in her eyes. He mentally cursed himself once more for his earlier arrogance and stupidity.

"It's better. Thank you," she told him shortly.

"I'm glad to hear that. I hope the staff here were helpful."

A stray lock of hair fell across her forehead. She tossed her head, and a look of annoyance crossed her features. "Yes, they were very helpful. Now, if you're done with the Mr. Nice Guy routine," she continued, striking what would have been a belligerent pose without the crutches, "would you mind explaining why you were so indescribably rude to me today? And why you neglected to tell me who you were yesterday? You led me to believe you were an employee here. And then you had the nerve to warn me against trusting strange men in hotels." Her eyes flashed with righteous anger. "I felt like an idiot when I realized who you were."

"I'm sorry about that. I realize you were at a disadvantage when we met in the hallway today. I assumed by then you knew who I was. In fact, I thought you were there solely to attempt to contact me."

"The only reason I wanted to see you again was to thank you. The hotel staff took very good care of me."

"I don't expect any more thanks. I only did what anyone would have done under the circumstances," he told her. "And as for today, I was surprised to see you there, and I jumped to a wrong conclusion."

She colored. "I suppose you don't get accosted by a crutch very often."

"No, we try to keep our halls free of stray crutches. Something to do with OSHA regulations." He allowed himself a brief smile, then abandoned the humor, though from the smile that tugged at the corners of her mouth, he gathered it was working surprisingly well. "You didn't mention on Sunday you were in town to interview with the Forrest Group."

"And you didn't mention your name," she reminded him.

"I apologize if I misled you. That wasn't my intention." That was met with a look of disbelief. "I do admit, however, that I deliberately withheld my identity."

She gave him a confused stare. "Is a name that important?" A sad blend of disillusionment and disappointment colored her voice, and he wished again that he could have preserved her first impression of him as a kind stranger out for a jog in the park. Even more, he wished the world were truly the pleasant place she seemed to believe it to be.

It wasn't often he came across someone who truly had no ulterior motive, and he felt an odd need to preserve such an innocent notion.

He couldn't keep the bitter regret out of his voice as he answered her. "To some people, it is." He looked away, out the window with the gorgeous view of the bay bordered by the Presidio. His hands in his trouser pockets clenched convulsively into fists. He didn't want to shatter her illusions, but at the same time, he felt compelled to explain his bizarre behavior.

He looked back at her. "A few weeks ago my name appeared in *Tattletale* magazine's list of top ten most eligible bachelors in the country. Since then, I've been the object of some rather odd proposals from an assortment of women."

Her eyes narrowed in indignation as she realized the implication of his words. "And you thought I was there to—"

"The thought occurred to me that you might possibly have planned your fall yesterday in an effort to make my acquaintance, or to gain your way into our employment office."

"Oh! Of all the ridiculous ideas—"

"Not so ridiculous, I assure you. You'd be surprised what some people are willing to do."

Her cheeks flushed. "Well, not me! I don't care how many millions you have or how wonderful the Forrest Group is, I want nothing to do with you or your company!"

"I realize I made a mistake, and I apologize. I should have known you weren't capable of such—" He stopped. He could see from her skeptical look that his apology wasn't as effective as he'd hoped. He let out a resigned sigh. "In the last two weeks I've had a woman strip in my office, a few others have mailed me their underwear, and now, suddenly, I've got enough kindergarten classmates to populate an entire school district." Weary disillusionment entered his voice as he added, "And I didn't even attend kindergarten."

She stared at him wide-eyed. "They actually mail you their underwear?"

His lips drew together in bitter acknowledgment.

"That's sick." She frowned. "You must be—"

"Cynical. Jaded. Distrustful of everyone I meet these days. There were a few other words you used earlier that fit the bill as well. Arrogant, obnoxious—"

"I won't argue with that," she agreed, a little too quickly, he thought, then she surveyed him in critical assessment. "You know what your problem is, Mr. Forrest?" She didn't wait for his response. "You've spent too much time in your gilded tower surrounded by Wall Street sharks who wouldn't hesitate to trade their own mother if the price were high enough. You've obviously forgotten that decent people still exist."

He couldn't help smiling at her blunt assessment of his associates. "Maybe you're right, although I do like to think that I know a few decent people," he admitted. Then with the instincts of one of the sharks she had just mentioned, he abruptly switched gears. "If you come work for me, you'll meet them."

"Oh, no, there's absolutely no way—"

"Is it the thought of working with all those 'Wall Street sharks' that bothers you, or is it the thought of working for me?"

"I—it's—oh, it's not you," she denied, glancing at him in reassurance.

He found her hesitation to offend him after her earlier tirade unexpectedly touching—and indicative of a forgiving personality he intended to capitalize on.

"Because I can assure you, I don't go around insulting my employees," he continued. "In fact, I'm normally quite civil."

"I—I'm sure you are, but—"

"Why did you interview with my company in the first place? Surely you'd heard good things about us?" Deftly, he steered the focus of the conversation off himself.

"Yes, I heard very impressive things about the Forrest Group—"

"And they're all true," he said with complete confidence. "I'm sure you saw that for yourself today." He paused, letting the thought sink in, then continued, his voice low with sincerity. "Normally, I try very hard not to let personal feelings intrude on work. I would hate to think that my mistake in judgment cost the company a first-rate programmer and you a job you obviously wanted."

He could see the indecision in her eyes before her gaze slid from his. "I believe you're sincerely sorry for what happened, Mr. Forrest. But nevertheless, I feel we got off to a bad start. After what happened today, I'm afraid my working for you might be awkward."

"Because the entire building is speculating about why I jumped down your throat this morning?" he said bluntly. "How about if I issue a memo stating there was a case of mistaken identity and the newest member of our technical staff was in no way to blame for my incredibly rude behavior?"

She gazed at him as if gauging his words. "It was more like 'boorish' behavior, and besides, I think I'd prefer the head on the platter bit myself. It's more dramatic." Her eyes began to glow with the humor he had seen yesterday. Humor in the face of adversity, once again.

"You've got it," he agreed promptly. "My head it is. I'm sure this is the first time since the Middle Ages an employment contract will require spilled blood, but if you insist—"

She held up a hand. "Wait, I haven't agreed to come work for you."

"Did I mention we pay moving expenses?" A slight smile lifted the corners of his lips, but his eyes remained sincere.

"Yes, I know, but—"

"And our health care package is second to none." He glanced down at her bandaged ankle. "I suspect that will come in handy."

Her lips twitched, then she gave him a look of mock severity. "Does anyone ever tell you no?"

"Actually, the last time someone told me no, I initiated a hostile takeover the next day. I now own the company."

He saw her face work through her emotions as she studied him, balanced on her crutches as she balanced his apology and his explanation. Finally, she held up her hands in surrender. "All right, I give up. We can avoid the hostile takeover, as well as the head on the platter. I know you're sorry about the misunderstanding, and that's all that matters."

He let out the breath he'd been holding in anticipation. "And you'll take the job?"

She hesitated only briefly, then offered him a warm smile. "Where do I sign?"

The sight of that smile made Connor forget momentarily why he was here.

He quickly recovered his wits. Business first, he reminded himself. "I'll have Martin send over the contracts. We should be able to wrap this up by this afternoon, in time for you to catch your flight back to Chicago."

CHAPTER THREE

Rebecca opened her desk drawer and found it was stocked with supplies: pencils, dry erase markers, and notepads featuring the FGI logo. She pulled out the employment manual she hadn't yet had time to read. Despite the fact she felt as though she had been plopped down in the middle of a football field, where everyone knew the game plan but her, her first day at FGI was going well.

The climate was relaxed, though she suspected that was unique to the fourth floor technical wing. Although they were all busy with their own projects and deadlines, several members of the staff had welcomed her to the Nerd's Nest, as they referred to their wing. Rebecca didn't have a problem with being called a nerd. She was familiar with the species and considered them loyal, hardworking, and, at heart, an irrepressibly mischievous bunch.

She had brought a few mementos to set on her desk. The Carmen Miranda doll would look right at home above her workstation, and remind her of the importance of irreverence. Whenever she had become frustrated at her previous job, she always used to imagine her boss with bananas on his head.

Somehow, as hard as she tried, she couldn't quite picture Connor Forrest with a bunch of Chiquitas resting on his glossy black hair.

Rebecca had read up on her new boss, the man of many moods.

Connor Forrest was a Wall Street *wunderkind*. Though he based his empire in San Francisco, his name was known throughout the financial world. Starting out as a money manager, investing other people's funds, he had soon amassed a fortune of his own. He bought into well-run companies and bought out completely those that were poorly run, turning them over to his own hand-picked managers. He had a reputation for meticulous research; it was said before he bought a company, he knew the exact square footage of the supply closet.

He purportedly possessed nerves of titanium. When the stock market had crashed a few years ago, he ignored the hand-wringing all about him and promptly snatched up a number of undervalued companies, consequently doubling his net worth a year later.

His personal life was a closely guarded secret. His image rarely appeared in a newspaper; when *Forbes* included him among their 400 richest Americans, they used his Harvard yearbook photo.

And when a supermarket tabloid published his name in a list of most eligible bachelors, the article was accompanied by a set of unflattering quotes: One ex-girlfriend had anonymously claimed he was "cold and distant," then added, "And exactly fifteen minutes after sex, he got up to check the stock prices on the Nikkei."

Rebecca wondered if she had ever been carried in his arms half a mile across a park…

Stop it, she told herself. She had given up romantic notions about the man shortly after realizing who he was—not a Good Samaritan but a ruthless financier who probably ate programmers like her along with his cold cereal.

Sighing, she shut the desk drawer and opened the manual.

Adrian knocked on the door to Connor's office and walked in, his suit rustling with a well-tailored whisper of success.

Connor glanced up. "How's our position on the commodities markets?" he asked.

"I instructed our managers to sell short on the gold futures, as you suggested."

"Good. The market's been tunneling since last month. I don't want to get stuck with gold bullion at bargain-basement prices. I know some might still swear by the gold standard, but with prices like these, I can't see the value. It's a risk better left in the vault, I think."

"If the market turns around, they'll be worth a fortune."

Connor shrugged, his attention on the numbers on his computer screen. "Unfortunately, I can't predict the future. Not even with the help of our excellent market simulation programs."

"But we're not talking soybeans here," Adrian argued. "It's gold. The weather in Arkansas doesn't affect the price."

"Exactly," Connor said, lifting his eyebrows above the computer screen. "Weather is at least somewhat predictable. The vagaries of the gold market, on the other hand, are too volatile right now for our portfolios. If you want to dabble in bullion on your own, go right ahead. But FGI is playing with investors' dollars, not Bitcoins."

If Adrian was disappointed by Connor's refusal to play daredevil, he hid it well. Connor had hired Adrian as his assistant two years ago. He was sharp and ambitious, and, with an MBA from Wharton plus an internship at FGI's biggest competitor, he was well trained in every aspect of the finance industry.

Adrian gave Connor a shrewd look. "Speaking of trading programs, we've got a new hire in Technical. I hear she used to work for CBOT."

"That's right. She wrote programs used to handle their e-trades." Connor returned his gaze to the screen. But for all he was aware, the numbers could be announcing a total collapse of the NYSE. He saw instead an image of Rebecca Evans, answering the door of her hotel room, a look of bewildered mistrust on her too-young face.

Adrian didn't seem to notice his distraction. "Well, if she can program half as good as she looks, I predict we'll have a commodities program worth its weight — in gold." He smiled at his pun, but when Connor didn't respond, Adrian cleared his throat and finished briefing him on the developments overnight at the Board of Trade.

When he was gone, Connor allowed his gaze to slide to the phone on his desk. Several times during the day, his hand had reached for the phone to call her. He was well aware it was Rebecca Evans' first day. Even if he hadn't been, the rumors circulating throughout the halls would have clued him in. He'd overheard Adrian and another analyst earlier discussing the new blonde in Technical. There was already speculation on who would be the first to land a date with her. He sincerely hoped Adrian wasn't in the running. He would hate to have to look at the guy on Monday morning during the weekly progress reports, wondering if he had spent the weekend in Rebecca's bed.

Even more reason to refrain from picking up the phone, Connor told himself. She was an employee, and, as such, out of his reach. He adhered firmly to the policies he had set up for the company, wanting to ensure the place was free of harassment in even the most subtle forms.

Connor couldn't help frowning at the thought of her working for Bob Steele. He had almost fired the guy last year when he got a little too close to a female employee.

Maybe he should issue a memo, reminding employees of the company policy on interoffice dating.

He tore his gaze from the phone, sighing in disgust.

His desk would be the first he would have it delivered to.

The next two weeks raced by at gigahertz speed. Rebecca spent almost every evening reviewing her textbooks as well as company materials. She had been introduced to several of the analysts who depended on the computer models she'd be working on to make their recommendations. They were an impatient bunch, never understanding why the system couldn't simply spit out the information they wanted after performing a mind meld. The success of her job depended as much on understanding what they needed as it did on persuading the computer to respond in the prescribed manner. Fortunately, Rebecca had always found computers easy to understand. They did exactly what she told them to do. It was people who were a little more unpredictable.

She stayed late most evenings, though most of the other occupants of the office left earlier. They arranged their flex time hours for earlier in the day, but Rebecca had a lot to catch up on. Plus, she found her work fascinating.

One evening, she was still at her desk well past seven, staring at the numbers and symbols marching across the monitor in a frantic parade. As she bit into an apple with a satisfying crunch, she wished she could just as easily take out the Apple on her desk. She'd spent three hours searching for an error in the code now displayed on the screen, and she was growing frustrated.

Frustration was nothing new; she considered it a job hazard. But this was her first solo project at FGI. Bob Steele had thrown the problem at her before leaving at his usual time, with a casual "Oh, by the way, if you have time, could you see what the hang-up is in the profit analysis program? We've been getting complaints from upstairs that it's overestimating the EP ratios by ten percent, but only when overseas earnings are involved."

It took an hour just to get the darn thing loaded into her computer. So many security measures were in place to prevent unauthorized personnel from gaining access to privileged information that Rebecca was beginning to feel like a spy herself. Her own security clearance wasn't enough to get her past the barriers, but Bob had provided her with the proper passwords.

She took another bite of the Granny Smith and began to chew slowly, thoughtfully gazing at the screen. If it only messed with overseas earnings ratios, the problem must be a glitch in the currency conversion process built into the program. Was it all overseas firms, or only certain ones? She'd have to check that...

Over the hum of her monitor, she could hear footsteps approaching her cubicle. Without lifting her gaze from the screen, she moved her wastebasket from under her desk and shoved it into the hallway. "It's full today. I finally caught up with Sheldon's junk mail."

A deep voice answered, "Who the hell's Sheldon?"

Startled, she let out a little scream. The man standing next to the partition wasn't the janitor she encountered every evening. Instead Connor Forrest was looking down at her, a bemused expression on his face.

"Oh, you scared me! I was expecting Tony."

"Who?"

"Tony. The janitor. You're not him."

"No, I'm not," he agreed, "although I've been told I was a janitor in another life. Perhaps that's why I have an aversion to clutter."

"Really?" Rebecca examined the man standing just outside her cubicle. In a well-cut suit, silk tie, and crisp white shirt, he didn't look much like the janitor who regularly emptied her trash.

He shook his head. "I didn't believe a word of it, but it would've been bad form to insult my host's mother," he said dryly. "Plus she could have put a curse on me. The Chinese can be so touchy." He glanced at the wastebasket she'd stuck in the hallway. "Now we've cleared that up, who's Sheldon?"

"Glenn Bascomb. The guy who used to have my job."

"Ahh," he said, but a puzzled expression lingered in his blue eyes.

"He looked like Sheldon. On *Big Bang Theory*. At least that's what they told me. I never met him."

"Yes, I remember him. He got married and moved to Salt Lake."

"That's right!" She beamed at him as if he had just got the answer right on a pop quiz.

Connor felt the effect of her smile clear down to his socks. He should be getting used to it; he had seen her around the place a few times during the last couple of weeks. Once he had spied her leaving the gym with Kevin Daniels, a towel hanging around her neck, clad in the same shorts and tank top she had worn in the park. She had greeted him cheerfully, clearly having forgiven his earlier rudeness. The sight of her dressed for a workout shouldn't have fazed him; the company encouraged employees to stay fit, and most of them took advantage of the opportunity to use the gym during work hours. Unfortunately, none of the other employees looked quite as appealing in workout wear as Rebecca. And apparently he wasn't the only one who thought so. Daniels hadn't been able to tear his gaze off her tanned legs — the same legs, Connor remembered, that had felt like warm silk under his fingers.

"Is there something I can help you with?" she prompted.

"Where's Steele?" he asked, glancing around the deserted office.

"He left an hour ago."

"Doesn't he realize EOQs are due tomorrow?"

"EOQs?"

"End of quarter reports."

"I'm sure he does."

She looked ill at ease, and Connor felt a moment's regret for putting her on the spot. And a growing annoyance with Steele.

"Is there something I can do?" she asked.

"What are you doing here so late?"

"Bob asked me to find the glitch in the PA program. It's been acting up."

"Yes, I've heard complaints. But you aren't cleared to have access to that."

"Bob gave me the passwords. If it's a problem —"

"No, it's not a problem. This time. I don't think you're about to run off with corporate secrets. But I'll definitely have a talk with Steele about allowing newly hired programmers access to vital trading information. He should have looked into this himself."

Rebecca began twirling a lock of hair around her index finger, her expression decidedly uncomfortable. "I don't mind checking it out. I once ran across something similar in Chicago. And Bob's wife just got out of the hospital. It's really no problem for me to stay —"

With the feeling she would have gone on making excuses for her boss all evening, Connor interrupted her. "It's late. This can wait until tomorrow. We're using the previous model for a backup anyway." He slid his hands in his pockets, eyeing her levelly. "Get your things together. I'll walk you out."

She glanced regretfully at the screen. With a sigh, she logged off the mainframe and shut down her computer. She picked up the scrap of paper on which she had jotted down the passwords and shredded it into tiny bits. Pausing before dropping it into the wastebasket, she looked up at Connor and whispered, "Should I eat the evidence?"

His mouth quirked slightly as he leaned closer. "Not unless you're starving." His eyes held hers for a split second before he straightened and looked away. A framed photo on the shelf above her desk caught his attention.

He stared at the image of two blond infants, one sporting a silly grin, the other a more woeful expression. Rebecca answered his unasked question. "Those are my babies. Aubrey and Alex."

"Your what?" He let his startled gaze swing around, encountering the affectionate way she looked at the photo. "I didn't realize you had children."

"Oh, they're not really mine, and they're not babies anymore, either. They're four years old. They belong to my sister. Technically, anyway. I was there when they were born. They needed an extra pair of hands. I held one, their father held the other." She smiled fondly at the memory.

"Your sister has twins." He emphasized the word "sister."

She nodded, then laughed. "She conveniently had an extra one so we could share. Unfortunately, she insists on raising them together, so I only get to visit."

"How inconsiderate of her," he said, then led the way through the maze of cubicles toward the exit sign.

On the way down the elevator to the main entrance, Rebecca filled the silence with what in most cases would have been considered appropriate chatter. "Do you have any brothers or sisters?"

"A brother," he answered shortly.

"Older?"

"Younger."

"Does he live here?"

"A couple hours north of here." Connor was surprised to hear himself replying. He never mentioned Rodney to anyone but his closest friends. For so long he had protected him — from the laughing kids on the playground, from the state authorities after their mother had died — and now here he was practically giving Rebecca Evans his coordinates.

"That's nice. You must get to see him a lot."

"I go up there once a month."

"Is he married? Any kids?"

"No." Then, opening the door to the lobby, he asked, "Are you parked in the ramp?"

"No, it was full when I got here this morning. I'm down the street."

He glanced at the sidewalk outside. "It's raining. Did you bring an umbrella?"

She shrugged. "I forgot. But don't worry; I'm waterproof."

"So's my car. I'll give you a lift."

During the short drive to her car, Connor asked politely, "How's the ankle? Giving you any trouble?"

"Oh no, it's good as new. I've still got the crutches, though, in case you ever rescue any more damsels." She grinned at him from across the front seat.

"I'm afraid I've reached my damsel quota for the month," he replied. "I assume you found a place to live?"

She nodded. "An apartment over in Oakland. It's small, but it's got character. There's this really neat Murphy bed—you know, the kind that comes out of the wall? I keep imagining I'm in one of those old Three Stooges movies!"

Connor gripped the gear shift tighter. He refused to picture her in a bed—any bed, especially his.

She apparently noticed the trouble he was having with the Jaguar's gear box. "It must be hard to drive a stick here, isn't it? All these hills."

He nodded, a little embarrassed she'd noticed. "I've had the damn thing two weeks." He gave her a wry glance. "It goes from zero to sixty in less than six seconds, but that seems to require getting it into fourth gear first."

She laughed. "The hardest thing for me is remembering whether to turn the wheels in or out at the curb. Here it is. The red Miata."

Of course she drove a Miata. Sporty, sexy, exuberant, like its owner. Rebecca Evans definitely didn't belong in a sedan.

There was an empty spot behind it, and he managed to pull in without disgracing himself too much. He'd drive up to Ukiah this weekend to visit Rodney and, on the way, put the Jag through the paces until he felt entirely comfortable driving the hill-strewn streets of San Francisco.

He left the engine running, but without the road noise, the interior of the car, warmed by the heater, was suddenly far too intimate for the relationship Connor had planned to establish with his newest employee. He tried to put it back on track.

"I don't like the idea of you working so late anymore. There's no need for you to take up the slack just because you're the newest on board."

"That's okay, I don't mind—"

"I do."

Rebecca was silent. Chastened, Connor thought, and he felt a pang of guilt.

He sighed. "I don't run a slave camp. I expect an honest day's work and a few miracles here and there, but burnt out employees aren't capable of either. That's why we have flex time."

She peered at him in the dark. "And what about you?"

"We're not talking about me."

"What time did you get to work this morning?" she asked, ignoring him.

He drew his lips in an exasperated line. He had been up at four thirty checking the overseas markets and in the office by six. "It doesn't matter."

She continued, glancing at her watch, "Let's see. It's seven thirty, and you were logged on when I arrived at eight…That's almost twelve hours."

"Minus the hour at lunch on the treadmill."

She shook her head. "Working out doesn't count. It's encouraged, according to company policy, remember?"

"I'm taking the weekend off."

"The whole entire weekend?"

"Forty-eight hours—" he glanced at his watch "—starting in exactly thirty-six hours and twenty-four minutes. Is that satisfactory, Miss Evans?"

"Perfectly." She gave him a wide smile. "Then we'll all expect miracles from you Monday morning, Mr. Forrest."

He frowned. "Only the *New York Times*—and a few competitors—call me that. I prefer Connor," he said, stifling the urge to remind her he had another year before he hit forty. He had a feeling it wouldn't matter to her if he were eighty or eighteen. She obviously spoke her mind, regardless of whom she was speaking to.

He had been wrong about her being chastened. Connor was surprised at how refreshing he found that. He hated being an object of awe, but somehow, over the years, his reputation had converted him into a figure that couldn't be argued with.

Except by this charmingly carefree woman, now poised with her hand on the door.

He suddenly didn't want her to get out of his car. But damned if he could think of a good reason for her to stay imprisoned with him, while the rain beat softly on the windshield, trapping them in an intimacy he didn't want…

At least he was ninety-five percent certain he didn't want it.

"Rebecca…" he began, and she waited, an expectant look on her face. "Be careful driving home. The roads are slippery."

She smiled at him—a smile so trusting, he was sure she had no idea of the thoughts that were pounding in his head with the same tempo as the rain.

"You too, Connor," she said, and she slipped out of the car and into the dark.

CHAPTER FOUR

"Hello, Rodney." Connor had found his brother in the back yard of the house where he lived with the Millers, the couple Connor had hired to care for him. He stood by a pear tree, staring intently at an insect crawling along a leaf. He was wearing the same gray cardigan he had worn the last time Connor had visited, and the time before that.

"Hello, Connor," Rodney repeated, not glancing up from his inspection of the insect. "CorTrans is up one point twenty-five. Nextel down two point six. MidTech—"

"Yes, I know. It took a tumble. Three dollars, wasn't it?"

"Two eighty five, Connor. AT&T is up point zero three. Lucent..." He continued reciting the day's stock quotes, with an accuracy that would have astounded anyone in the industry had they overheard. His voice remained a flat monotone, but Connor wasn't expecting animation. Rodney had been diagnosed as autistic when he was five. The most emotion he ever showed was when someone tried to turn off the television during *Jeopardy*.

He could quote every stock price that came across the board and had memorized half the Ukiah phone book, but he had absolutely no idea what any of it stood for. For Rodney, numbers existed for their own sake. They had no connection to human beings, and stock prices had nothing to do with dollars won or lost.

Standing next to him, watching the insect make its way across the leaf, Connor let himself enjoy the slow pace of life in Rodney's world. He rarely pitied his brother. Sometimes he thought it was better that Rodney had no concept of the intricacies of the world that surrounded him, the world that saw him as an oddity. And no memory of the father who had left them the day he found out his second son had a disability.

Beside him, Rodney continued to sing-song Friday's closing quotes. Connor was familiar with the routine. Eventually he interrupted. "So, what's your opinion of TranStar?"

"Down point three eight March sixteen. Up point zero five March seventeen."

Connor let him go on, then inserted another question midstream. Anyone overhearing their conversation might think they were two investors discussing their portfolios. But this lopsided exchange of information was the closest Connor and Rodney ever came to familial companionship.

Finally, his own thoughts far from the stock prices, he interrupted again. "What do you think about Rebecca?"

Rodney paused. "Rebecca. Rebecca Adams. 322-8998. Rebecca Arrowsmith. 325-4658. Rebecca—"

"I'm thinking of asking her out."

"Rebecca of Sunnybrook Farm. Connor's going to ask her out. Rebecca of Sunnybrook—"

Connor smiled. "Yes, you're right. Definitely not the woman for me."

Instead of agreeing, Rodney returned to quoting the NYSE.

Connor decided Rodney was probably much smarter than anyone figured. At least he knew enough to stick to what he knew.

He, on the other hand, famed for his intellect, was having a hard time figuring out exactly what he wanted when it came to Rebecca Evans. He'd never had this problem before. If a woman he found attractive was off limits, he simply made do with another. There were more than enough women eager to spend the evening with him, on his terms. He preferred knowing in advance what a woman wanted from him. If the terms were acceptable—dinner, tickets to the occasional play or art opening, followed by sex if both parties agreed—then he closed the deal.

The arrangements rarely lasted more than six months, but he had heard no complaints. He always made sure a nice gift was delivered the day after breaking off a relationship.

He just wasn't capable of more than that. It wasn't in his physical makeup, he had decided long ago.

Connor had no desire for emotions and the problems they caused. He'd seen first hand how his mother had suffered after his father had left to get a drink one night and never returned. She'd waited, her heart broken, year after year, for the man to show up. He never had, but Maggie had kept a photo of him on her bedside, a pointed reminder that true love was a commodity in short supply. His mother, who had once planned to become a nun, was one of the few people he had known who was selfless enough to love unconditionally.

She'd died of breast cancer five years ago. A home health nurse who had devoted her life to her patients, and to Rodney, as well as the husband she never forgot, Maggie had spent her last day on earth at home with Rodney, reluctant to upset his routine by leaving for the hospital, though her pain was severe.

If love demanded that kind of sacrifice, Connor had decided he wasn't prepared to make it.

If there were times he longed for companionship, he simply filled in the hours with more work or called one of the entries in the database of suitable companions his secretary maintained.

That's exactly what he would do now, he decided, watching as the insect made its way to another leaf. He would have Peggy arrange for tickets to the opera on Saturday. Lauren Rostaman would be an ideal date.

She even looked a little like Rebecca.

Rebecca spent the weekend sightseeing. She watched the seals lazing on the rocks at Fisherman's Wharf, then took a charter boat out into the bay, photographing the lacy underside of the Golden Gate Bridge. She drove down the famed twisty turns of Lombard Street, stopping at the bottom to take more pictures. She would send them to Kim and hope it would help convince her to bring the kids out for a week in the summer.

She missed her niece and nephew more than she'd thought she would. Though Kim and Randy lived out in the Chicago suburbs, almost an hour from her apartment in the city, Rebecca had managed to visit often. An evening babysitting, watching *Frozen* and playing Legos, was her idea of fun.

On Sunday, she made a return visit to Golden Gate Park. She decided it was her favorite place in San Francisco. Strolling along the park's wide walkways, she saw lots of family units. Grandparents, pregnant mothers, fathers with their kids. At twenty-six, her biological clock had barely started ticking, but still...she longed to have her own child.

She really should make an effort to date, she thought as she sat alone in the Japanese tea garden, sipping lotus tea. If she ever wanted to start a family of her own, she'd have to get over her feeling of dissatisfaction when it came to the opposite sex.

She wasn't looking for Mr. Right. She was looking for Mr. Perfect, her sister had told her. Kim had tried to fix her up with Randy's brother. They had had one date, and when he tried to kiss her goodnight, Rebecca had glanced out the window and reminded him he was double parked. He had seemed annoyed, but not too annoyed to call her the next week and ask if she wanted to buy a whole life policy.

Rebecca sighed. Most of the guys she worked with were too shy to ask her out, and they became friends instead. The guys who did ask her out were more interested in getting her into bed than in carrying on a conversation — unless it was about themselves.

Of course, she could always work up her nerve and call up the guy of her dreams herself. Women had come a long way, baby — if only men had done the same, she thought, frowning.

Kim was definitely right. Her standards were just too high.

The problem was, the only man who intrigued her was her employer, and he was entirely wrong for her. He was too stuffy. Too rich.

Too tall.

Gazing down into the pond, she sipped her tea and wondered what he was doing on his vacation. Probably holed up with a good book on economic trends. Or maybe he was spending his weekend with a woman. She remembered the parade of names linked with his: models, socialites, even a princess from a small European country.

There hadn't been a single computer programmer on the list.

She sighed, put her teacup and cookies on the tray, and resolved to put Connor Forrest from her mind.

Later, in the de Young Museum of Art, located on the grounds of the park, she was reminded of him again. While viewing the Central American collection, she noticed a few objects donated by the Forrest Foundation. The man was obviously a supporter of the arts, as well as several charities, she had read in one of the articles.

The more money he gave away, the more he made, the article had said, somewhat facetiously.

For a guy who had everything and then some, he didn't seem too happy. She pondered this as she examined the Tibetan figurines. He had a lonely look about him, a man trapped by his own wealth. She remembered what he had said about women throwing themselves at him.

The Buddhists believed that material wealth made it harder to find happiness. If this was true, poor Connor must be miserable.

Rebecca didn't stop to think how ridiculous the idea of feeling pity for a billionaire was. Instead, in her book, the thought required action.

She puzzled over the problem as she left the museum. She'd make it her business to brighten his day, she decided, to bring a bit of happiness into his life. A cheery note, a book…a plate of home baked cookies…

Her sister had sent her a recipe for whole-wheat carob chip cookies that sounded scrumptious. Guaranteed to bring a smile to even the most curmudgeonly face. She'd make a double batch, bring some in to the other guys in the office. Their diets needed some fine tuning, she had noticed. Most of them thought a healthy meal choice was extra lettuce on a Big Mac.

When a niggling little thought told her she was substituting her co-workers for the family she missed, she ignored it.

What were co-workers for, after all, if not to eat your extra cookies?

On Monday, Connor was surprised when a plate of home baked cookies was delivered to his desk, along with a note that read "Hope you enjoyed your vacation!"

No signature, just a smiley face that reminded him an awful lot of a certain computer programmer.

He wondered if this was some new form of flirting he was unaware of. Come hither looks replaced by chocolate chips?

He bit into one. It tasted healthy. And much too rich for his blood. He could almost imagine Rebecca Evans, owner of a red Miata and a pert ponytail, standing in his state-of-the-art kitchen, with a Winnie the Pooh nightshirt and legs that belonged in an art museum.

Wanting something he wasn't prepared to offer.

Suddenly the cookie tasted like sawdust on his tongue.

He instructed his secretary to write Rebecca a polite thank you note and take the plate of cookies to the child care center on the first floor, along with a gallon of milk. When she returned, he would remind her to put in that call to Lauren Rostaman.

Lauren had probably never baked a cookie in her life and wouldn't know Winnie the Pooh from Tweety Bird. But she made excellent dinner conversation, played tennis like a pro, and after two divorces, wasn't the least bit interested in marriage or emotional commitment.

Exactly the woman for him.

CHAPTER FIVE

Over the next few weeks, Connor managed to put thoughts of Rebecca Evans out of his mind. He concentrated on work and his upcoming trip to Europe, where he planned to finalize a deal with a Greek shipbuilder.

If all went well, he would own his own shipping company in a very short while. Why that thought failed to make his blood race he hadn't a clue, he realized on Friday afternoon while going over Sunday's travel arrangements.

Perhaps it was because he'd run into Rebecca Evans earlier, getting on the elevator. She had a cup of yogurt and an apple in her hand and was wearing a vintage sweater, paired with a plaid miniskirt. Although it probably hid more than the gym shorts he'd seen her in before, he still had to resist the urge to mop his brow.

"Hi, I was just going to send you an email," she said, punching the button for the fourth floor. "I've made the final improvements to the commodities market simulation program. Whenever you want to take it for a test spin, give me a call." Then her eyes went dreamy. "It's based on neural network algorithms I wrote at MIT. It includes some really sophisticated pattern recognition and data analysis tools, plus built-in animation. I think you'll like it."

"I'm sure I'll be impressed," he said, but at the moment, it was her legs that were making an impression.

"I'm still tweaking the recurrent backpropagation algorithm. Maybe I should wait until I have that worked out—unless you're in a hurry?" She glanced up at him and blinked, as if she'd just remembered he was there.

"That's all right. Take your time. Backpropagation is crucial, I always say." He wasn't quite sure what she was talking about, but she seemed very enthusiastic.

"Oh, sorry. I guess I'm having a nerd moment." She gave him a sheepish grin, looking nothing like any nerd he'd ever seen.

The elevator stopped on the third floor, where his meeting was. But instead of getting off, he stood there, frozen with inexplicable indecision. She looked up at him, young, beautiful, and smart as hell. She could probably program her way out of deep space and still have a free hand to beat off the men who flocked to her like flies to jelly. So, what was Connor doing hovering in her orbit?

"Anything else?"

Several possibilities ran through his mind. He thought of saying: *We could go to dinner sometime.* Or perhaps: *Let's do lunch—naked.* Or simply: *Why don't we find the nearest conference room and screw ourselves silly?*

But he was her employer, and she was too young, and he was too jaded.

He'd told her instead to have a nice afternoon and left the elevator, his honor intact and his libido on fire.

Now, sitting at his desk, he shook off the hesitancy that had gripped him earlier. He'd invite her to lunch, he decided, jotting a note in his Day Timer. They'd talk business, of course. He wanted to hear more about her work for the company—preferably in English—and then, broaching the subject very carefully, he'd find out if she was amenable to the sort of relationship he had in mind. A brief affair, to get over the obsession that had gripped him since he'd first seen her in the park. They'd have to be discreet, of course, and when the relationship was over...

There was no need to think that far in advance. For now, he'd concentrate on getting what he wanted. A shipping company in his portfolio and Rebecca Evans in his bed.

"Call Rebecca Evans in Technical and set up a date for lunch," Connor said to Peggy ten days later as he walked through the corporate reception area to his private office.

"Any particular day?"

"Yesterday?" he said wryly, knowing Peggy was as unaccustomed to his impatience as he was. He picked up his messages, glancing through them for word from Bourgikos on the final agreements they still needed to sign. "Any day this week is fine—no, make it today. Rearrange my schedule if you have to." He wanted to leave himself plenty of time to arrange a date this weekend—if things worked out the way he planned.

"Today it is. Anywhere special?"

"The Greens, out at Fort Mason." He'd thought this over carefully. It was a twenty-minute drive, provided the traffic was heavy, and he'd have plenty of time in the limo on the way back to pin her down on weekend plans.

"I'll make the reservation. If she can't make it today?" Peggy glanced up at him, pen in hand.

"Then make it tomorrow. And then get Bourgikos on the phone. Tell him the six percent still stands, and we'll take over the inventory upon signing."

"Right."

"Oh, and, tell Rebecca—" He paused. "Explain to her I'd like our meeting to remain confidential."

As he expected, Peggy asked no questions, merely put the calls through.

If he had any sense, Connor thought as he pulled the files he needed from his briefcase, he'd simply fire Rebecca, offer her a position as his mistress, and find a new computer programmer. There were dozens graduating every day, weren't there?

Of course, she'd probably object to that. She wasn't the mistress type, unfortunately.

He'd just have to negotiate around whatever objections she had. He sat back in his chair, staring reflectively at the painting on the wall. He'd been in trickier situations. Managing to snag a ship-building plant from a crafty Greek shipping magnate hadn't exactly been without complications.

Surely getting Rebecca Evans right where he wanted her would be a simpler proposition. But a voice inside his head, a voice he rarely ignored, told him the matter might not be as simple as he wanted it to be.

"Oh! You knew!" she said when he told her where they were going.

"Knew what?"

"That I'm a vegetarian. I've been dying to try The Greens."

He held open the door to the limo. "Lucky guess. I figured a woman who risks her neck dodging squirrels in the park probably wouldn't go for a ribeye."

As he slid into the back seat, she looked at him like he'd just put an end to world hunger. "You know, Connor, underneath that dour expression, you're really a very thoughtful person."

He wondered what she'd say if she knew that right now he was thinking about her naked, lying prone on the backseat of the limo… "And you're too easily impressed," he said with a half-smile.

"No, I'm not."

"Yes, you are. Most women your age are at least a bit jaded."

"Oh, I'm jaded," she assured him. "Plenty. Why do you think I stopped dating?"

"You've stopped dating?" His head jerked around in surprise.

"Well, pretty much. The last guy I went out with tried to pump me for information about the automatic trade program I was working on."

His gaze narrowed. "You're kidding. Did you report him to the SEC?"

Her gaze hit the floorboard. "Oh, no. It wasn't that big a deal."

It *was* a big deal, but not the deal he wanted to focus on right now, so he changed the subject. "So, one bad apple and you've sworn off men for good."

"Actually, it was more like a bushel."

"That many?" He raised his eyebrow.

"Well, for a long time, I was hung up on this one guy, you see…"

Connor's throat felt suddenly dry. "Oh?"

"My best friend's brother. He didn't know I was alive. He was older, kind of quiet…A lot like—" Connor had the feeling she was about to accuse him of being old, then she glanced up quickly. "You're not a Virgo by any chance are you?"

"No, a Pisces. And don't tell me you put any stock in astrology."

"Of course. Don't you?"

"Never. Give me a solid earnings report any day."

"But I'm talking about people—"

"So am I. Behind every company, there's management, which is 'people,' personalities. And people are predictable, without the help of astrologists and soothsayers."

"You really think so?"

"Of course."

She pondered that for a moment. "You must find us an awfully dull bunch. Us humans."

He smiled. "Every once in a while, I'm surprised."

Their gazes met, tangled briefly, then she looked away, as if afraid he might read her thoughts.

Rebecca stared out the window at the stalled traffic. She was very much afraid she was, predictably, becoming besotted with another guy who was totally wrong for her.

Unfortunately, she couldn't keep her eyes from sliding over to where he sat, perfectly at ease beside her. His suit, a smooth navy wool, seemed made to fit his body. The blue silk tie he wore must have been chosen by an artist to match his eyes, and the crisp white shirt underneath looked as if it would crackle if he moved—or if she ran her hand over his chest.

She swallowed a sigh. Occasionally she thumbed through *GQ* while waiting at the hairdresser, and Connor, she decided, would look right at home on a two-page spread on "Proper Attire for Corporate Raiding."

"Mind if I make a phone call?" he asked, interrupting her thoughts.

She shook her head, then watched as he handled his cell phone with all the finesse of a Viking wielding a sword.

Fortunately, the car arrived at Fort Mason before she had a chance to imagine what a Viking wore under his armor.

The restaurant overlooked the marina, where sailboats were scattered among the docks like overgrown toys. Their waitress seated them at a quiet table by the window, handed them menus, and disappeared. Rebecca decided on tofu brochettes, and then helped interpret the menu for Connor. "Seitan is a meat analog made from wheat gluten," she told him.

He glanced up at her. "That sounds…filling…but I think I'll have the salad with roasted baby vegetables."

She thought corporate raiders were probably used to heartier meals. But then, he likely had no intention of plundering this afternoon. In fact, she still had no idea what his agenda included for their lunch date or why he had asked her to keep it secret.

He probably wanted to quiz her on one of the new programs she was writing. She'd been working overtime, consulting with the various fund managers. She had to remind herself he was her boss, not her friend; otherwise, she'd find herself making more embarrassing confessions or, worse, imagining herself the object of his latest takeover.

She gazed out at the marina while he ordered and tried not to notice how the sky reflecting off the water matched his eyes.

Appetizers of grilled portobello mushrooms arrived, accompanied by a balsamic-laced marinade. Connor stabbed a mushroom with his fork, placed it on her plate, then asked Rebecca about her family back in Chicago.

"My parents divorced when I was twelve. My dad traded in my mom for his secretary. For a long time, Kim and I swore we'd never get married." She sipped her water, looking at him over the rim of the glass. "But then she met Randy and changed her mind."

"And you?"

"Well, it's kind of hard to get married when you've given up dating, remember?"

Connor put down his fork. "Yes, I suppose that does present a problem."

Suddenly his proposed arrangement didn't sound so farfetched after all. She had just admitted she didn't want marriage. Didn't even want to date. Perhaps he should just ask her if she wanted to stop for sex on the way home.

"Of course, men do have their uses." She gazed at him from under her lashes.

"I like to think we do," he said, picking up his glass of white wine.

She leaned back in her seat and tilted her head. "But then, there's always a turkey baster."

He almost choked. "A what?"

She grinned. "My mother told me I could just use a turkey baster. To get pregnant."

He blinked. "You want to get pregnant?" Suddenly he wasn't having the conversation he thought he was having.

"One day. Eventually." Then she sighed, and her eyes filled with a wistful look. "Oh, Connor, there was the cutest little girl in the park the other day."

His gaze narrowed. "You want kids. But no husband."

"Well, if the right guy came along…" Then she laughed. "Actually, I'm holding out for the perfect guy. You know, the one who makes your heart go pitter-patter, the one who steals your breath away, the one who makes you want to jump off a cliff into the unknown."

"The one the glass slipper fits." His fingers absently traced the stem of his glass.

"Exactly!" Her eyes lit up. "The one in a million, absolutely right for me, Cinderella-man."

"And in the meantime?"

Her gaze met his, and she grinned. "Well, not to mix metaphors, but I've kissed my share of frogs, and they still keep on croaking. Until I find one that sweeps me off my feet—"

"I see." He had the odd feeling his voice came out a croak. Somehow, he had just been placed firmly in the category of "frog," and he was damned if he could figure out where to go from here.

Then she laughed. "How on earth did we get on this subject?"

"I haven't the faintest. Would you care for another mushroom?"

During the rest of the meal, he did a better job of keeping the conversation on safe topics—the food, the view, even the weather. Finally, in the car on the way back to the office, Rebecca turned to him and asked, "By the way, Connor, what was the purpose of this meeting? I got the impression from your secretary—"

"I wanted to thank you for the cookies."

"Oh."

"They were delicious."

She beamed. "You liked them? The guys in the office said they tasted like concrete mix."

She had probably baked cookies for the entire building. A whole building full of frogs, croaking and munching chocolate chip cookies baked by a woman who had sworn off kissing frogs.

He should have listened to his instincts all along and ignored his libido. An affair with a woman who wanted a family more than she wanted a quick fuck just wasn't feasible.

Even Rodney would have clued into that.

He swallowed what felt suspiciously like disappointment and lifted an eyebrow. "Concrete mix? Definitely not. I'm not a regular consumer of cement, but I'd imagine it's a little more — moist."

She laughed. Thankfully the traffic was light, and they made it back to the office in time for his next meeting.

CHAPTER SIX

It took Connor only a moment in his closet to find the things he needed to pack for his trip tomorrow. He knew he could come in here blindfolded and still find exactly what he needed. Every item had a place from which it didn't dare stray: stacks of crisply folded shirts, arranged by shade; suits lined up on one side, exactly four inches apart. The shoe rack held only a half-dozen pairs of shoes; Connor didn't see the need for more. Once he found a pair he liked, he stuck with them until they showed signs of wear, then they went to charity along with his other castoffs.

He set the bag on the bed with his briefcase. His housekeeper, Mrs. Pascal, would double-check the contents and have it delivered to the car that would take him to his jet.

The phone next to the bed rang. He glanced at the caller ID before answering. "Hello, Aunt Helen. How are you?"

"Hello, Connor dear. I'm not calling at a bad time, am I?"

"Not at all. I planned to phone you anyway. I'll be coming up there this weekend, on my way to Tokyo. I wanted to stop in and say hello."

"I didn't realize Ukiah was on the way to Tokyo!" She laughed. "I'd love to see you. In fact, there's a problem you could help me with if you have time."

"Of course. What can I do for you?"

"It's Craig. He still hasn't found a job. He's been looking, but you know how the market is. He wanted me to loan him a bit to tide him over. I wanted your advice before I wrote him a check."

Connor knew the advice he'd like to give her wouldn't be heeded. He sighed. Helen wasn't really a family member; she was the older woman who had employed his mother for years, first as an aide to her bedridden husband, then after the death of Peter Tannehill, as companion and friend. She'd long ago instructed Connor to call her Aunt Helen, and out of courtesy, he had. Besides, he had no other family claiming the title. His mother's family had cut all ties when she'd left her native Ireland with Mitchell Forrest, an American soldier who had captured her heart.

"I seem to remember you loaned him five hundred grand less than a year ago," he said, rolling a tie into a circle and tucking it into his open suitcase.

"Yes, but he invested that in — what did you call it?"

"A hedge fund."

"That was it. He lost it all. You know Craig. He's got no head for business."

Unfortunately, he did know her son. In Connor's opinion, Craig Tannehill was a professional freeloader whose main goal was to empty his mother's bank account before he turned forty.

When her husband died, Helen had inherited several million in stocks and CDs, which she had asked Connor to invest shortly after his graduation from Harvard Business School. It had been her assets that had spearheaded his own financial empire. Connor had never forgotten the trust she had placed in him, nor the fact that Helen had given him his first job, mowing her lawn for twenty dollars a week.

Now, due to his careful managing, her fortune was worth substantially more, despite the fact that her son made regular withdrawals on his inheritance.

"I can liquidate more funds for you, but Aunt Helen —"

"That would be wonderful. I'm sure one of these days Craig will be just as successful as his father. I only wish Peter were here to give him advice. You know he doted on Craig."

Again, Connor kept his opinion to himself. It was her money, and even if Craig managed to waste the entire portfolio, Connor had already made sure Helen would be taken care of for the rest of her life.

"Oh, and Connor, if you're coming up here this weekend…"

"Yes?"

"Would you mind seeing about the elm tree in the back yard? The gardener thinks it should be cut down, but I think there might still be a little life left in it. You remember your mother and I used to sit under that tree and drink our lemonade on hot afternoons? I would hate to see it go."

"I'll call a tree service and have them give you a second opinion."

"Of course. Why didn't I think of that?"

Connor heard her laugh over the phone. He really should have called and checked on her before now. God knows she was probably lonely. Her son only called her when he needed a handout.

"Are you all right, Connor? You sound a little…down."

"Back to back overseas trips. I was in Europe just last week, and I'm due to visit our Asian affiliates in Tokyo on Monday."

"Oh, I always loved Japan! And Tokyo is so lovely this time of year. All the cherry blossoms. I remember when your mother and I went that year…"

"There's plenty of room on the corporate jet if you'd like to come along," Connor said.

He heard her delighted laughter.

"Imagine that, inviting an eighty-year-old woman along on your business trip! You should have one of your young women friends join you."

"I'm afraid this trip is strictly business, Aunt Helen. No time on the schedule for sightseeing, much less entertaining. Although, if you'd come, I'd gladly set aside a few hours to swing by the geisha district. I hear you made quite a stir there when you went with Mother."

"Oh, dear, did she say that? Maggie oughtn't tell tales." Then she gave a creaky sigh. "Oh, Connor, I do miss your mother!"

"So do I." He rarely admitted that, though it was true. He cleared his throat. "I'll see you Saturday, then. Goodbye, Aunt Helen."

He gave the phone a thoughtful frown as he hung it up. He'd make sure the tree service saved the tree, or else planted a replacement. Craig was another matter, another reminder that families didn't make for good investments, emotionally or financially. He was glad his only family was a brother who didn't care how much money he had, or even if he were alive, as long as his routine wasn't interrupted.

Playing surrogate son to Aunt Helen was a role he felt he owed her, for her trust in him as well as the friendship she'd offered his mother at a time when Maggie needed both a job and a sympathetic shoulder.

Of course, his reputation as a ruthless corporate raider would be in question if the truth were known. And if it got out how much he burned to have Rebecca Evans in his bed, his reputation as being equally detached when it came to sex would also be suspect.

It was precisely the fact that he wanted her so much that he refrained from going after her. Wanting something so much put him in danger of losing his perspective, losing control of a situation that could very easily become messy. Excess emotion invariably left a bad taste in his mouth, like a dessert laced with too much brandy.

He picked up the economics journal on his bedside table and stuffed it into his briefcase. If he got bored, he'd read the article about cyclical Asian markets, rather than fantasize about tanned legs topped by red running shorts.

Perspective. Control. Focus. He reminded himself of his guiding principles, but strangely, the mantra didn't satisfy the craving he had felt at the mere sight of the pink-smudged rim of Rebecca's water glass while she went on about turkey basters and frogs.

She wanted to get pregnant; he wanted to get her into bed.

Maybe, he thought, picking up his suitcase and smoothing the wrinkles from the bedspread, they could compromise.

Rebecca yawned and shut down her laptop when the clock on the display screen blinked midnight. Once again she had filled the lonely weekend hours with work, ignoring Connor's admonition not to work overtime. Bob's wife still hadn't fully recovered from surgery, and she knew he was needed at home, so she willingly took on extra tasks. Kevin was busy troubleshooting the system glitches that arose like weeds among the terabytes of information, which left Rebecca to fine-tune the tricky programming that made the work of the analysts more efficient and productive.

She had started having lunch with a few friends from work. After a quick workout in the gym, they grabbed snacks from the cafeteria and traded woes and company gossip.

Unfortunately, Rebecca had found, Connor Forrest seemed to be the main topic for gossip.

The man was an enigma even to the rest of the employees at FGI, though there was no shortage of rumors. It was said he had been involved with one of the retail analysts, Claire Porter, and when their discreet affair was over, he had transferred her to Philadelphia.

Another reason not to fantasize about him. Not only was he out of her league, but she had no desire to move to Philadelphia.

Once asleep, however, her mind wasn't influenced by cold hard logic. Last night, she had dreamed he rode a white horse, and he whisked her from atop her desk and insisted on calling her Cinderella. Then when she kissed him, he gazed at her tenderly, told her he loved her, and wanted her to be his bride.

What silliness, she thought, throwing back the covers on her bed and trying not to imagine Connor there. She had no idea what she'd do with him if he were, anyway. At the age of twenty-six, she was, she sometimes suspected, the oldest virgin alive outside a convent. She'd come awfully close a couple of times, but at the last minute, she'd chickened out. Or more precisely, come to her senses. The guy she was with wasn't the one she wanted to spend the rest of her life with, and the idea of sharing such an intimacy with anyone else just didn't turn her on.

Sex, to Rebecca, was a life-time commitment, and she hadn't met a man yet she was prepared to change her life to accommodate.

But there were times, like now, when she wouldn't have minded the company.

Before she could turn out the light, the phone rang. She picked up the receiver on her bedside table, and within a few short minutes, her world completely upended.

Thoughts of Connor, and innocent dreams, flew from her mind, and it was a long time before they came back.

CHAPTER SEVEN

The trip to Tokyo was, as Connor had predicted, successful. During the week, he had consulted with his Tokyo-based analysts, reassured his major Japanese investors with a few well-chosen facts, and explored several lucrative investments. He'd met with economic advisers to the Prime Minister and was certain he knew the future — of the Asian markets, at least. He'd had no time to admire the cherry blossoms; in fact, he doubted he'd even caught a glimpse of the Tokyo streets as his limo had whisked him from one meeting to another.

Now, in his office Monday morning, he emptied his briefcase, automatically sorting the files his secretary would need. She appeared just as he added the last file to the stack on his desk.

"Peggy, everyone needs hard copies of these. They offered to make them before I left, but I knew you wouldn't mind having them made." He was also confident she knew who "everyone" was. After ten years in his employ, she could almost read his mind.

"Of course. Did you have a good trip?" she asked, without a glance in his direction. He answered with a non-committal murmur, scanning the stack of messages she handed him. All of them were important, of course; nothing but the most urgent problems ever reached his desk.

Peggy took the files and left him alone. He knew she would be back with coffee and more correspondence momentarily.

On the twelve-hour flight from Japan, Connor had allowed himself to contemplate the problem of Rebecca Evans. He'd have to be up front with her, spell out exactly what he wanted. He was certain they could reach an agreement. He was considered something of an expert at negotiating, as a shipping magnate in Greece could testify. After a long week of give and take, they had both walked away from the table satisfied.

He had never given this much thought to the process of seducing a woman, but never had anyone intrigued him the way Rebecca did. Never had the thought of a woman lingered in his mind long after she had left the room. Other women seemed dull in comparison, including Lauren Rostaman, whom he still hadn't called.

Maybe this attraction was the result of their unorthodox meeting in the park and subsequent misunderstanding. They had gotten off on the wrong foot — or was it the right foot? He was no longer certain.

All he knew was that he was impatient to talk to her, to make plans.

When Peggy came back with coffee and messages, he glanced up at her, and said, "Would you get Rebecca Evans on the phone? And then I'd like you to call back Bruce Westphall and tell him—" He stopped when he noticed the stricken expression on her face.

"Rebecca Evans isn't here. Didn't anyone tell you? Her sister died last week. She was killed in Chicago, along with her husband. A car crash. They both died instantly. Rebecca's gone to be with her family."

Rebecca tossed the dying carnations into the wastebasket and placed the card in the basket on the dining table, along with the other sympathy cards. Her mother's house was empty for the first time since the horrible tragedy that had brought her back home to Chicago. Her mother had driven the twins over to Randy's parents' house in the northern suburb of Evanston, and all the aunts, cousins, and well-meaning friends had finally stopped dropping by with food and offers of help. Rebecca had gotten used to the constant commotion these last few days; she welcomed it, in fact. It was the only thing standing between her and a wall of grief she didn't want to face.

She was holding herself together, staying strong for her mother and, most importantly, the twins. The babies she had helped bring into the world needed her now more than ever. Fearful and confused, they had turned to Rebecca for comfort.

Today Randy's parents had insisted on a visit; otherwise she wouldn't have let them out of her sight. Plus, she knew the twins needed to maintain the close connection they'd had with their grandparents while their parents were alive. Though their lives would never return to normal, she wanted them to realize the people they loved weren't all disappearing from their lives.

She stuffed her own grief into a cold place deep in her heart. One day, she'd take it out and let it thaw, let herself grieve properly, but for now, the twins, and her mother, needed her. She slid open the envelope on another card. A spray of jonquils adorned the cover — Kim's favorite flower, she thought sadly. She opened the card and read the inscription three times before she realized it was from Melvin Dailey, the man who was driving the car that had swerved into the wrong lane and smashed Kim and Randy's minivan beyond recognition and ended their lives instantly.

For a moment, she imagined what he must be feeling. A stupid mistake on his part, resulting in irreparable damage to a family he didn't even know. She could almost feel pity for the man, but something held her back.

Ugly black anger threatened to consume her and fill her with foreign thoughts of revenge, except retribution wouldn't take the place of Kim. All the angry thoughts in the world wouldn't give the twins their mommy and daddy, making sure they were safe in their beds when dreams got too scary. Revenge wouldn't replace the sound of her sister's voice on the phone on the weekends when she called to chat.

She folded the card with a sigh. The anger was still there, but its color had turned from black to a healthy shade of red, an emotion she could deal with — had to deal with — if she wanted to heal from the wound Melvin Dailey had dealt her family.

When the phone rang, she reached for it gratefully, afraid her own thoughts were dragging her down. She was surprised to hear Connor's voice. "Rebecca. I just heard the news."

"Oh. Hello, Connor. I thought you were in Japan."

"I was until last night. Peggy should have contacted me, let me know what was going on."

"That's all right. You couldn't have done anything." But hearing his voice was doing something now, wasn't it? She suddenly felt achy and tender, like she wanted to lay her hurt at his feet and let him carry her to a place where sorrow didn't exist.

"God, I'm so sorry, Rebecca. I know how close you were."

"Yes." She swallowed the tears she had become adept at keeping at bay. "We got the flowers from FGI. They were very nice."

There was silence on the line for a moment, but not the awkward kind. She was used to his contemplative way of speaking, as if he carefully measured each word to make sure it fit the situation perfectly before he uttered it.

Finally he spoke the words everyone else had said, but somehow she knew he was truly interested in the answer. "How are you?"

"I'm fine." She paused, then amended that. "I'll *be* fine. I have to be. I'm going to have the twins now. Full time."

"You mean their parents named you as their guardian?"

"Yes. We had discussed it before, but I never thought—"

"No one ever does, Rebecca."

She sighed. "I suppose not. Kim's husband, Randy, co-owned an insurance agency, and they had a friend who was a lawyer. He drew up their wills. So, I guess they were more prepared than most."

"And what about you? Are you prepared for this? Raising two children?"

She let out an exasperated breath. "Everyone keeps asking me that, like they think I'll want to back out or something. Of course I'm not prepared. I don't even have a backseat! But I love them more than anything, Connor."

She knew the adjustment would be hard for them, even though they had been in daycare during the last year while Kim had worked part time at her husband's company.

But there was no other option. Her mother had taken all the time off from her job she could afford, and Rebecca's aunts and cousins all had full time jobs.

Their grandparents had tried to insist that the twins live with them. George Severson worked at the insurance agency along with his two sons, and his wife stayed home. But Rebecca had firmly and politely told them no. Kim had disagreed with her in-laws on child raising issues in the past, and Rebecca knew that had been on her sister's mind when she asked her to be the children's guardian if anything should ever happen.

She clutched the phone with determined resolve and said to Connor, "I can get a bigger car, a bigger house. But they can't get a new mother. I'm all they've got. And they're all I've got, too."

When Connor hung up the phone, he sat gazing out his window at the last remnants of the morning fog. He couldn't even begin to imagine the pain she must feel, losing her sister. How did one go about picking up after a blow like that? Losing his mother after her long fight with cancer had been hard, but losing a parent couldn't compare to losing a sister.

A knot of emotion lodged in his throat. Suddenly, his feelings toward Rebecca seemed to shift, reordered in a pattern he didn't recognize. He no longer wanted to ask her out, or get her into his bed. Oddly, all he wanted was to offer comfort—a commodity he'd never before valued. The emotion felt strange, thick and sweet like molasses, and just as likely to stick.

Peggy buzzed him on the intercom with news that Westphall was on the phone. With a sigh, Connor put his thoughts away and got back to work.

A week later, Rebecca sat at her desk long after everyone else had left the office, taking care of the loose ends she'd left untied when she'd left abruptly. She had returned to California alone, knowing she had to make a few changes in her lifestyle if she was going to take over the care of two four-years-olds. Fortunately, daycare wasn't a problem. The onsite facility run by the Forrest Group was more than a convenient employee perk, she had found. It was staffed by caring, well-qualified teachers. Parents were welcome at any time during the day, and many chose to have lunch in the pint-sized chairs of the center.

There was an opening for the twins. Apparently it was company policy that all employees would be accommodated at the center, although two weeks' notice was necessary to ensure the availability of staff.

She sighed. At least that had gone well. It was proving more difficult to find a house that fit her budget. She was determined the twins should have a back yard, with plenty of room for all the toys and play equipment that littered their yard in Illinois. She wanted them each to have a bedroom; although, since their parents' death, they had been sleeping together in Rebecca's old bed at her mother's house.

She had pored over the want ads, checked the listings on the Internet, with little luck. Even though her salary was competitive, housing costs in San Francisco were among the highest in the country. There were still a few possibilities. A house in Richmond, though the rent was steep, sounded promising—although she couldn't help but wonder just what kind of house could be described as "cuddly."

Maybe if she lived further out…A two-hour commute wasn't so bad, was it?

She clicked on another ad and picked up the phone to call, but then she heard footsteps in the hallway. They stopped at her cubicle.

She glanced up. Connor stood by the partition, hands in pockets, staring at her as if he'd forgotten what she looked like. Finally he said, "I heard you were back. I thought you told me you were planning to take a month off."

"I'm only here for a few days. I had some things that needed to get done. Then I'm going back to Chicago."

His gaze narrowed. "For good?"

She gave him a tired smile. "No, just to pick up the twins. I'll be driving them out here as soon as I find us a place to live."

"I thought you had a place in Oakland."

"My apartment's only a studio. There was barely enough room for me, much less two four-year-olds."

"I see." He continued to stare at her, his gaze thoughtful. He settled his arm along the top of the partition and rested his face against two fingers. "And what about a backseat? Have you found one of those yet?"

"I'll be keeping my sister's car. It's a sedan. Mine's for sale now. Know anyone who's interested in buying a low-mileage Miata?" Then she sighed. As much as she'd loved it, she had no need for a frivolous set of wheels now.

Connor frowned, feeling a stab of regret at her words. He had a sudden image of a little red sports car and the carefree woman who drove it—a contrast from the subdued woman sitting in front of him. "How are the twins?" he asked.

She glanced at their photo above her. "Not so good. Aubrey doesn't talk at all. She's started wetting the bed. Alex—he's more verbal, but he's still confused. They're too young to understand what happened."

"They're only four. It must be terribly confusing."

She nodded. "It is. Alex asked me if I had a very tall ladder. He wanted to climb up to heaven." She managed a smile. "And Aubrey just sits and stares, her thumb in her mouth, those big, sad eyes staring off into space. I don't know what she's thinking." Her voice broke. "How am I ever going to make things right for them? What happened was so unfair!"

"It wasn't fair to you either."

"But I'm a grown up. I can handle it."

"Can you really, Rebecca?" He stepped around the partition, then settled himself against the desk, facing her. Compelled by an emotion he wasn't sure he'd ever felt, he reached out and gently pushed a stray lock of hair from her forehead. "I know what it's like to lose someone. No matter how old you are, it still hurts."

She gazed up at him, her eyes glowing gold with tears. Her lips trembled despite the wry smile she offered. "You're right. It hurts like hell!"

Without thinking about what he was doing, he pulled her up from her chair, into his arms, against his chest. He held her and felt her shake, while her tears wet his shirt.

Her ragged voice broke through her sobs. "I've been trying so hard not to do this! There was always someone else who needed me."

"I know," he said, one hand smoothing her hair against the vulnerable spot on her neck, not certain what to do with a weeping woman in his arms. He searched for something to say, but words seemed too much.

A memory surfaced of himself, five years ago, staring at the urn containing his mother's ashes, unable to cry. He had thought then he was incapable of emotion, but maybe he just hadn't had anyone to share it with.

His arms tightened around her. More than anything in the world, he wanted to ease her grief, but he knew that was impossible. He was helpless, as helpless as he had been years ago to stop his mother's pain.

But his mother's suffering had finally ended, bringing release to her, and to him the beginning of a silent anguish he'd never acknowledged.

Connor's throat constricted, his eyes stung, his heart quaked like a tremor along a fault line far below the earth. As he held Rebecca's shaking body against his, he found himself grieving with her, her emotional outburst breaking loose his own pain from the cold, dark place he'd hidden it.

Slowly her sobs grew less urgent, until at last she was still, wrapped securely in his arms. Her tears had soaked the fabric of his shirt, and her face was stuck to the dampness. He half-sat, half-leaned on the top of her desk, her body pressed against his. His hand stroked the gold strands of her hair, his palm bunching its length together then releasing it. It felt like silk in his hand, and when he breathed in the scent, it smelled like Japanese patchouli.

A tiny spark of desire started to build in him. She felt so good against him, nesting snug against his body. He wanted to go on holding her, but now he knew his motives were going beyond the simple offering of comfort he had first intended.

With a gentle grip on her shoulders, he moved her back, mere inches from him. He slid a hand to her chin, tilting it up so he could see her tear-stained face.

Her eyelids fluttered open. For a moment, he felt trapped, blinded by the wet gold of her gaze, a twenty-four carat prison he wasn't sure he wanted to escape. He couldn't speak, couldn't move, couldn't think what his own name was.

Then he lowered his gaze to her still trembling lips, so close to his, and his good intentions warred with his instincts.

He reached in his pocket and pulled out a monogrammed handkerchief. She took it, and dabbed at her face, then gave him a sheepish look.

"I'm sorry. I ruined your shirt. And now your handkerchief."

"I've got extra of both. Do you feel better now?"

She nodded.

"Then it must be true. A good cry is reputed to do wonders," he told her.

"Reputed to? Haven't you ever cried?"

"Not since the last market crash." He straightened and noticed a local rental search website on her computer screen. "Any luck with the house hunting?"

She grimaced. "Not so far. This place on Eubank sounded promising, but Kevin told me that was one of the worst neighborhoods in the city."

"Maybe I can help you there. I know a real estate agent who specializes in residential property."

"Oh, I couldn't afford to buy."

"They often handle rentals. If there's something available, it usually goes through word of mouth. Why don't I call him, see if he knows of anything?"

"Oh. Well…"

Before she could come up with a reason to refuse his offer, he took a phone from his pocket and placed a call. When Howard Brietmann answered, he quickly explained the problem, though the figure he quoted for rent was far below the going rate for two-bedroom condos in the city. "She'd like at least—what, three bedrooms? Four?" He sent a questioning glance toward her.

"Three," she said, "and a back yard. It doesn't have to be too big—or new. Maybe a Victorian," she added with a hopeful look.

"Perhaps there's something in Buena Vista," Connor suggested. He kept his face expressionless as the voice on the other end scoffed.

"Are you kidding?" Howard said. "For that amount, you couldn't afford an outhouse over there."

"Is that right? Why don't you check that out, and I'll get back to you in, say, twenty minutes?"

"I'm telling you, there's nothing—"

"Good. I'll give you a call." Connor pocketed his phone. "He thinks he may know of something. Why don't you meet me in my office in half an hour? By then I should have heard from him, and we can go from there."

Rebecca nodded, a glimmer of her usual optimism finally showing through the tear stains. "Does he really think he can find something?"

"I'm certain he can." With a reassuring smile, he turned and left.

As soon as he was on the elevator, Connor pulled out his phone and tapped the redial button. When Howard answered, he made his request, this time in a firmer tone. "Find a place that meets the requirements.

At any price, for sale or rent, it doesn't matter. In fact, I'd prefer if it were for sale, as long as it's available immediately. The transaction will have to be made anonymously—I don't want her to know I'm footing the bill. Then we'll make sure the rent is in her price range.

"And make sure it's in good condition," he added. "I don't want her to have to worry about repairs."

"Right, a Victorian with a yard. As long as price is no object, I think I may know a place. It belonged to an old lady whose family wants it sold fast so they can split the estate."

"Fine. Call me back with directions, and we'll meet you there to look at it. Remember, I don't want her to realize the place is out of her price range."

"I'll tell her whatever you want, boss."

Connor drove Rebecca to a place on Carroll Street, a charming three story Victorian. Rebecca told him it reminded her of the Painted Ladies she had admired while sightseeing. He agreed; with a fresh coat of paint, it could easily be as picturesque as one of the "grand dames" coloring the nearby hills.

Howard met them there, and he explained as he opened the door that the house had belonged to an older woman who'd recently moved into a nursing home. Though a "for sale" sign was in the front yard, the agent told them the market was soft and the family would be grateful if they found a trustworthy renter.

Rebecca seemed to accept that, Connor was glad to see, without asking any questions about why the rent was so low—although the condition of the house had him wondering if it shouldn't be lower.

She and Connor walked through the house, their footsteps echoing against the hardwood floors. Connor looked on silently while Rebecca admired the first floor, exclaiming every few minutes when she found an unexpected bonus.

"Oh, look at the cute little telephone nook," she said as they climbed up the stairs.

"Just the right size for a cell phone," he replied dryly, but Rebecca didn't notice his sarcasm. She seemed to be too busy falling in love with the house.

The wallpaper in the bathroom was old and stained, but Rebecca thought the twins would love the ducks stuck to the tub.

"Reminds me of the green mushrooms my mother stuck on our tub — back in the seventies," Connor told her, jiggling the handle of the toilet. "The plumbing's probably ancient."

"As long as it works when Alex stuffs his dinosaurs in there," Rebecca replied.

There were two large bedrooms, plus a third smaller one. "We can turn this one into an office," she said. "Until Aubrey is able to sleep by herself. Then I'll separate them and put Alex in here."

It was clear she was thinking long term. Connor had been half-afraid she would decide to return to Chicago, to be near her family. He didn't want to lose a valuable employee. "What about all that space on the third floor?"

"Oh, that will be the playroom. They can put their castle there."

"They own their own castle?"

She nodded, then pulled back the lace curtain to gaze out the window. "A big plastic one they got for Christmas. I was going to put it outside, but this is better."

Then she turned to him, eyes shining. "Did you see the marks in the bedroom closet? Children grew up here, Connor. I bet the woman who lived here really loved this place. She must have been sad to leave."

"Or perhaps she was tired of the responsibility of taking care of it. It must be over a hundred years old."

"Oh, do you think so?"

"Most likely. This section of San Francisco sustained little damage in the nineteen-oh-six earthquake and fire."

"That's a good sign, isn't it?"

He wiped a finger on the dusty windowsill. "I suppose. You're sure you wouldn't prefer a modern apartment, or at least a house that's been renovated in the last half century?"

"Are you kidding? And give up all this charm?" She pulled the crystal knob dangling at the end of the light chain. The small chandelier hanging in the middle of the room lit up, then one of the bulbs flickered and went out.

Connor glanced up. "You'll want to make sure the wiring is up to date. The house was probably originally equipped with gaslights."

"Oh, Connor! I can just imagine this place glowing." She got a faraway look in her eyes. "Wouldn't that be romantic?"

"If there's a surge, your computer could get fried."

"Oh. You're right. But that can be fixed."

On the way downstairs, Rebecca admired the oak banister. "Just think how many hands have held on to this!"

Connor was looking at her, admiring the way the golden strands of her hair fell every which way to her shoulders. He ignored the urge to smooth his hand over it and replied, "You're right. It should be sanitized. It feels a little wobbly, too."

Howard was waiting for them in the living room, standing next to an old chair with crocheted antimacassars on the arms. "The few pieces of furniture are included," he told them. "I can have them hauled to the dump for you."

"Oh, no!" Rebecca cried. "I love that chair! And the iron bed frame upstairs is a treasure. Don't you dare have it hauled away!"

Connor glanced at the fireplace, where gas logs were attached to a pipe that led behind the wall. "Is the fireplace a safety hazard?" he asked. "And how about the wiring?"

"I'll check—on both." He made a note on his cell phone.

"Do that. And the banister felt a little loose."

When Rebecca disappeared into the kitchen, Connor said to him in a low voice, "I'd like a full inspection done tomorrow. Then have anything fixed that's broken or needs replacing. I take it we can close the deal tonight?"

"I'll have to contact the owners, but I'm sure that won't be a problem. The asking price—"

"I'll pay it. Cash."

Rebecca called from the kitchen. "Oh look, the back yard has a rose trellis! And it's fenced. I even see signs of kids next door. This place is perfect!"

She seemed to want this somewhat shabby house more than anything, and Connor felt an unexpected thrill of satisfaction that he could give it to her.

He'd just have to make certain she never found out he was her landlord. Somehow he knew she would see his motives behind the gesture, although he wasn't even certain himself what they were. He just knew he liked seeing the light again in her eyes.

Before they went back to the office and Rebecca's car, they stopped at a restaurant in Chinatown. Over dinner, Connor listened while she talked about the accident's aftermath.

"The prosecutor is charging the driver with vehicular homicide. He could go to prison for twenty years."

"That must be a relief."

"Not really. It won't bring Kim back. And it probably won't even make anyone else stop and think before they get behind a wheel drunk. I'd rather see the guy sentenced to a lifetime of community service. I want him to go to every bar in the country and tell anyone who thinks they can drive after a few drinks what happened." She leaned across the table. "I know he feels remorse. I called him the other day—"

"You spoke to him? The man who killed your sister?"

She nodded. "Yes. I had to. I saw him on the news—he looked devastated. Even though I wanted to hate him for what he did, I knew he would have taken it back if he could."

She absently shoved a broccoli floret with a chopstick, worry creasing her forehead. "I don't think I could ever forgive him. I'm still angry. I just knew he needed to hear from a member of her family. Not to know we forgave him for what he did, but to let him know…" She shrugged. "I don't know. It's just like there's a connection there. He was suffering, too. He feels terribly guilty. He said he wished he could have been the one who died."

"Probably part of his defense strategy."

"No, it was genuine. I'm sure of it."

Connor shook soy sauce on his Szechuan shrimp and gave her a skeptical look. "Haven't you been fooled before? You were the one who said your last boyfriend tried to pump you for inside information."

She lifted her shoulders. "So, I make a mistake now and then. I still know when a person's sincere."

"Do you really?" He met her gaze, then fished for a shrimp with his chopsticks.

She nodded. "Like you, for instance. When I met you in the park, and when you apologized later—"

Connor frowned. "I could have just as easily been hitting on you."

She smiled. "No, you would never take advantage of a helpless woman. You're too…kind."

Connor swallowed the shrimp. "Kind?"

"Yes. You could never hurt anyone. You're a gentle man, Connor. You just hide it under those formal frowns and dark suits and that—that ruthless look you're so good at."

He glanced up sharply. For a minute, he thought she knew about the real estate transaction he had just finalized over the phone while she was in the restroom. But as she gazed softly at him, her expression all too open, he realized she truly believed, without a shred of proof, that he was still her Good Samaritan, capable of performing random acts of kindness for no reason other than goodwill.

Suddenly he hoped she never found out the truth of what he'd done today. How he had hoped to find a way to get her into his bed.

He felt like a cad. For weeks he had plotted and planned how to have sex with her without paying her price: love and marriage. Impersonating a perfect prince beneath the frog suit.

She, on the other hand, obviously saw him as a trusted friend, and now, that seemed more valuable than all the casual sex in the world.

He'd been blind, so intent on getting what he wanted, he hadn't stopped to assess what the true value of her company was, to see where the true profit lay. The unconditional trust she offered, the belief that he was better than he was, was suddenly an investment worth having. He couldn't throw it away on something as fleeting as a sexual relationship.

He drove her back to her car, silently contemplating his new role as Rebecca's friend. Though he'd had plenty of female friends, none of them had ever stirred up quite the reaction he had to Rebecca. She sent his senses into confusion. He wanted to take care of her but, at the same time, felt oddly comforted by her presence, a sense of peace he'd never had with a woman.

She got out of his car near the parking garage where her car waited. "Thanks for dinner, Connor. I'll return the favor one day, I promise. You can be our first guest in our new house!" She shut the door and hurried to her little red car, her skirt blowing in the evening breeze, wrapping around her legs like plastic wrap.

He groaned. How the hell was he supposed to be a friend to a woman he desperately wanted to fuck?

CHAPTER EIGHT

Rebecca tossed the wet sheets in the washing machine and added a capful of bleach. Ten weeks after their parents' deaths, and after a month of therapy, Aubrey still wet the bed, and Alex was constantly putting his action figures into cars and colliding them head-first. Rebecca no longer cringed whenever she heard the crash of metal on metal.

Their therapist had told her it would take time for them to deal with the loss of their parents. There would always be scars, but with time, the twins would resemble the happy children she saw at the daycare each day.

They had been going for half days, as Rebecca arranged her schedule to work part time at home. She knew she couldn't continue that forever, though, and next week she intended to make it a full week.

"Oh, Kim, why didn't you just stick around!" She sighed and turned on the washer. Since crying on Connor's shoulder, she had given in to tears only late at night, and then she went into the bathroom and turned on the water so the twins wouldn't hear.

She hadn't thought it was possible, but since becoming responsible for the twins full time, she had grown to love them even more than when she only saw them occasionally. She loved them so much it hurt—a fierce, physical ache deep inside whenever she kissed them goodnight or handed them peanut butter and jelly sandwiches, cut in precise triangles for Aubrey, squares for Alex.

As she shut the door on the washer, his voice called from the living room. "Rebecca, Aubrey wants to watch *Peter Pan!*"

"Aubrey wants peanut butter? Okay. Be right—"

"No! She wants to watch *Peter Pan!*" Giggles accompanied the request, a sound that made her smile. Laughter had been absent from their world for too long.

"Right. Peter Pan peanut butter. Coming right up. On graham crackers or saltines?"

"*Peter Pan* the movie! With the pirates!"

"Pirates? Did you say pirates?" Rebecca stuck her head in the living room, where Alex sat surrounded by toy cars, then looked around as if searching. "Where? Where'd they go? I wanted to talk to that Captain Hook."

Alex giggled. "You're silly, Rebecca."

"No, you're silly, goose."

She and Alex continued playing word games, while Aubrey sat on the couch watching with wide blue eyes. This was Rebecca's latest strategy for encouraging Aubrey to talk. Despite her attempts to draw her out, Aubrey only occasionally spoke, in a small voice, to either Rebecca or her brother, who often seemed to read her mind. Rebecca suspected he often misinterpreted his own wishes as Aubrey's, but Aubrey didn't seem to mind.

Finally Rebecca picked up the DVD and stuck it in the player. "Okay, a movie and a snack. How's that?"

Later, after the twins had been bathed and the mountain of books they had brought to her were read, Rebecca made herself a cup of herbal tea, lit a tranquility candle, and cleared room for herself among the toys on the couch. She'd moved in barely a month ago, and already the Victorian she was renting was starting to feel like home.

There were a few boxes left to unpack, but she could do that in the morning, before the annual company picnic in the afternoon.

It would be held at a park in Sonoma, about an hour north of downtown. Food would be catered and games set up for the employees and their families. The annual FGI tennis tournament was going on during the event, but Rebecca wasn't planning to participate. She'd taken tennis lessons in high school, and she soon discovered she didn't possess the killer instinct to finish off her opponent.

She had to admit she was looking forward to seeing Connor again. Even after bawling on his shoulder, she still thought of him as an enigma, a puzzle of a man. An emotional dichotomy: caring and compassionate one minute, cold and aloof the next. Like the Dr. Jekyll and Mr. Hyde she had first accused him of being.

Unfortunately, puzzles had always fascinated her, as had tall, dark, and handsome men.

One thing was clear: she was certain he thought of her only as a friend. That was just as well, she told herself. She didn't have time for romance right now.

Although occasionally, she still had dreams...dreams of a dark-haired knight on a white horse, galloping to her rescue there in the middle of Golden Gate Park.

She sighed and put down her herbal tea. On the table lay a card from her friend Molly, who'd laughingly quoted the advice from a book on feng shui: "To bring romance into your life, toss a pair of red panties into your Relationship corner." Right now there was a naked Barbie sprawled in her Relationship corner.

Maybe that would do the trick.

Or maybe Barbie would get lucky, and Rebecca would just have more action figures to pick up.

The next day turned out to be a gorgeous day for a picnic. Rebecca had dressed the twins in matching khaki shorts and red checked shirts, and without thinking, had pulled on a pair of khaki shorts and a red top herself. It wasn't until Kevin had remarked on the resemblance that she realized they all looked like a trio of hikers wearing Italian tablecloths.

Alex had already found his new best friend and gone off to the swings with Jared and his mom, but Aubrey hung back, clinging to Rebecca's hand. Several of her co-workers had stopped and talked to them, and she'd met some of the other daycare parents. They all assured her that Aubrey would settle into the routine, eventually.

"Hey, how about a veggie dog?" Kevin came weaving through the scattered groups of families and friends, balancing three plates in one hand and a couple of drinks in the other.

"Thanks. Which is mine?"

"The one with everything. I hate onions, remember?"

"Oh, right." She took one of the plates, then motioned toward the empty space beside her. "Would you like to sit?"

"Sure. I just got creamed on the tennis court," he said, plopping himself down on the picnic blanket she had brought. "Our boss shouldn't be playing on this amateur circuit. He belongs at Wimbledon."

"Is he really that good?"

Kevin shrugged as he stuffed one end of the hot dog into his mouth, then wiped a dot of ketchup from the side. "I've never played Federer, but I have a hard time believing Connor Forrest couldn't give him a run for his money."

"I thought he usually only played doubles at these tournaments."

"Yeah, but his partner moved to Philly. Claire Porter—you didn't know her. She runs a department store out there now, and she recently announced her engagement to Matt Grayson."

"That's Claire Porter? I thought Matt Grayson's fiancée was a former actress."

Kevin shrugged again as he finished off the hot dog. "I don't keep up, but apparently she was involved in some kind of scandal years ago, ended up changing professions. She was a damned good analyst too, from what they tell me. She was sort of Connor's protégé."

"Oh. I see." Then, unable to resist, she added, "I heard they dated while she was here."

"I don't know. Ask Bob. He knew her better than I did. Their kids played on the same soccer team or something. You want another hotdog?"

"No thanks. I'd better—"

Suddenly she heard a scream. She jumped up and, with Aubrey in tow, rushed in the direction of the playground. Alex had fallen off the jungle gym, Jared's mother explained when she arrived. A little trickle of blood decorated his knee.

From the screams, she'd thought he'd lopped off an arm, or a finger, at the very least. "It's okay, sweetie. It's only a little scrape."

"No! It's bleeding! I'm gonna die!"

"Oh, Alex, you're not going to die!" Rebecca bent down and looked him in the eye. "A little bit of blood won't hurt you."

"But it does hurt!" Another wail erupted full force, and Rebecca did the only thing she could do. She plea bargained.

"I bet we can find a bandage for that."

"I want one with Scooby-Doo on it!"

Before she could talk him down to plain old tan ones, a deep voice replied, "I think the Scooby-Doo ones were all sold out. We have a fresh box of SpongeBob, though. I remember seeing it at the first aid table."

She stopped, looked around, and saw Connor, tennis racket slung over his shoulder.

"Here, I'll take that," he said, and took Alex from her arms.

Alex was too fascinated by the new entrant in the bandage discussion to protest. "Who are you?"

"I'm Connor. You must be Alex."

Fortunately, Alex seemed to have forgotten his wound. "Why are you carrying that thing on your back?" he asked.

"It's a tennis racket. Do you know how to play tennis?"

Alex shook his head. "No. But I can play Monopoly!"

"No kidding? That's my favorite game. We'll have to play sometime."

"Okay! I'll let you buy all the purple ones!"

With a happy grin soaking up the tears, Alex let himself be carried in Connor's arms, a position all too familiar to Rebecca. She pulled Aubrey into her own arms, and together they walked down the sidewalk toward the pavilion, Alex chatting all the way. The tears quickly dried, and Rebecca thought he might forget about the promised bandage by the time they reached the pavilion, where a first aid kit had already been opened to attend to the various cuts and scrapes that had accumulated during the picnic.

"How's the new house working out?" Connor asked her, his steps slowing as the path sloped upward.

"Oh, fine! Aubrey's thinks it's cool to live in a Painted Lady, don't you, sweetie?"

Aubrey dug her face into Rebecca's neck.

"I noticed it needed a coat of paint. Perhaps your landlord should see to that."

"They already have. A contractor was out last week with paint samples. They're even letting me pick the colors."

"My favorite color's red!" Alex put in, peering down at his knee.

"I'm partial to red myself," Connor said, his gaze on Rebecca's collar. "What about Aubrey? What's her favorite color?"

"She likes red too," Alex informed him.

Aubrey twisted her face, and briefly her eyes met Connor's.

"Is that right?" he asked.

She whispered in Rebecca's ear.

"What was that?" Rebecca said, pretending not to hear.

Aubrey whispered again, louder, and Rebecca announced, "Polka dots. Aubrey's favorite color is polka dots."

Aubrey giggled, while Alex said, with an indignant wiggle in Connor's arms, "Polka dot's not a color!"

And when Aubrey whispered again, louder this time, Rebecca finally *got it*. "Purple. Aubrey likes purple."

Connor nodded. "Purple and red it is, then. For the house. Perhaps a nice polka dot pattern."

Connor watched as Rebecca bandaged her nephew's knee. It was obvious she cared for the kids, and equally obvious she had her hands full—literally. The little girl seemed anxious not to let her out of her sight. Her big blue eyes followed Rebecca's every movement, as if she were terrified she'd lose another person she loved.

Again Connor cursed the accident that had killed Rebecca's sister. He'd made a substantial donation to MADD, anonymously, in Kim's name, and been assured it would go toward programs to increase awareness.

His own father had been an alcoholic, Connor had realized as he grew older, but the knowledge didn't excuse the fact that Mitchell Forrest had abandoned his wife and sons when the going got tough. Connor had never forgotten the sting of poverty, of knowing his mother had accepted handouts from Helen Tannehill when she couldn't stretch her paycheck to cover Rodney's medical bills as well as the care and feeding of two growing boys. That was no doubt the source of his own infatuation with the money industry. "Understand your enemy" was the one lesson his father, a sergeant in the army, had taught him before he split. Connor, convinced that the key to the unattainable was a thorough knowledge of financial markets, had done just that, with a dedication and drive that would have made the old man proud had it been focused on the battlefield.

Connor eyed the dozens of employees milling around him. They all looked relaxed, but he knew they'd all be eager to get back to conquering the market on Monday morning, with him leading the charge.

The picnic was winding down, and as he headed down the path toward the parking lot, he tried to convince himself he'd done exactly what he'd set out to do. He was respected throughout financial circles; some had even mentioned his name as a potential Treasury Secretary.

Still, he felt a tinge of dissatisfaction. Not even a job in the cabinet would take away the strange hole he'd felt in his life lately, a nebulous feeling that crept through his mind occasionally like early morning fog and disappeared whenever he tried to grab hold of it. He felt at loose ends, as if he had too much time on his hands, though he was busier than ever. He had a sense that his life wasn't exactly the one he wanted, despite the fact he'd achieved much more than most his age. Some discovery he still searched for, some knowledge he had yet to accrue.

Connor crossed the parking lot and unlocked the door of his Jaguar, impatient with this unaccustomed self-examination.

It was probably just a reaction to the fact his fortieth birthday was coming up next year.

Connor flung his tennis racket in the back of his car. A midlife crisis didn't sound appealing. Maybe he just needed a new hobby.

Wasn't this the right time of year for climbing Everest?

CHAPTER NINE

Lauren threw off the sheet and strode naked across the room. Connor watched with a mere flicker of interest from the king-sized bed in his penthouse.

"Sure you don't want me to stay?" Lauren asked, returning with a silk robe he kept for guests.

"I've got work to do."

"Ah, yes. The markets in Japan open in, what, an hour?"

"They're already open. The European markets open in an hour."

"Oh, then I'm keeping you." She pretended to be contrite.

He didn't answer, just let his gaze slide over her bared breasts. They'd had hot sex, with few words as accompaniment — the impersonal touch, as one of his previous lovers had put it.

Connor appreciated a woman who didn't mind if he didn't call her name, who didn't feel offended if he didn't lose himself in passion. Sex was purely a physical release for him, and he'd never bothered to hide the fact it was his body that was being satisfied. His mind was usually half-occupied elsewhere. Though he wouldn't want anyone to know, he'd often thought about business while caressing a woman to orgasm.

As he'd kissed Lauren's breasts earlier, he'd been planning his next day's stock purchases. When he'd entered her, he'd envisioned his next takeover, and driving fiercely toward climax, he'd been calculating whether or not the market for semi-conductors had peaked.

Lauren didn't seem to care that she didn't have his full attention.

"I have tickets to a play at the Curran next weekend. Would you want to go?" she asked.

"What is it?"

"Neil Simon. Another one of those midlife crisis stories."

"Sounds boring. Let's get together during the week. I can carve out time on Wednesday. How about dinner...here?"

"Hmmm. And we'll have sex for dessert?" She sat on the edge of the bed, pulling on the black stocking he'd recently removed with his teeth.

"Unless you're busy."

"Never too busy for you, darling. In fact..." She turned and spread her palm on his chest. "I was hoping..." Her fingers made a trail through his chest hair, down toward the sheet that covered his lower half.

"What were you hoping, Lauren?"

"That we could...indulge ourselves — again — before I go?" Her fingers struck gold under the sheet, caressing him until he had a full erection. "After all, I am ahead of you. I came...let's see now...three times, was it? Or four?" Her bland gaze met his as she stroked him.

"I believe it was four. In the shower, remember?"

"Ah yes. Then I owe you, don't I? And I do like to pay my debts." She leaned over, her mouth found him, and within minutes she'd paid him back, and more.

Afterward, he lay still while she dressed. Sex had been great — each time. He should feel satisfied, but there was an itch he couldn't scratch. Deep in a part of him he didn't acknowledge, he knew Lauren wasn't the one who could scratch it.

He had no solution for that problem, so he let it go and concentrated on problems he could solve — like what was hot on the Asian markets.

Connor fingered the tickets in his hands. His secretary had just let him know Lauren had canceled their date this evening. A board member of his foundation had offered him tickets to the opening of a play at the Mason Street Theater — an experimental adaptation of an Edward Albee play. He'd been planning to take Lauren, to make up for the Neil Simon he couldn't stomach, but she had just called and canceled, saying she had the flu.

She'd sounded terribly sorry, but Connor wasn't. He didn't particularly want to take Lauren. Though she was dynamite in bed, the rest of the time she had all the personality of an attractive dinner plate.

He wondered if Rebecca liked experimental theater.

She needed a diversion. Earlier he'd almost run into her as he'd been stepping off the elevator. She'd been too busy wiping her tears to see where she was going.

He'd put out a hand and stopped her.

"Hey, what's wrong?"

"Oh, hi, Connor. I'm sorry. I'm—it's…Oh—" She sniffed, searched for a tissue, and when he handed her a handkerchief, she dabbed at her nose and looked at him sheepishly. "I don't need to bother you with this. I know you're busy."

"I've got a few minutes. Come in here, you can tell me all about it." He steered her into a nearby conference room. "Obviously there's a problem. Is it something I can help you with?" he asked as they sat down at the table.

She swiveled her chair to face him. "Oh, no, it's Aubrey. I just hate telling her goodbye. I think this is harder on me than it is on them. It's just so sad, the way tears well up in her eyes, but she never makes a sound. I thought she'd settle in soon, but so far…"

He resisted the urge to take her in his arms. Instead, he angled his elbow on the table and propped his chin in his hand, one finger against his cheek.

"I thought you were working part time at home."

"I was, but this week I decided to start back full time."

"I see. Any particular reason?"

"Well, there is a matter of paying the bills. Part-time salary won't cover it."

"Aren't you entitled to four months of family leave?"

"Only if I give birth or adopt—and then only after I've been employed six months."

"Then perhaps the employment policies here need to be adjusted."

"Oh, Connor, it won't make any difference. Sooner or later they'll have to get used to going to daycare. And Alex is fine; it's just Aubrey. She's always been the more sensitive of the two. It's just so painful for me to see her so sad."

"That's one reason we have corporate child care on the premises. To make it as easy as possible for employees with young children."

"Yes, and I appreciate that. I really do. I don't think I could stand knowing they were far away."

"You're really attached to them, aren't you? Most young women would see the addition of two four-year-olds as an unwanted complication."

She looked shocked. "Of course they're not a complication! They're my—they're my kids! I love those guys, Connor!"

"Then there must be some way for you to stay with them. How about a six month leave of absence? We could—"

"Connor." She stopped him with her hand on his arm. "I can't quit, even temporarily. I love my job here. I don't want to give it up, even if I was willing to dip into savings."

For the first time in a long time, Connor was stymied. A problem he couldn't solve was right in front of him, and he didn't like the feeling.

He frowned. "There must be some solution. Perhaps a full time nanny—"

"It's not that. I think they like the daycare. Aubrey's just so fragile right now. Her world crumbled, and she needs to know it won't happen again. My being able to pop down and see them twice a day helps."

"I'm sure once a routine is established, they'll feel more comfortable."

"I imagine so. I've tried to stick to a schedule, but it's hard. I've always been…" She hesitated, then, making a vague gesture with her hand, stated, "…a little less programmed."

"So was my mother," Connor told her. "But she adjusted. My brother craved routine, and she saw that he got it. Personally, though, she always remained a free spirit. The two are compatible, especially when you're doing it for someone you love." And Connor had an idea a woman who dodged squirrels in the park would give up a lot of spontaneity for these children.

Rebecca smiled. "I guess you're right. Your mother sounds like an interesting person. I wish I could've met her."

He gave her an assessing look. "I have a feeling you would have gotten along great. And you probably wouldn't have been at all shocked when she introduced you to the leprechauns who lived in the orchard behind our house."

Rebecca grinned, enchanted. "Your mother believed in leprechauns?"

"She was from Ireland. They're not just a marketing tool there."

Rebecca laughed. "How on earth did you turn out so...so normal?"

"I had no choice. Someone had to. The job fell to me."

Her expression turned sober. "Poor Connor. You have a lot of responsibility, don't you? All this—" her hand swept to indicate the surroundings "—and you'd really rather go off and play with the leprechauns, wouldn't you?"

"Actually, I was considering climbing Everest."

"Oh?"

"But I suppose I'll just start up a new fund instead. Something risky. 'The Everest Fund,' we'll call it. Heavily invested in outdoor equipment," he said, half seriously.

She laughed, and Connor realized he had accomplished one thing: Her eyes shone with laughter now instead of tears. Suddenly a sharp ray of desire raced from his throat to his toes, lighting up the places in between, and Connor wondered what she'd do if he tossed her atop the empty conference table, lifted her short skirt and—

"I think you're on to something," she said. Looking at her watch, she added, "I'd better get back to work." She rose, and Connor's brief foray into erotic fantasy was cut short.

Now, sitting in his office, he realized he had the perfect excuse to ask her out. She needed a lift; he needed a date.

He picked up the phone and called her extension.

"I'm in need of a date tonight. I was hoping you'd be interested."

"You need a date?" He heard the slight emphasis on the word *you.* Or was it *need?*

"I have tickets to a play, and my date just called and canceled. She has the flu."

"Oh. That's too bad. I heard that was going around."

"Yes, well, you seemed to be in need of some cheering up earlier today. And as I was really hoping to attend the play."

"I'm not sure I can go with you. I don't have a babysitter. I've never left the twins with anyone."

"I could help you there. My housekeeper, Mrs. Pascal, has five grandchildren. She must be good with kids. I'm sure she wouldn't mind coming over and watching them."

"Well…" She hesitated, but Connor knew exactly how to get her to say yes.

"I'm really desperate. The tickets were a gift from a board member—Henrietta Dove. She'll be devastated if I don't use them."

"Oh, dear."

"I'll give you Mrs. Pascal's number. You can call her and make arrangements for her to arrive in plenty of time to meet the twins and learn the routine."

Connor could almost hear her biting her thumbnail.

"Well, there was this article I read the other day at their therapist's office. It said children need to see their parents nurturing their own interests occasionally." Then, with a sigh, she capitulated. "I suppose, if you're sure she wouldn't mind—"

"She'll be glad for the overtime."

"Will she?"

"Yes. I pay her peanuts."

Rebecca laughed. "Right. Well, I'll give her a call."

"Great. I'll pick you up you at seven thirty, then."

Connor arrived promptly at seven twenty-nine. Mrs. Pascal, who was exactly as Rebecca had pictured, had been there an hour, and the twins had already bonded with her. Even Aubry had taken her thumb out of her mouth long enough to examine the children's books Mrs. Pascal had brought along. She reminded Rebecca of her own grandmother, though she was still young enough to get on the floor with Alex and help dig his cars from their "garage" under the sofa.

Connor was wearing a dark suit. Rebecca had donned the only thing she owned that was remotely appropriate: a black knit dress that ended mid-thigh. She didn't have a suitable jacket, but fortunately the evening was warm.

"You look nice," Connor told her as she opened the door. He glanced around. "And so does this place. You've certainly improved the property."

Rebecca had decorated with a mix of antiques and new, some of Kim's things she'd brought from Illinois, and some of her own college kitsch.

"Thanks. Would you like a drink?" Rebecca asked, hoping he liked apple juice. It was all she had in the fridge.

He glanced at his watch. "No, we'd better go, if you're ready." About that time, a streak of orange and white fur pounced on his leg.

"Sam!" Rebecca disengaged the cat's claws from Connor's wool pants. "Sorry. He thinks he's a Rottweiler." She gave the cat an admonishing look and handed him to Alex. "He's really just a kitten. We got him at the animal shelter a couple of weeks ago."

"A security system wouldn't be a bad idea. Perhaps you should mention that to your landlord."

"Why? We've got Sam. He's capable of inflicting severe damage to any intruder," she said, inspecting the damage to Connor's pants. She didn't notice any snags, thank goodness.

She hugged and kissed the twins, who had already been bathed, pajamaed, and read to. "You look pretty, Rebecca. Is Connor going to kiss you?" Alex asked in a loud whisper.

Wiping the embarrassment off her face, and the juice off his, she answered, "No, honey, Connor's just a friend." But she avoided his gaze nevertheless.

Does he think of this as a date? she wondered as they walked to his car.

He opened the door for her, just like a real date, or maybe he was just being a gentleman.

Then she remembered: She was only here because his real date had canceled and he felt sorry for her.

She slid into the seat, relieved she'd solved the puzzle.

After they arrived at the theater and settled in their seats, Rebecca called to check on the twins.

"Everything all right?" Connor asked after she disconnected.

"Yes. Alex has only asked for water twice since bedtime. Mrs. Pascal must be a miracle worker. She's really very good with them. She told me her granddaughter is the same age."

"I didn't know that." Of course, he had never taken the time to find out. He had the feeling Rebecca already knew more about his housekeeper than he did, and he'd known her for eight years.

The play started, and they sat in silence, but every now and then, Connor felt her gaze on him. Every time she moved beside him—and she seemed to fidget a lot—his attention was jerked back to her. When she brushed his arm, he felt the effect through layers of suit and shirt, right through to his pounding blood.

He crossed his legs and tried to avoid contact, but the theater was old, built before a few generations of good nutrition gave humans larger frames. By the time the play was over, Connor was ready to claw his way outside his skin and into hers. But he merely stood and politely applauded his way through three curtain calls.

The play must have been a hit. Unfortunately, he couldn't remember a single line.

He hurried her through the lobby and to his car, avoiding the few acquaintances who tried to capture his attention. He wished he'd had his limo drive them. He didn't want to concentrate on driving the damn stick shift. He wanted to concentrate on what he was going to say to Rebecca.

"Would you like something to eat? Or perhaps a drink?" he said as they got into his car.

She looked at her watch. It was almost eleven. "I should get back. Your housekeeper is probably tired of twin patrol."

"I told her we'd be late."

"Well…"

The hesitation in her voice caused his eyebrow to lift questioningly. "Is that Rebecca-code for yes?"

"It's Rebecca-code for 'my better nature insists I see to my obligations rather than my own wishes.' Don't you ever have that problem?"

"Yes, but I'm used to telling my better nature to go to hell."

She laughed, a warm trickle of sound more vibrant than the classical music on the sound system. Connor felt like a kid on his first date, wondering how the evening would end. Suddenly the car felt too warm. He reached over and turned up the air conditioning.

They were driving down Haight Street. When they passed a Ben and Jerry's, Connor asked, "How about ice cream?" Rebecca made a sound of agreement, so he found a parking space a block away.

They walked up the street, past eclectic storefronts where the sweet scent of incense still lingered in the doorways. "Wouldn't it have been fun to have lived here during the sixties?" Rebecca asked as they passed a bookstore brimming with New Age materials.

"You would have been a protester, wouldn't you? Protesting the wearing of fur in Vietnam or something."

"And you'd have been part of the Establishment."

"Undoubtedly. I was part of the Establishment at six years old. I opened my first lemonade stand and sold shares to my mother's employer."

She laughed. "I can't imagine you as a child."

"I was much shorter."

He held the door open to the ice cream shop, and a wave of cold air greeted them. They spent a few moments looking over the selections behind the freezer case, then placed their orders with the dreadlocked server behind the counter.

When their bulging waffle cones were handed over, they walked to the corner and sat down at a scarred table. Rebecca tossed him a teasing glance while her tongue made a circle around the ice cream. "So, I bet you were cute. When you were six."

Connor swallowed and felt his brain freeze. "Not cute enough," he answered after a moment. "Sally Colfax didn't return my affections."

"Oh, well, that was her loss."

"Probably not. I was five years younger than her at the time. She sat in front of me on the bus."

Rebecca smiled. "So that's it. The reason you've never married. Heartbroken at the age of six by an older woman."

He concentrated on his cone of Cherry Garcia. "No. I never married because I never found a woman I'd want to wake up with for the next forty years."

"That doesn't stop some people. They just figure they'll get divorced when that time comes."

"Then why bother marrying at all?"

She nibbled off a nut from the mound of ice cream. "What about children?"

"They're cute. But I've never had a burning desire to procreate."

"No biological clock ticking?"

"No. Just an impending midlife crisis."

She slid her tongue around her cone. "Really? Are you having hot flashes?"

"Yes. Right this moment, in fact." He nodded toward the street and said, "Why don't we take this outside?"

They strolled down the block, toward the car, the only people on the street whose clothes weren't held together by safety pins.

Rebecca was too busy keeping her cone from dripping all over her dress to talk. Finally they stopped at his car.

"What about you?" Connor asked, leaning casually against the parking meter. "Still sold on the idea of a turkey baster rather than a man?"

She laughed. "It appears I don't need it. I mean, I've already got the children, and there's no turkey on my Thanksgiving menu."

"So, you've got no need for a man *or* a turkey baster." He finished off his cone in one bite.

She glanced up at him. He was staring at her with an unfathomable expression, making her unsure again whether or not he considered this a date.

But even if he did, she reminded herself, she was his second choice. Or maybe even third or fourth.

"Actually, I wouldn't say that. I mean, if the right man were to come along…"

"The one the shoe fits."

Her gaze met his. "The one who wants me more than his kingdom. Or a pair of shoes, for that matter," she said, biting into the rim of her cone.

"Are you worth a whole kingdom? Or even a good pair of Cole Haans?"

She smiled. "The right guy wouldn't have to ask."

He thought about that for a moment, then tossed his wrapper in a nearby trash can. "And what if a guy wanted to take a risk?"

"I guess he'd have to be pretty fearless."

"Or have a big ego."

She shook her head. "I prefer self-confident; no ego."

"Maybe you should make a list of requirements."

"You're one to talk. Apparently no one's measured up to Sally What's-her-name on the bus in the last three decades."

"And I have a feeling even Sally would have been a disappointment after a few trips to the ice cream store."

She sighed. "What's wrong with us, Connor? Are we just too picky? Is it hopeless? Should we compromise our principles and settle for second best?"

"I certainly have no intention of doing so."

"Yes, well, it gets lonely at the top, doesn't it?"

"Not at all. There're always companions available—on a temporary basis."

"One-night stands, you mean."

"Or longer."

"How long?"

"A few weeks. Months."

Rebecca bit through the bottom of her cone, pondering his statement. "You mean you know going into a relationship it's only going to last a short while?"

"I don't have the same kinds of needs you do. I don't want emotional attachment. Perhaps it's a fault of mine. God knows that certainly runs in the family."

"What do you mean? From the way you spoke about your mother, I would have thought—"

"My mother attached herself quite easily. That was the problem. My father didn't have any problem un-attaching himself. He left home without a word as soon as he found out my little brother was handicapped."

"Oh, Connor, I'm sorry! What happened?"

He hesitated, and Rebecca wondered if she'd overstepped, but then he replied, "Rodney's autistic. He was diagnosed when he was five. Up until then, we thought he was some kind of child genius. It turned out he operated more like a computer. He has amazing memory circuits, but he can't interpret the millions of bits of information stored up there." He tapped his head. "He's frustrating as hell to talk to."

"Who takes care of him?"

"I've hired a couple who live there with him, in the same house where we grew up. Rodney hates for anything in his environment to change. So, I've made sure it doesn't."

"You must love him a lot."

"I take care of him. Financially. That's really all Rodney needs. That and a television with a hundred and fifty channels."

"Then why do you go visit him once a month? Is it for him, or for you?"

"Someone has to make sure things are running smoothly. Besides, as you pointed out, it's a nice vacation. I have a house not far from there, within hearing distance of the ocean. Very few people even know about it. It's a great place to get away."

"By yourself?"

"What's the point of getting away if you bring someone?"

She shook her head and smiled. "Don't you ever need anyone?"

"No. I don't think I ever have." He looked at her through the light-sprinkled night. "Not in the emotional sense. I've got physical needs, yes. Unlike you, I do see the need for sex every now and then." His mouth curved in a half smile.

"Sex without love?"

"Yes."

She was quiet.

"I take it you wouldn't be interested in that."

"I don't know. I've never tried it."

"You mean you've been in love with every man you've dated?"

"No. I've just never had sex with them." She glanced up and waited, amused, for the fallout that line got every time.

"Are you telling me you've never had sex?"

In the darkness, she could just make out the look of stunned disbelief on his features.

She folded her arms across her chest and gave him a faint smile. "That's right."

"That can't be normal."

"You've never fallen in love. In my book, *that* can't be normal."

"It's perfectly normal. It takes much more effort to fall in love than it does to have sex."

She shrugged. "How would you know?"

He continued to stare at her while a couple of leftover hippies strolled by, trailing the scent of pot. Finally he agreed. "You're right. We've both obviously got problems. You can't find the perfect man to have sex with; I can't find the perfect woman to fall in love with."

"The difference is, you—" she pointed a finger at him "—aren't even trying."

"You're right. Why search for something you haven't lost?"

"Why climb Everest?" she pointed out with a shrug. "Because it's there. There's love out there, too, Connor. I may not have found it yet, but I'm willing to accept the notion it exists. And that it's worth having, and worth waiting for."

"The Buddhists say we should give up our attachments. Even to people. Attachments are simply a cause of unhappiness, because we can never truly have another person."

"And a car is a good substitute? Or a hotel? Or whatever company you've bought this week?"

"I never said they were substitutes. Merely diversions."

"Maybe you wouldn't need so many diversions if you truly cared about someone."

"Perhaps. But as long as I can afford the diversions…" He shrugged. "Why not?"

She sighed. "Because cars don't crawl in bed with you at night and wrap their arms around you so tight you can't even breathe."

"Sounds dangerous."

"It is. Loving someone is always risky. Just ask the twins. But they're willing to give it another go. You, on the other hand, prefer safe investments like…like shipping companies and blue chip stocks."

"Precisely. But I don't see you taking any risks, either, Miss Evans. Afraid passion might lead your heart down the wrong path?"

"Maybe. I do have a tendency to fall for losers."

"So did my mother. Look where it got her."

"She had two sons she loved—"

"And a husband she never stopped waiting for. Don't do that to yourself, Rebecca. Trust me, it's a no-win situation. It's much easier not to care."

She shook her head. "Sorry. I'm not buying that. And I don't think you do either. You're just afraid you'll end up like your mother. Not every relationship results in one person being hurt, Connor."

She put her hand on his arm. His eyes, despite the streetlight reflecting in them, were dark as nightfall, and just as unfathomable.

"Are you saying you'd take that risk yourself?" he asked her. "The risk you'd eventually be hurt?"

She was quiet a moment. She was familiar with hurt, on a first-name basis now. Hurt had eaten a hole in her heart and left it bleeding, aching…and then filled it with another pint full of love. Two pints, actually.

Slowly, she smiled at him in the dark. "Yes. I'd risk it. In a heartbeat."

Connor was quiet a moment, his gaze opaque and unbending. Somewhere a traffic light turned green, reflecting off the parking meter beside them, and finally he spoke. "Are you sure about that?"

Suddenly, Rebecca was aware of something new bubbling in the air between them, as wispy and nebulous as incense smoke. Up until now, she had been convinced this was a hypothetical situation they were discussing—a vague possibility, a perhaps-one-day thought to ponder. Yet now, as she felt the dark heat of his gaze, she realized there was a distinct possibility that not only did Connor consider this a date, but that he wanted it to end in bed.

Had this been what they were dancing around? All those cordial, yet oddly intimate moments these past few months—in his car, in her office, on the elevator—and at the theater, when she could feel his attention on her, her nerve endings pirouetting in response.

She inhaled sharply, a little giddy at the thought.

"What are you saying, Connor? Is this some kind of dare you subject your friends to? A game of emotional chicken?"

"No. It's not a game. I'm totally serious. I have been for some time now."

"Serious about—?"

"Wanting to have sex with you."

"Ahh."

He continued to lean against the parking meter, unmoving, as if they were discussing the price of downtown parking. "Don't tell me you're surprised."

She smiled weakly, as self-consciousness found a familiar pit in her stomach and crawled in. "Sometimes I'm clueless about things like this."

"Maybe that's how you've remained a virgin all these years."

She laughed. "Possibly," she agreed.

"Of course, if you're still waiting for the right man…"

"Maybe you *are* the right man."

"That's doubtful," he said with such an air of finality, Rebecca was instantly on edge.

"You think it's impossible?"

"I think it's highly unlikely. We're two entirely different people. We don't want the same things out of life. I'm older than you—and much more experienced."

"True. But I wasn't looking for a clone."

"I know what you're looking for, Rebecca. And believe me, I'm not him. I won't woo you with phone calls and chaste kisses while you make up your mind whether or not you want to go to bed with me. I won't send greeting cards full of false sentiments on your birthday, or the anniversaries we'll never get around to having. I won't ever grow old with you in our mortgaged house with a view of the soccer field," he said, his voice flat, then he continued relentlessly, as if determined to expose the truth. "I will, however, take you to the best restaurants—anywhere in the world; see that you receive equal—or greater—pleasure in bed; and when it's over, send you a token of my esteem. Usually a watch, sometimes diamonds. Once a car."

"My God, Connor! You talk about sex like it's just another business deal!"

"I honestly don't see much difference."

She laughed bitterly. "You'd better keep an eye out for the vice squad. It sounds like you're talking about high class prostitution."

He shrugged. "If both parties are satisfied, I see no problem."

"Well, I do. What you're describing is…is…the farthest thing from love."

"Which is why I never use the word. In my experience, most people who claim they experience it are thinking primarily of themselves and their own needs."

"And your mother? She was thinking of herself all those years she pined for your father?"

"Yes, in a way. My father apparently filled some need in her, a need to take care of someone—an undeserving someone, in this case. She was a nurse, after all. It was in her nature to care for others."

"You honestly believe that. You think human beings are incapable of total, selfless love."

"Not all of them. Mother Teresa comes to mind. I'm just saying I'm not equipped for that kind of emotional investment."

"Maybe you are and you just don't know it."

"That's the kind of thinking that will get you into trouble."

"Not unless I fall in love with you myself," she pointed out with confidence she didn't feel.

"Don't do that, Rebecca." He sighed. "That's exactly why I haven't floated my 'business proposition' before now. I know you're the type to imagine yourself in love with whomever you're with—and I don't want to be the lucky guy who takes your virginity and breaks your heart."

Rebecca wanted to protest, but a part of her knew he was right. He could break her heart; she was already close to falling in love with him—and not totally convinced he was as coldhearted as he claimed.

He turned and opened the car door. "It's late. I should be getting you home."

She got inside, and when he'd joined her, she turned to him and asked, "So, what does this mean? Are we friends, Connor?" She swallowed a sudden stirring of pity, then added, a bitter edge to her voice, "Or is even that sentiment too much for you to handle?"

Ignoring the sarcasm, he started the ignition. "Of course we're friends—if you wish. I never should have told you that I viewed you as anything else." He slid the car in gear, then continued, "As a matter of fact, I think you should forget about ninety percent of the conversation we just had."

She was quiet as they pulled away from the curb, then she said, more rhetorically than combatively, "Why is it you who gets to decide the nature of our relationship? Why shouldn't I have a say in the matter?"

He glanced at her. "You're the smartest woman I've ever met, Rebecca. You should be able to figure that out," he said with a wry smile.

Rebecca gave an exasperated sigh as he drove into the night. The compliment should have appealed to her ego, if she'd had one, but she was just a little irked. She wasn't at all sure she wanted to forget his words, especially the part about wanting to go to bed with her.

She was pretty sure she was ready for that—and pretty sure she wanted Connor to be the one, even if the relationship didn't end happily ever after. Since Kim's death, she'd been all too aware that life was far too short, and love far too elusive. She could settle for attraction—and that flutter she felt tickle her tummy whenever Connor looked at her.

She'd always been attracted to older men; Kim had sworn she was trying to replace a father figure. But Rebecca knew it was because guys her own age were more interested in shopping for electronic gadgets than searching for enlightenment.

Connor, on the other hand, was mature, thoughtful, intelligent. She watched as he skillfully maneuvered the car through its gears. There was something sexy about a man and a stick shift. She shivered, thinking of those hands on her...stroking, caressing.

Maybe, she thought as they neared her house, it was time she stopped waiting for a man to seduce her and learned to do the seducing herself.

CHAPTER TEN

*U*nfortunately, the next few days gave her no time to learn any seduction techniques. Bob was out on vacation, and the twins were invited to a birthday party. They also had doctor appointments as well as therapy once a week.

Then there was the fact that Rebecca was chicken. She admitted it while getting ready for bed on another Friday night she'd spent with the twins for "dates." Every time she started to pick up the phone and call him, she lost her nerve at the thought of risking her heart in a game where the odds were already stacked against her. This was a man who'd told her he had no intention of falling in love, a man who wore armor around his emotions and kept his heart in cold storage.

The same man, she reminded herself, who held her tenderly when she cried, who made her laugh in unexpected moments, who insisted he didn't want to hurt her.

He'd been very polite about it, she remembered, pulling down the covers and climbing into bed alone, but he was still adamant that he'd do nothing to further a sexual relationship.

She sighed and punched her pillow. Damn it, why did she have to fall for someone who was too nice to break her heart?

The next morning, Rebecca was awakened by a cold foot. She rolled over and almost crushed Aubrey, who must have joined her sometime in the night, as she often did.

"Good morning, sweetie," she said, yawning.

Aubrey didn't answer; she just stared at her with big blue eyes, her thumb stuck firmly in her mouth. She must have had another bad dream, Rebecca thought, remembering the therapist's advice to encourage Aubrey to talk through her fears.

"What did you dream about last night?" she asked.

Aubrey removed her thumb just long enough to whisper, "I dreamed my mommy came back."

Rebecca wanted to cry, but instead she gave her an encouraging smile. "Tell me what happened."

"We went to the park to see the windmills."

"Just you and your mommy?"

"And Alex and you and Sam." Then her eyes filled with sadness. "But Sam got lost, and I cried."

"That would be sad," Rebecca agreed. "But look, Sam's right here, at the foot of the bed. See?" She peered up over the blanket and nudged the sleepy cat with her foot. He woke up and yawned, then began licking his paw delicately.

Aubrey's thumb went back in her mouth, and Rebecca knew it wasn't the fear over losing Sam that had prompted the dream. Aubrey still missed her mother and father. But at least she was talking about them. For a while, she had never mentioned either of her parents. The psychologist had told her that was an indication that she hadn't fully accepted their loss.

"I wish your mommy *could* come back," Rebecca said, stroking Aubrey's damp hair from her forehead. "And your daddy too. We'd take them to see the windmills and the beach and the dragons in Chinatown."

Aubrey shook her head.

"No? No dragons? Okay, then, we'll skip Chinatown and go see the Painted Ladies instead." Then she stopped. She didn't want to give her the impression she really believed her parents would come back. "You know we can't really do all that, but I think they would like to know where you live now. I think they'd like to hear all about Sam, and your ballerina book, and our new house, and your friends at daycare," she went on, "and everything else that you're doing. Maybe if you close your eyes and think real hard, your mommy and daddy will hear you up in heaven."

The thumb stayed in the mouth, but the big blue eyes staring at her held a trace of hope.

"I tell your mommy stuff all the time, just like I used to."

"Does she hear you?"

"I don't know." Rebecca had to be honest with her. "But it makes me feel better." That was the truth, too. Rebecca did feel better after "talking" to her sister, and she felt sure Aubrey needed to retain a connection to her mother, and her father, no matter how tenuous. That's why she made sure their names came into the conversation naturally, whenever possible. Though they weren't here physically, she knew the twins hadn't forgotten them any more than she had.

Aubrey closed her eyes, and her face screwed up in concentration. Eventually Rebecca felt her little body relax, and the thumb edged from between her teeth. When Sam got up and came toward them, Aubrey opened her eyes and smiled. Then Sam poked his nose under her chin and tickled her with his whiskers, and she giggled.

After breakfast, the phone rang. It was Jo Severson, Randy's mother. Rebecca sighed. She knew what this was about. Her mother had warned her there'd be fallout.

"I couldn't believe it when I heard what you'd done! After what that man did, you'd think you'd want to see justice done."

"He feels guilty for what he did, and he's paid enormously for it these last few months. Now it's possible he could do some good in the community service program."

"The man killed our son! He hasn't suffered nearly as much as we have. He deserves worse than the slap on the hand you recommended in your letter to the judge. How could you, after what we've all been through? After what those children — my grandchildren —"

"The twins need to get on with their lives. We all do. There's no point in dragging this out in a long trial when both sides are willing to plea bargain."

She heard a disgusted sniff. "You expect us to get on with our lives with a murderer running loose?"

"I have. And the twins are starting to —"

"They've lost their parents! Surely you don't expect them to just go on like nothing happened."

"No, of course I don't—"

But Jo Severson had worked herself into a state. "I have to wonder if you're really committed to those kids. Maybe you just wanted the money."

"I haven't touched the insurance money. That's for their education." She glanced out the window. The twins were playing on the swing set in the back yard, enjoying the summer afternoon.

"If you're worried about their education, then why on earth aren't you sending them to kindergarten in the fall? They'll be old enough by the time school starts."

"Kim and I talked about it months ago. She didn't feel they were mature enough, emotionally, to handle the transition. And I agree. Aubrey still sucks her thumb—"

"I told you how to cure that."

Rebecca wasn't about to take her advice to put noxious ointment on Aubrey's thumbs. But she didn't want to antagonize Jo Severson further, so she replied lightly, "The doctor says she'll stop eventually—at least by the time she gets to college!"

When Rebecca finally hung up the phone, she sighed with relief. She'd known she'd anger the Seversons with the letter she'd written to the judge responsible for sentencing Melvin Dailey. He'd pled guilty to charges of vehicular manslaughter, a lesser charge. Rebecca, as well as her mother and Randy's parents, had been asked to provide testimony on the impact of his actions for the sentencing. Instead, she had written a letter to the judge in the case, explaining her belief that the man's own guilt would punish him the rest of his life. Locking him up for twenty years, leaving his own family without his income, wouldn't do as much good as requiring him to perform community service. With his heartfelt regret, he would be the perfect person to illustrate to others the serious consequences of drinking and driving.

Her own mother disagreed with her. But Rebecca couldn't help her feelings, and though she didn't want to minimize the impact of the tragedy on anyone, she wanted some good to come out of it. If Melvin Dailey could convince even one person to think twice before getting behind the wheel, in her opinion, he ought to be given the chance.

However, the Seversons didn't see it that way. They wanted to throw the man in prison for a lifetime, and watch while he performed hard labor. They were entitled to their own opinions, of course, and

Rebecca wanted the twins' grandparents to have some influence in their lives, but she was ultimately responsible for their welfare. Kim would want her to stick to her guns where her mother-in-law was concerned.

Looking out at the two of them, playing Peter Pan and Wendy in the back yard, Rebecca had to believe she was doing an okay job with them.

Just then Alex roared and jumped from the top of the slide. Rebecca winced, but then he scrambled up, charging after an imaginary Hook. She smiled and went outside to warn Peter Pan about the effects of gravity.

While the twins were taking their naps, she tried to catch up on some work she'd brought home. Her mind kept wandering away from the computer screen in front of her, from the industry simulation she was working on to another problem she was determined to solve, another "script" she intended to write.

She wished she could talk to Connor about the letter she'd sent to the judge, and the Seversons' reaction to it, but she'd bothered him enough with her problems. And after their conversation the other night, she wasn't sure how to proceed with him. Either he wanted to sleep with her or he wanted to be her friend. Apparently, he couldn't accommodate both.

That same giddy excitement tightened her stomach muscles, just thinking about the possibility of spending a night in Connor's arms. He'd be a good lover — she instinctively knew that, knew he'd be careful, considerate — and remembering how calmly he'd stated he wanted her, she felt another jolt of longing, just at the thought of unleashing the passion beneath the smooth surface.

The price of that passion would be losing the friendship that had come to mean a lot to her. But a part of her — the part that craved red sports cars and short skirts and tightrope walking across the clothesline — that part wanted to jump in the deep end and see where she bobbed up.

The part of her that climbed trees to rescue kites and took in stray kittens and kissed bandaged knees, the part that baked cookies for lonely bachelors — that part wanted to rescue this emotionally stranded man who looked at her with well-concealed longing, like a little boy who knew better than to want a second helping of dessert.

Could she give him both? The friendship, companionship he seemed to need, and the unencumbered sex he claimed he wanted? And would he take it if she offered?

She suspected Connor was capable of much more than he knew. She'd seen evidence of a loving, caring man beneath the formal business suits and stiff reserve. Away from his own turf—in the park, for instance—he seemed a little more relaxed, a little more carefree.

An idea formed, one that seemed to make perfect sense. Leaving the twins for any length of time was out of the question; for the sake of convenience, if nothing else, she would have to make her move here, at her house—on her own turf.

She smiled and typed in the password to log on to the FGI computer. All she needed now was the right moment.

And a few aromatherapy candles.

Connor skirted an outcropping of rock, his running shoes digging in the wet sand where the waves sucked at his footprints. He'd come up north to see Rodney this weekend, but also to get away from the temptation of Rebecca.

He'd made a mess of things the other night.

Not only had he not succeeded in getting what he wanted, but he'd thrown a nice little kink into their friendship.

He just hoped he hadn't ruined it by admitting he wanted to sleep with her. He still didn't intend to do anything about it. He knew, inevitably, any sexual relationship they had would eventually turn sour, and a friendship that was beginning to mean a great deal to him would be lost.

He didn't like losing. If this were a business deal, he'd figure out how to get exactly what he wanted without giving up too much in return.

But he had a feeling Rebecca would probably balk at a thirty-day option to purchase.

He dodged a dead cormorant, cursing himself for stupidity.

He'd wanted to quash any illusions she'd had about him—and in the process, he'd practically admitted he viewed women as prostitutes. Any female in his acquaintance would have immediately called him out. Rebecca, however, had merely given him a look of pity along with her pique.

Then there'd been an almost superior edge to the smile she'd given him as she'd gotten out of his car. He wasn't used to being the recipient of superior smiles.

Up ahead, a group of seals were sunning themselves on a large rock that rose up from the ocean. Deciding he didn't want to disturb them, Connor turned around and headed home.

He crossed the highway and jogged along the wooded path that led to his secluded home, designed with glassed-in angles and cedar decks that jutted aggressively into the rocky hillside. He thought of it as an ascetic monk's retreat, and though he'd had it furnished with modern appliances and comfortable Scandinavian furniture rather than bare cots and dusty incense holders, something of a Spartan monastery environment remained. He never brought guests here, though Rodney had a room for the few occasions he stayed over.

When he reached the house, he phoned Adrian to make sure things were on track with Bourgikos, then made himself a quick omelet.

After breakfast, he called Helen and made arrangements to visit her while he was in town. The Millers were planning to visit their daughter, and Connor had agreed to stay with Rodney for the night. Though Rodney was mostly self-sufficient, Connor didn't like to leave him alone. There was always the chance he'd leave the stove on and burn down the house.

They'd play a game of Trivial Pursuit, and, as usual, Rodney would win. Connor couldn't compete when it came to memorizing minutia. Then he'd work on the shareholder's report due Monday.

As he packed his bag for the visit, Connor decided he was overdue for a vacation, a real vacation. He thought of his beach estate in Maui. He hadn't been there in a year. He could pull out time from his schedule for a quick trip, but the thought of enjoying the slice of paradise alone seemed indulgent.

Maybe he'd invite Rebecca and the twins—provided she forgave him for the obnoxious way he'd behaved the other night. His throat tightened at the thought of Rebecca in the lush Hawaiian setting, lolling on his beach in a bikini.

He'd never brought a woman there, either, but there was always a first time, he decided as he zipped his bag shut and slung it over his shoulder.

CHAPTER ELEVEN

After lunch in the courtyard, Rebecca and the twins were walking back to the childcare center when Alex spotted a trail of ants crossing the sidewalk. They all stopped. The twins had been fascinated recently with insects, and Rebecca had a few minutes before she needed to return to her office.

As they peered down to watch the tiny team of dirt movers, Rebecca heard footsteps, then a familiar voice.

"Lose something?"

"Oh, hi, Connor. We're just looking at the ants." Rebecca squinted up at him, her heart racing a little faster at the sight of him outlined in the sunlight.

"Ahh. Of course." He didn't seem to find it the least bit unusual to find them squatting on their haunches in the middle of the courtyard, staring at a line of ants forging a path to the rock garden. Instead, he knelt down on one knee to join them.

Rebecca breathed in the scent of soap and something indescribably sophisticated—Asian spice, she wondered? His hair was a bit damp, and she guessed he'd just come from the gym. He was wearing her favorite blue silk tie again. She bit her lip.

He glanced up at her. "Are things going better this week?"

She nodded, glancing down at Aubrey's bent head. "No more tears. You were right. A routine helps."

Blue eyes continued to gaze at her, questioning. "Peggy said you stopped by."

She blinked. *Time to execute program.* She smiled brightly and said, "I wanted to invite you for dinner." He didn't say anything, and she plunged ahead. "I owe you one, remember? After my house hunting trip? I told you, you could be our first guest. How about this weekend?" He still didn't say anything, so she went on, determined to convince him. "I bought this great Italian cookbook. I've been dying to try it, but these guys don't appreciate pasta that comes from anything but a can." She laughed. "Although they love dessert. There's this peach thing—"

"I don't think that would be a good idea." Connor straightened, his hands in his pockets, and she remembered this was a man known for his shrewd maneuvering. With a barely perceptible sigh, he continued, "For all the reasons I mentioned the other night. We have different goals here. You want companionship, commitment. I want…something else."

She rose. "Maybe I want the something else too," she said, meeting his gaze squarely.

"The problem is you want them both. It would be impossible—"

"Nothing's impossible, Connor."

He frowned. "Believe me, if I thought there were a chance…"

Her heart took a little dive. He didn't even think there was a chance? But she went on bravely, "All I'm doing is inviting you to dinner. You know, friends do that sometimes. It's a simple gesture, really. No need to make it all complex with hidden motives and agendas."

He almost smiled. "You're incapable of hidden agendas."

That's what you think, she wanted to say, but returned his smile instead, lifting her arms in a shrug. "So, what's the problem?"

He merely looked at her, his expression inscrutable.

"How about this weekend—Saturday night? That will give me a chance to go grocery shopping, clean up the place." She laughed as if she had no intention of buying a black negligee and a dozen Romance aromatherapy candles for her bedroom.

He waited a beat, long enough for Alex to chime in. "Hey! You could come over and play Monopoly with me! Can he, Rebecca? Please? You always let me win."

"I do not!" she protested. "I just never roll double sixes."

Connor's eyes creased with mock seriousness as he gazed down at Alex. "I warn you: I don't let anyone win. Not even four-year-olds."

"I'll be five in — how many days, Rebecca?"

"Twenty-eight. That's four weeks."

"And we're having a party. You can come if you want to. We're having two cakes."

"Two cakes?"

Alex nodded. "Aubrey wants a ballerina cake, and I want one with trucks on it. So, we're having two. You can have some of mine if you want."

"That sounds nice. How about I check my schedule and get back to you?" Connor told him with a serious look, and Rebecca knew he'd do just that.

The man really was wasted as a bachelor. He should have an armful of kids. That was useless thinking on her part, and no doubt she wasn't the first woman who'd had the thought, but Rebecca couldn't get the picture out of her head.

Step one, go on the offensive. Red wine, black lace, and Romance candles turned up high.

"So, Saturday's okay?" she prompted.

He looked at her for a moment, as if weighing the danger. Finally, with just a note of reluctance, he said, "Saturday's fine."

When the doorbell rang on Saturday night, Rebecca sent Alex to answer it. She'd put on a gauzy black sundress that showed off the tan she'd acquired in the backyard wading pool she'd bought for the twins.

She heard footsteps on the hardwood floors, and then Connor was in her kitchen, a bottle of wine in his hand. He was dressed casually, in a navy polo shirt and khakis. She almost missed the office look. She'd grown fond of his suits.

She took the bottle from him: a California merlot. Probably expensive, but it would go well with the seduction she'd planned for dessert. "That's nice. But you didn't have to bring anything."

"I picked it up from the sommelier at the Towers. He assured me it went well with Italian."

She smiled. "Dinner is almost ready. Aubrey, could you find the corkscrew for Connor? You were operating on your doll with it earlier."

After dinner, Connor helped clear the table and stuff the few dishes into the small dishwasher. Rebecca was impressed. She didn't think there were too many billionaires who knew how to load a dishwasher.

Alex found the Monopoly Junior game and set it up, carefully counting out the cash for each player. They sat around on the floor, and then Connor proceeded to trounce them. Alex and Aubrey didn't seem to mind, but Rebecca decided he needed a handicap.

Keeping her gaze on the board, she hiked her skirt up a little higher—enough to show a healthy amount of her new tan. Then she threw the dice, and landed on Connor's cotton candy stand. Connor didn't notice, even though he'd placed a ticket booth there and she owed him ten dollars.

She handed the die to Alex and cheered as he landed on Aubrey's Ferris wheel. When Connor's gaze kept straying to her own "property," she felt a tiny thrill of victory, despite the fact that now Alex was racking up the cash. On her next turn, she rolled doubles. She took a third turn just to see if Connor was paying attention, but his gaze was firmly fixed on her left thigh.

"Hey! You had too many turns, Rebecca!" Alex, unfortunately, was keeping count.

"Sorry," she said, and started to hand the die to Connor. She managed to drop one—and had to lean over his knees to retrieve it. As her breast brushed his thigh, she heard his sharp intake of breath.

She straightened, and with what she hoped was a seductive smile, murmured, "Your turn." It wasn't, but he went anyway.

When they ended the game, Aubrey had the most money. Rebecca had "accidentally" landed on her Ferris wheel twice, and Connor, she was pretty sure, had slipped her an extra five when he paid her rent on her haunted house.

Amid yawns, the twins put the game away. Then it was time for the nightly shuffle: bath, books, and bed, in that order. The twins were capable of handling the first without Rebecca, but the second—reading two books of their choice—required her help. Connor waited patiently downstairs as she hurried through, then switched on the nightlight near the door, and left them nodding off among a pile of stuffed animals.

Connor was downstairs with a drink in his hand, staring at a photo of Kim.

"Aubrey looks like your sister," he said, picking up the frame and studying it closer.

Rebecca was glad he didn't avoid talking about Kim; sometimes she desperately needed to say her sister's name.

"Yes. Kim got my dad's blue eyes; I'm a throwback to my Italian great-grandmother."

Connor replaced the photo frame. "It's been over three months. Is it any easier?"

She took a sip of the wine she'd saved from dinner. "It's easier, I suppose, if you mean by that my chest doesn't feel like it's caving in every time I wake up and realize I'm facing another day without my sister in the world. But am I ever going to stop missing her?" She shook her head. "I don't think so. I have conversations with her in my head all the time. The only problem is she can't answer. She always knew just what to say when I couldn't figure out the latest development in my life. Like you, for instance." She took another sip of the wine and watched his face. "She would have put in overtime telling me to forget all about you, that you're not the right man for me."

"And she'd have been right. Rebecca, I told you—"

She shook her head. "I've decided I don't want to listen to your good advice. This time I don't care if I'm making a mistake. If I want to have an affair with someone who just might break my heart, then I will." She kept her gaze on him as she sipped her wine. For courage, she told herself.

"If you won't take my advice, then take your sister's."

Rebecca's gaze fell to the picture. "She played it safe, and look where it got her. You know, they were both wearing their seat belts when they were killed. They weren't speeding; the car was equipped with airbags." She shrugged. "So I want to jump without a safety net. Big deal. I've been hurt before, Connor."

He smiled faintly. "I don't go around sleeping with women who aren't equipped for the fallout."

She raised an eyebrow. "You make it sound like a nuclear reaction."

"I think it's been described that way a few times."

She turned and walked to the couch, hiding a smile. "Okay. Show me what you've got."

"Excuse me?"

"I want a demonstration. Who knows, we might not even be compatible. I might think your nose is too long, for example, or maybe you kiss cold—without any warm up. That always irritated me, you know, when some guy just expects me to want to share his saliva without so much as a 'get acquainted' pat on the knee."

She plopped down on the couch and gazed at him with what she hoped with a sexy pout— she was in entirely new territory here. But she was convinced, if all his sidelong glances during the game were any indication, that he really, really wanted a physical relationship, regardless of all his earlier protests.

Connor blinked. "You want me to audition?"

"Sure. Why not? If I'm risking my heart here, I ought to at least know if you're worth it. Think of it as a business deal. I get to inspect the goods before I sign on the dotted line."

He looked down at her, feigning calm for all he was worth. "I generally prefer calling the shots, Rebecca. In business deals and in the bedroom." In fact, just the thought of not being in control sent shivers of fear skittering down his spine.

"Don't tell me you're one of those guys who always has to be on top."

She smiled innocently, but her eyes glowed with seductive challenge. She crossed her legs and stroked a fat red candle on the coffee table with one bare toe. Connor had to remind himself he was dealing with a virgin. Or else a multiple personality. He had a feeling she was about to whip out the handcuffs and black silk, and he'd be doomed. Just the thought of Rebecca's legs encased in black silk stockings…

"Actually, I have no preference as to position." He did, but he wasn't about to give her details—yet.

"I bet you plan it all out. Step one: Take off tie. Step two: Pull down the sheets. Step three: Unbutton her blouse." She toyed with the buttons on her dress and gave him an inviting look.

He crossed his arms and smiled from across the room. "You forgot the shoes. They're always the first to go."

"Ahh. See? I'm learning something already."

"And I think you've learned enough for one night. I'd better be going, anyway." He glanced pointedly at his watch. "I have a meeting in the morning."

She shook her head. "Uh-uh. I don't think so." She sat on the couch, looking at him with those gold-tinted eyes that came from some Italian ancestor. Probably a courtesan involved in Caesar's downfall. He had a feeling he was next on the list, unless he managed to get out the door and off her porch and into his very fast car in exactly—

"I bought condoms."

He closed his eyes and pinched the bridge of his nose. "All right. That's it. Thanks for dinner, Rebecca, but I'm really not planning—"

"Then you *were* lying before. When you said you were serious about wanting to take me to bed."

He considered lying now—honesty be damned, when the truth came with attachments. Instead, he hedged. "The thought had crossed my mind a few times, that's all. But it was a bad idea, as I pointed out. And since I don't tend to hang onto bad ideas, with your permission I think I'll say goodnight. Now," he said firmly, setting his wine glass on the coffee table.

She sighed. "You know how long it's been since anyone's kissed me, Connor? Really kissed me?"

He glanced at her over the flame of the candle. "If the critique you just issued is any example of your prelude, I would imagine it's been a while."

She looked crestfallen. "Oh dear, did I intimidate you? Damn. I always screw this up. See? I told you. I'm not very good at this." She gave a short laugh. "It's really not any wonder I'm still a virgin after twenty-six years."

"You've never gotten that far, have you?"

"No! And from the looks of it, I won't be getting that far tonight, either." She gave him a grumpy look that was quite at odds with the siren look she'd thrown at him earlier, and which, oddly, he found more attractive. She pulled a pillow in front of her. "What is it about me, Connor, that makes me always say the wrong thing at the right time?"

"Maybe you're not as ready for this as you think you are."

"I'm twenty-six years old! Don't tell me I'm going to hit thirty without knowing what it's like to…to…"

"There's no deadline." He moved a doll-sized automobile and sat on the opposite end of the sofa from her. "Your biological clock hasn't even gone on the downswing yet."

"It's not my biological clock. I told you, there's no hurry to have kids. But I want someone to share my life with, Connor, even if it's only a few hours."

"You don't want to settle for that. I know you, Rebecca. You want commitment."

"I've got commitment! Those guys —" She pointed upstairs. "They're all the commitment I need right now. I want someone to touch me, to make me feel like I'm a woman instead of a machine that goes around programming computers and wiping stuffy noses and reading two-minute bedtime stories every night."

Connor's take on the situation suddenly shifted. Perhaps she was right. Maybe what she needed from him, what he wanted from her, were exactly the same. But then he wasn't sure anymore what it was he wanted from her. A quick roll in the sheets didn't seem appropriate for a woman who had saved herself this long, waiting for the perfect guy. "I could give you that. Anyone could. But in the morning, you'd wonder why you settled for less."

She gave him a perplexed little smile. "Why are you raising so many objections, Connor? Aren't I offering you exactly what you want? Sex with no strings?"

He'd just tried to tell himself exactly that, but his mind wasn't buying it. She'd want more from him than he could give her, more than a hot night of passion in whichever bed he took her to.

Her eyes were still turned on him, full of needs he knew he could satisfy, if only for one night. He dropped his gaze to her mouth. Her lips parted slightly in invitation, and he felt his self-control slipping. It had never failed him before, but he'd never had to battle the image of Rebecca in black silk before.

She slid closer, then reached out and laid her hand on his knee, her fingers caressing his kneecap through the material of his pants, and suddenly he was in second gear without having hit the clutch. Unless he took over very soon, they'd be hurtling down the hillside at neck-breaking speed.

"Kiss me, Connor," she said, her voice husky with longing, and he found himself in third, wondering if he'd buckled his seatbelt.

Maybe he should do as she asked. Maybe he should prove to her that he was far too experienced for her. Too old.

But he didn't feel old. He felt like he had the first time, at the age of seventeen, when he'd dropped by Jennifer Gorman's house and found her parents conveniently gone and a long comfortable couch nearby.

His blood pounded in his veins. Rebecca leaned toward him, eyelids dipping low over her eyes, clearly intending to make the first move if he didn't.

He remembered what she'd said about warm-up. He reached out and touched her behind the ear. Her hair was piled on top of her head, leaving the territory open for exploration. A few tendrils, though, had escaped and teased the back of his hand as he trailed his fingers around her neck. She shivered, her eyes never leaving his.

They were warm gold now, lit with anticipation, and he wondered if she had any idea what he wanted to do to her.

Her hand on his leg moved.

Desire raced through his bloodstream, and he'd yet to do more than touch her neck, her ear. He took a breath, his usual calm threatening to desert him.

Lifting her hand from its wandering journey along his thigh, he caressed her fingers, then brought them to his mouth and kissed the pads of her fingers, nibbling on the ends.

Somewhere a clock ticked, its heavy tocking like a metronome to his heartbeat. He heard her sigh, and he forgot everything: the twins upstairs, the meeting he had in the morning, the Japanese markets, and his objections to taking her to bed. All he wanted now was to lose himself in this attraction, plug into the current of pure electricity that flowed between them, white hot and dangerous.

With a quiet groan, he bent his head and crushed his mouth against hers. Soft warm lips met his, opened, and he tasted peaches, wine, and sweet, urgent, desire.

She knew how to kiss. God, she might be a virgin, but the woman definitely knew how to kiss. Her tongue played with his, a teasing game of tag he didn't want to win, while her fingers raked through his hair, sending the current directly to his groin. She was all fire and raw emotion, throwing herself into the act, holding nothing back. He felt the urge to lay her down and meld with the heat, for just a moment…until sanity reared its cool head.

He pulled back, relieved to find a thin thread of control still within his reach. "I told you this was a bad idea," he said, struggling to breathe evenly.

"Umm-hmm. You were right. It's a very bad idea." Her leg came up and trapped him on the sofa. "Kiss me again," she demanded, bringing his head down toward her mouth.

He obliged, free falling toward the abyss.

He didn't know how it happened. One minute they were upright, the next they were lying on the sofa, their bodies pressing into the soft cushions. Her legs tangled with his, her bare foot stroking his calf and sending a little lick of fire racing along his body, eating at his resolve.

Feeling as if he were in the path of a controlled burn, one that had quickly gotten out of hand, Connor let himself be consumed. Just a moment longer, he told himself as he kissed her again, meeting her heat with his own.

She moaned, and his muscles clamped with desire.

Then a heart-stopping scream from above doused the flames.

CHAPTER TWELVE

"It's Aubrey." Rebecca jumped up and raced upstairs to the room the twins shared. Thankfully, Alex still slept, curled into a ball next to Aubrey, who sat upright in bed, eyes closed, loud wails coming from her tiny mouth. The dim glow of the night light was enough to see that there was no blood, no intruder, and no apparent reason for the screams.

Rebecca held her on her lap, smoothing her damp hair from her face, murmuring softly. Finally, the screams subsided, and Aubrey relaxed into sleep.

Rebecca looked at Connor, who stood in the doorway, concern etched on his face. "She's had these since she was a baby—night terrors. The pediatrician said she'll outgrow it." She glanced down at Aubrey, now sleeping peacefully with her thumb in her mouth. "But it always stops my heart to hear that scream in the middle of the night."

"She doesn't wake up?"

"No, and Alex usually sleeps through it too. Though how he does, I can't imagine."

"It *is* rather heart-stopping."

Rebecca smiled, stroking Aubrey's hair. "Nothing like a scream to alter the mood, huh?"

"It's just as well. Things were getting a bit out of hand."

Their eyes met over Aubrey's head, and she remembered how he'd touched her, just a few moments ago, with barely contained passion. How close she'd come to breaking through his reserve.

And how she'd responded. Unlike other times she'd been in similar situations, Connor's kisses didn't leave her filled with vague disappointment, like the taste of sugar-free chocolate.

Connor's gaze was unreadable, but Rebecca thought she saw a touch of regret.

She laid Aubrey gently down on the bed and followed Connor down the stairs. "She'll sleep all night now. They both will."

"I'd better be going."

She shook her head reproachfully. "You're pulling the plug, aren't you? What happened earlier—"

"What nearly happened."

"What *nearly* happened was good. It was fantastic! I've never—" She started to say she'd never felt that way with any man, but thought better of it. She didn't want to alarm him.

"We'll talk about it later." He stuffed his hands in his pockets and turned to go.

"But—"

"I'll be busy tomorrow, but I'll call you on Monday," he continued, his expression mild. "I'll free my schedule. We'll discuss…the terms of our relationship then."

She frowned. "The terms? What do you mean 'the terms'?"

"We'll discuss it on Monday."

She halted at the bottom of the stairs. "Either you want to make love to me or you don't."

"It's not that simple. There are others to consider. The twins, for example—"

"They don't care if we make love."

His gaze skittered off, and she realized, with a start, that he was afraid. Frightened of what he was feeling. What she made him feel.

A tender glow spread through her, leaving a feeling of power in its wake. Maybe she had accomplished more than she'd thought. At least she'd made a good start.

She smiled softly and moved closer, slowly, giving him time to react. He didn't move. She slipped her arms around his neck and kissed him gently on the lips.

"It's okay, Connor, I'll go easy on you," she said lightly. "If you want to set parameters, fine." She had no intention of following them, but he didn't have to know that. She gave him another kiss, on the cheek this time, a non-threatening peck, meant to reassure him, but he turned away. She followed him to the door, and they said a quick goodbye.

After he left, she passed through the living room, picking up the wine glasses as she went. The candle was still burning, wafting seductive aroma throughout the room despite the fact the intended target had just slipped out the door with his virtue intact.

So, her plan needed a few adjustments. At least she knew one thing: Connor wanted her.

And she wanted him, more than she'd ever thought possible.

His passion was as intense as his intellect.

When it was unleashed, it scared him. She smiled and bent over to blow out the candle, watching its thin trail of smoke dissipate into the air. A piece of wick had dropped into the hot wax, and as she dug it out, she realized that what he'd been afraid of was his own passion, his own desires, his own hopes and dreams. As long as he kept them bottled up, his life would be manageable, on his own terms.

There was hope. He had, after all, ordered a car equipped with a stick shift. Maybe, she thought, stacking the wine glasses in the sink, he was tired of driving through life on automatic.

Monday morning, Rebecca strode through the tech wing after dropping off the twins. She almost collided with Bob Steele as he came around the corner formed by the office cubicles. He reached out and steadied her.

"Slow down. Don't tell me you're eager to get to work on a Monday."

She flashed him a grin. "Of course. I love my job. Doesn't everyone here?"

He eyed her suspiciously. "You're in a good mood. Should I ask what you did this weekend?"

"No, you shouldn't. What's on the agenda for the week?" she asked, unloading the contents of her bag onto her desk.

He lifted his brows. "Since you're only going to be here three days, I didn't think you'd want to start on another project. I handed it to Kevin."

"Three days? Is there a holiday I don't know about?"

His brow furrowed. "You're taking some vacation time, remember?"

"Vacation time?" She stared at him blankly.

Bob laughed and waved a hand in front of her face. "Hello! Earth to Rebecca? I came in early, and there was a note on my desk. You're taking off Thursday and Friday."

"I am?"

He stroked his goatee thoughtfully. "Split personality, right? I read about this once. A woman spent half her time as a hooker; the rest of the time she was a computer programmer."

Rebecca laughed. "There must be some mistake. I'm not taking any time off. I can't afford to. I used all my vacation days for the next ten years, remember?"

He shrugged. "It's already been approved. If you want to change it, talk to Martin Grainger."

"I will."

She stuffed her bag under her desk and sat down, puzzled but not overly concerned. Mix-ups happened, even at well-run corporations.

She'd call Martin just as soon as she'd talked to Connor. Fortunately, she had an excuse to go up to his office. The twins had hand-drawn an invitation to their birthday party. She was having it at her house, in the back yard. A swimming party, with veggie dogs, carrot sticks, and plenty of Juicy Juice.

She took the elevator up to the eighth floor and found Adrian outside Connor's office.

"You're just the person I wanted to see," he said. "I've been using your commodities market simulation program. Works great. Made a million yesterday on pork futures."

Rebecca gave him a weak smile. "That's what it's supposed to do. Help you guys predict the future."

"We'll have to do lunch sometime. Talk about the possibilities. You know, you could market a commercial version—"

"A commercial version?"

"Sure. Designed for Mom and Pop investors. Based on what I've seen, yours could outperform the bestsellers."

She shook her head. "That's okay. I've got enough on my plate without giving Mom and Pop a leg up on pork futures."

"I'm sure we could interest a venture capitalist in something like this."

Rebecca listened patiently. There were already several commercial products out there that promised investors "scientific forecasts of the future" based on everything from Elliott Waves to astrological signs. None of them were foolproof, and eventually someone lost money. She didn't want to be responsible for anyone losing their life savings.

"It's a great idea, Adrian, but the commercial potential is limited. Without the data FGI has available, the programs would be useless to the average investor."

"But you could get around that." He smiled confidently. "Besides, all we need is endorsements. It doesn't matter if it actually works."

She gaped at him, but apparently he was serious. "Well, in that case, why don't you develop your own software? It's really easy. They've even got programming languages for four-year-olds now. You should see the twins. Why, just yesterday they were programming their laptops to corner the market on Kool-Aid." She smiled brightly, hoping the subject was dead. She glanced toward the closed door that led to Connor's private office. "Is Connor in there?"

"Sure, but—"

She ducked into the doorway before he could recruit the twins in his get-rich-quick scheme.

Peggy looked up and gave her a warm smile. "Go on in, Rebecca. He said you'd be stopping by."

"He did?" So much for surprises. Life in the corporate world was becoming more confusing than a game of Monopoly.

She opened the door and walked in. Connor looked up, then put the finishing touches on his phone conversation. Rebecca had been in his office before, for a meeting he'd arranged with the tech staff. It was decorated simply but elegantly, with subtle Asian influences. Warm shades of red dominated, with two maroon leather sofas facing off in front of the desk. A pair of geometric paintings on the wall caught her attention: devilish blue circles danced in one frame, while another held an unyielding yellow square.

From the wide windows behind his desk, she could just see the edge of the Transamerica Building, a monolithic sculpture that fit the décor perfectly. A beam of light illuminated a glass globe on his desk, where a replica of Earth was trapped inside.

A man who had Earth suspended on his desk. Definitely a man who liked to be in control. Rebecca smiled to herself, wondering if he'd mind very much if she upended his world.

"Hello, Rebecca," he said, hanging up the phone. "I had a feeling you'd be by."

"Don't tell me you've already heard about the big bash." She passed him the card in her hand. "It's an invitation to the twins' birthday party."

He frowned. "I thought that was another four weeks."

"It is — three weeks from Saturday. I'm getting the invitations out early. Four-year-olds have busy schedules these days." She smiled. "I know you said you'd try to come, but if a birthday party with a bunch of kids isn't your style, I'll make your excuses to Alex."

"Actually, there is a potential problem."

"Oh?"

"I assume you'll be inviting other kids from the daycare. I would prefer it not get out around the building that I'm seeing you."

She felt a little thrill at the words "seeing you," but then realized what he meant. She bit her lip. "You think someone would think... we're more than friends."

"We *are* more than friends." He gave her a mild look. "I think we crossed that line right about the time you slipped your hand around my kneecap."

A funny little feeling filled her tummy. "Umm. That was good, wasn't it?"

He cleared his throat. "I think it's a given we both want to continue in that vein."

She perched on the arm of the nearest leather sofa and tilted her head. "Yes, I'd say that's a given." Then she grinned. "I'm free tonight."

His lips curved in a half-smile. "How about this weekend?"

"Actually—" She laughed. "It looks like I'm on vacation this weekend, according to the personnel office anyway."

He rose from his chair and came to join her on the couch. "Yes, I know."

Rebecca watched him, her gaze narrowing at his words. "You know? You mean it wasn't a mix-up, was it?"

"No. I cleared it with Martin and had him send a note to Bob."

"With Martin? You couldn't have cleared this with me first?"

"I knew what your objections would be, so I took care of them beforehand."

Rebecca suddenly felt like the object of a takeover, so quickly and thoroughly had he maneuvered her. An echo of resentment in her voice, she replied, "I suppose you've made plans for the twins too."

"I've contacted a babysitting service in Maui."

"Maui? What's in Maui?"

"Some rather nice beaches. World class restaurants. Excellent weather. And my estate."

"You have a home in Maui?"

"Yes. And I've decided it's time I took a vacation. You and the twins are invited. For an extended weekend."

"You want us to come on vacation with you? To Maui?" She couldn't seem to stop repeating everything he said.

"We can leave Thursday afternoon. I've carved some time from my schedule."

"What about my schedule? I have work to do, too," she pointed out.

"Don't worry—"

"I *am* worried about my job! Just because I may be having an affair with my boss doesn't mean I can slack off at work."

He smiled. "No one's about to accuse you of slacking off at work. On the contrary, you've done an excellent job since you've been here. I hear from the managers the system's working perfectly, requests for information are being met on time…Frankly, it sounds like the whole department's working quite smoothly now, despite Bob's frequent absences. And like I told you before, I don't expect my employees to perform the miracles they do without adequate down time."

"Advice you don't take yourself."

He lifted a shoulder. "Which is why I'm taking a vacation. Three nights, four days in Hawaii. With you. Unless you can think of another objection?"

She thought for a minute. She knew she had one; she just wasn't sure what it was right now.

Connor watched her, his gaze guarded. "The twins will be with you, of course, except for in the evening. I've hired a nanny to stay at the house. She can watch them if we want to go out. There are several nice restaurants on the island, or you might like to attend a luau. There's also a national park with trails for hiking. The beach is nice, and very private."

There was a key element he'd left out. "And at night? Who sleeps where?"

"That's up to you." He met her gaze steadily.

Rebecca paused. She'd wanted him on her turf, but his turf included a lush tropical paradise. It might just be the perfect spot for throwing off inhibitions—hers, and his.

"Before you agree, there are a few other items we need to get straight."

"Like what?"

"I'd like for this to remain quiet. I don't want the whole building buzzing with gossip. For your own sake."

"I don't like the thought of having my private life gossiped about either. But don't you think someone will eventually figure out what's going on?"

"If they do, they won't have any confirmation from us. Peggy will know, of course; she's already made the arrangements." He crooked his arm along the back of the long couch, resting his chin on his hand.

"Oh. That explains the look she gave me when I came in."

"What look was that?"

"Umm...encouraging," she decided.

"Ahh." The phone on his desk buzzed, but he ignored it. "Then if I have your agreement on that—"

"You want me to agree to keep mum about this? Should I sign in blood, or will ink do it?"

"Actually, I'd like your promise that whatever happens..." He paused, his expression a little uncomfortable. "We'll remain friends. If nothing else, I hope we can continue to have a working relationship. You're an excellent employee, not to mention a trusted friend, and I'd hate to lose either one."

She softened. "Oh, Connor..." She slid over to where he was sitting, then reached up and kissed him on the cheek. "You're the best friend I've got. Do you think I'm going to let a little sex get in the way of that?"

"I hope not."

Mesmerized by his gaze, she moved closer, slid her arms around his neck and kissed him again. Without touching her, he responded, hard and hot and making her eager for the end of the week.

She groaned. "Do we have to wait until Thursday?"

He moved her away, untangling her arms from his neck. "Yes. We have to do this my way. I want to be alone with you, without any distractions."

"You mean like night terrors and telephones and—"

"And objections to making love to virgins." He still held her at arm's length. "I want your promise, Rebecca, you won't expect more commitment than I can give. I'm not your Prince Charming, I'm not even a date for the office Christmas party. All I want from this is sex. Pure and simple."

She almost smiled. He was so wrong. He wanted more than that; he'd just told her. But he was too blind to see where his heart was leading him.

So, she'd let him find out on his own.

She nodded. "No expectations. I promise. But you have to promise something too."

"What's that?" His gaze narrowed.

Rebecca wanted to wipe away the wariness she saw reflected in his blue eyes, but instead she swallowed the tiny lump in her throat and took a breath. "I want you to be honest. Totally honest."

"Of course."

"I meant…" What she meant was, she wanted him to be honest with himself. But somehow she knew he wasn't ready for that, wasn't ready to face what might be happening between them. So, she smiled instead, and said, "I'm a big girl, Connor. I can take it. If you decide you want out, all you have to do is climb out of the water." She shrugged. "And the same for me," she added. "If I decide the water's too hot—" She felt herself growing warmer at the thought of what he'd do to her in just a few days. "I'm free to jump out anytime. Deal?"

He nodded. "Deal."

Then her gaze dropped to the firm mouth she'd kissed the other night, the memory making her cheeks flush pink. Drawn like a magnet, she reached over and brushed his lips with hers. A second later, he was kissing her back.

This time he touched her. He slipped his hands under her jacket, sliding around the silk of her blouse to her back, sending shivers along her spine. His hand lightly grazed her breast. "Oh, heaven," she managed to murmur when his lips left hers to trail down her neck, setting off a cascade of desire.

He lifted his mouth from her skin long enough to murmur, "Make no mistake about it: I want you, Rebecca. As much as I've ever wanted anything. Trust me, I'd never risk losing what we have if it weren't for the fact I…"

"You what?"

He met her gaze, his eyes burning with a blue flame, the hottest part of a fire, she'd read once. He didn't answer her question. Instead, he dropped his gaze to her mouth, and then bent his head and kissed her again, expressing without words how long he'd wanted this, his lips, his tongue, speaking more eloquently than his vocal chords.

Rebecca let him take over. He wanted to be in the driver's seat, needed to feel in control—she understood that—but she also understood he needed to be stood on his head once in a while. Shaken from his predictable routine.

Every so often, he needed his ruts repaved.

She loosened his tie, pushed it aside, then began unbuttoning his shirt, until three buttons in the middle were open. She slid her hand beneath the starched cotton and caressed him over the smooth undershirt he wore. His chest was warm, his heartbeat strong.

"You're not a cold unfeeling statue, are you, Connor?"

"I get turned on just like any man, when a beautiful woman looks at me like she wants to rip my clothes off."

She laughed, then licked the skin exposed at the top of his undershirt. "I could have you naked in seconds. You don't have any appointments, do you?"

He glanced at his watch, then pulled her into his lap. "You've got half an hour."

She went for it. Taking advantage of her position atop his lap—just enough leverage to allow her to reach his mouth with ease—she devoured him, with her mouth, her hands. He returned her kiss, but she could feel him holding back, not letting completely go. That was okay; she had to go back to work soon herself and didn't want to look thoroughly kissed.

Although she was. Definitely. His technique was flawless, his moves measured and meticulous, precisely designed for maximum impact.

She shivered. He was way more advanced in this than she was, but she didn't mind losing the upper hand. She just enjoyed sitting on his lap, necking like she was a teenager in the backseat of a very elegant car.

The phone in his pocket rang again, and with a sigh she let him go.

While he spoke into the phone, Rebecca refastened the buttons on his shirt. She gave him a farewell wave, then went back to her office on the fourth floor.

When she saw Bob, she said, with a chagrined smile, "You were right. I don't know how it could have slipped my mind. I'm visiting a friend this weekend."

"Oh. I see." He gave her a strange look, and Rebecca realized her ditz quotient had just gone up, but she didn't care. She just hoped he didn't ask her where the friend lived, because she would have a hard time explaining how she'd forgotten she was going all the way to Maui.

CHAPTER THIRTEEN

On Thursday afternoon Rebecca drove the twins to the small airfield where Conner's private plane waited for them. He was already on board, talking to the pilot.

The flight attendant helped Rebecca and the kids settle into the passenger seats and went over the safety procedures as the plane took off. While Connor worked at his laptop, Rebecca kept the twins entertained until they fell asleep, overdue for their afternoon naps.

Then she unhooked her seatbelt and crossed the aisle to the table where he was jotting notes. "How long have you had a home in Maui?" she asked him, settling cross-legged in the chair opposite him.

"Since my mother was diagnosed with cancer. I wanted her to have a place to get away, from the chemo, from Rodney occasionally—"

"Your brother."

"Yes. He can be rather time-consuming."

"You must have been devastated to find out she had cancer."

He looked up at her, his expression guarded. "I called every expert in the country—in the world. The cancer was too advanced by the time they discovered it. In the end, she only managed one visit to Hawaii. But she enjoyed it. I think you'll like it too. There's plenty to do, even for the twins. And the scenery's spectacular."

Rebecca let him change the subject. For a man who craved control, his mother's death from an unstoppable disease must have been doubly hard. She could relate to that. After more than three months, Kim's death still didn't make sense to her.

Right now, though, her goal was to enjoy the unexpected vacation.

Maui stole her breath at first sight. From overhead, the island looked like it had been squeezed in the middle by a giant fist, with lush green mountains leaking out from either end. Rocky cliffs and ecru sand beaches outlined the spectacle. As they neared, the mountains grew larger, and she could make out individual buildings. She was surprised to see what looked like cattle ranches and plantations in addition to the hotels clustered on the western end.

Across from her, Connor snapped his laptop shut. "The first sight of it is always somewhat breathtaking." But he was looking at her, Rebecca noticed, not out the window on his left. "The island was named after the Polynesian demigod Maui, who they say pulled the Hawaiian islands out of the ocean with his fishhook."

"He must have been very powerful."

"And not afraid of much. He also threatened the sun by chopping off its legs one by one until it promised to stay in the sky longer."

Rebecca smiled. "Sounds like a real take-charge kind of guy."

"He also turned his daughter's lover to stone, supposedly the mountain now known as the Needle." He glanced out the window to where the airport runway stretched out ahead. "We'll take a drive to Iao Valley, and you can see the poor guy for yourself."

After they landed at a small commuter airport, a man Connor introduced to her as Kimo helped load their luggage into a white Land Rover. Connor spoke to him in Japanese, then turned to Rebecca. "Kimo and his wife live on the property full time. If you need anything while you're here, all you have to do is ask. Sheila speaks English."

Rebecca nodded at him over the top of Aubrey's head. She hadn't wakened, and as it was already eight o'clock, their time, Rebecca didn't expect her to.

Connor held the door of the Land Rover open for them. "*Aloha nui*. Welcome to paradise," he said as she got in.

His eyes shone blue as the tropical sky, and her breath caught. She'd almost forgotten the reason she'd agreed to come here to paradise. Her stomach flipped at the thought. She was tired of looking over the precipice. It was past time to take a plunge, and if a few bruises were the result, the thrill of a free fall, she hoped, would be worth it.

After a winding trip along the coast, they turned onto a side road that wound through a grove of ohia trees. By then Alex was yawning again.

"There're ten acres, with a couple hundred yards of beachfront. It's mostly rocky, but the previous owner had sand hauled in for a beach and roped off a small swimming area. The pool might be safer, though, at least for the twins."

The house came into view, and Kimo parked the Land Rover in the curve of the driveway. Doors painted Chinese red opened, and two women stepped out onto the small porch. The older woman was Kimo's wife, Sheila, who introduced Mona, the babysitter Connor had hired. Mona's dark hair glistened in the last rays of the sunset, and white teeth flashed as she smiled at Alex, then bent to his level to talk to him. Rebecca was instantly charmed, as was Alex.

Mona was a part-time student at the university, majoring in early childhood education. It was clear Connor had done more than instruct his secretary to make a phone call. Not only did Mona know the twins' names, their birthdate, and their favorite colors, she also was aware that they had recently lost their parents.

Rebecca hid a smile. Connor could put a few demigods to shame when it came to wielding power, yet he'd been thoughtful enough to ensure the twins had the best of care on his island retreat.

The inside of the house was fit for a Polynesian king. Roomy enough for ten, yet cozily decorated in earth tones of sandalwood and jute. Local artwork hung on the walls, exotic prints of flowers and hula dancers and enchanting green valleys.

Sheila showed Rebecca to the bedroom the twins would share, which adjoined the room where Mona had already unpacked her bags. Rebecca was just down the hall in a room decorated with white muslin — on the bed, over the French doors leading to the patio, and on the pillows bunched on the inviting settee. Three crystal vases brimming with fresh flowers filled the room with the fragrance of frangipani and jasmine.

Connor had disappeared, she assumed to his room upstairs. She'd promised to meet him in an hour, after the twins had been settled in for the night with Mona.

She checked her watch. It was too late in Chicago to call and let her mother know how to reach them. She'd call in the morning, just to reassure her Connor hadn't already sold them into white slavery, as she seemed to think might happen.

"You hardly know him!" her mother had said two days earlier when Rebecca had told her their plans. "And now you're flying halfway around the world with him?"

"Mom!" Rebecca laughed. "We've known each other for months, and I'm pretty sure he's never had any dead girlfriends turn up. Believe me, the worst that can happen is he'll send me to Philadelphia."

"Phila—oh, never mind. I just hope you know what you're doing. I worry about you, Rebecca. You always did go around with your heart on your sleeve."

But she'd never given it away completely, though she wasn't sure Connor didn't already have a tiny piece of it. "Connor's not going to break my heart, Mom," she had told her mother firmly, and now, as she dressed to go downstairs and meet him, she hoped she was right.

They had dinner at a Japanese restaurant, located a few miles away in Hana. They ate al fresco, with nothing but tiki lights and the soft candle glow from their table to interrupt the romantic star-cast night.

It was better than anything she could have planned for a seduction scene. Here, far removed from San Francisco, their relationship took on a subtle difference. He was no longer her employer, she no longer a harried single parent. Instead, they were just a couple of romantic souls on a moonlit night in paradise.

After dinner, Connor suggested a walk along the beach. They held hands and strolled beside the moon-soaked water, the perfect image of lovers, except they weren't. Not yet.

"It's not too late to back out," Connor told her as they stopped near the edge of the beach and retrieved their shoes.

"Do you want me to?" she asked, looking up at his shadowed face.

"No, of course not."

A thought struck her, and she smiled. "Are you nervous, Connor?"

"Why should I be nervous? I've done this before."

"Is it always like this, then?"

"Like what?"

"Romantic strolls in the moonlight. Candlelit dinners for two. This attraction pulling us together like a magnet. Or maybe magic."

"There's no magic to it. Simply biological urges, in this case surrounded by all the trappings you just mentioned."

"Of course. Simple biological urges," she mocked. "The kind that drive birds across a continent in search of mating grounds, the same kind that lead men to fight a Trojan war for the love of Helen —"

"The same kind that urged Marc Antony to take on Caesar — and lose," he supplied.

"Exactly. 'Simple biological urges.' That's all this is, right?" She gazed up at him, watching the moonlight wash his hair with rays of silver.

Instead of answering, he leaned down and kissed her, and their biological urges surged into life, there on the beach.

Rebecca's toes dug into the sand, as she fought for purchase amidst a swirling wave of desire. Connor's mouth fed her passion-starved soul, and underneath his ice-cold reserve, she could feel the hot trickle of longing. His fingertips traced the seams of her dress, the same one she'd worn the night of their first "date," when she'd first realized the potential — and the limits — of loving this man who challenged her soul, who made her heart shake with just a look.

She would have let him take her right there, on the beach just a few yards from the crowded restaurant, but Connor led her toward the car.

It was a thirty minute drive back to the house, during which Connor proved to be well-versed in Hawaiian folklore. As he recited the legends of Hana, Rebecca couldn't help smiling. For a man who didn't believe in magic, he seemed to know an awful lot about the local myths.

Finally, they turned on the road leading to the house, and Rebecca's heart began to canter in anticipation. Connor parked in the circular drive, then held the door open while she climbed down from the seat. He held her hand as they went through the wide red door, then stopped at the threshold.

Her palms suddenly felt damp.

"You can get ready for bed. My room is upstairs. I'll wait for you. Unless you change your mind."

He was going to leave the options open until the last minute, she realized.

But as far as she was concerned, the die had been cast the minute she agreed to come here to his own personal slice of paradise.

In her room, she pulled on the black nightgown she'd bought for just this occasion, brushed her teeth, and tied on a robe. She left her hair up in the loose knot she'd pinned it in before dinner.

As she left her room, she took a breath for courage. Then, as she looked up at the wide staircase, she almost giggled. She felt like a heroine in a gothic novel, minus the cold English moor.

When she stepped into the doorway of his room, she paused. The whole room glowed, lit by dozens of candles set in silver trays placed here and there, making the space seem cozy despite its size. A large four-poster bed sat square in the center, intricate Chinese carvings trailing up the posts. Shiny dark sheets were already turned down, and on a table near the bed was a bottle of champagne with two glasses waiting to be filled.

It was the ideal setting for a honeymoon, but the "groom" seemed to be missing. Rebecca glanced around and spied him on the balcony, his back to her.

She moved closer, her bare feet silent on the carpet. In the distance, she heard the sound of the ocean crashing against the rocks he'd warned her about. He'd also warned her not to fall in love with him, but looking at him now, a stoic figure surveying the darkened paradise he'd brought her to, Rebecca felt her heart burst with longing, and with something she very much feared was love.

He turned when she reached the doorway. His gaze dropped to her waist, then back up. His eyes were shadowed, but she thought she saw warmth there. Or maybe it was the glow from the candles.

He nodded toward the room. "Sheila's idea of a romantic setting, apparently."

"This wasn't your doing?"

"I told her we'd want champagne. The rest, she improvised. Native islanders tend to be a romantic lot."

She wanted to tell him girls from the Chicago suburbs had romantic inclinations as well, but she figured that wasn't what he wanted to hear.

"I suppose we can just ignore all the candles…and the flowers…" She glanced around. "…and all the other trappings and pretend we're on my couch, surrounded by Fisher Price."

"Or we could just make the most of it." He moved closer, until he was almost touching her.

She swallowed. "We could do that, too."

His gaze held hers for a moment, then he motioned toward the table. "Would you like some champagne?"

"That sounds nice." *And it wouldn't hurt to be slightly drunk.*

He walked over to the bed and filled the flutes. Holding one up to the candlelight, he examined it, then murmured, "No, it's not quite as dark."

"What do you mean?"

"Your eyes. They're darker. I always thought they were the same shade as mellow champagne. But they're darker. More intoxicating."

She shivered and took the glass he offered. "For a guy who hates romance, you've got a way with words."

"Just observant."

"Or maybe you want to distract me. Ply me with champagne and romantic words until I'm incapable of defending myself from your onslaught of passion." She took a sip, her gaze meeting his over the rim of the glass.

He laughed. "You've got a way with words yourself. Maybe I'm the one at risk here."

"You mean you're not going to slaught me with passion? I'm disappointed." She gulped a too-large sip and winced as bubbles filled her throat.

He smiled and lifted his hand to her hairline, where wisps of hair had escaped the knot. Gentle fingers caressed her nape, behind her ear—a new erogenous zone, Rebecca decided—then slipped beneath the robe to her shoulder. "How exactly does one go about slaughting?" he asked, all the while doing a fine job of it.

She sighed. "Oh, you seem to have the general idea…" She closed her eyes and swayed in his direction. His hands caught her to him and pulled her closer against his hard body, silk against silk, heat against heat.

She clutched the glass, wishing she'd drunk more of it. Connor had already set his glass on the table, and he began slipping the pins from her hair, one by one, watching as it fell in bunches to her shoulders.

"There's a drink made by monks. Frangelico. It's the same color as your hair."

She glanced up at him, amused. "You sound like you've given this a great deal of thought."

"I always think through my acquisitions."

She frowned. "I'm not an acqui—" she began, bristling, but then she noticed the way his eyes crinkled at the corners.

"Gotcha," he said with a small smile.

She arched her brows. "Maybe I'm the one acquiring you. To add to my collection."

"Your collection?"

"Of frogs." She leaned up and kissed him lightly, and their mouths caught, the kiss growing deeper, more urgent. Cold flames raced along her nerve endings, and she hoped with all her heart she had found a prince this time.

She set her glass on the table next to his, then pushed aside his robe and slid her fingers through the dark smattering of hair. He stood still while she explored his hard chest, his skin warming her chilled fingers. Her hand paused over his heart and captured the beats in her palm.

Their eyes met, and she read desire, impatience, and something else she hesitated to name. She reached up and nuzzled his cheek with her lips. He smelled like shaving cream, male and sexy, and her heart quickened at the image of him shaving again, for her. He kept saying he'd hurt her, but the signs said differently.

He bent to kiss her again, and this time he was firmly in control. He held her head in place, and explored her mouth, slowly, meticulously, as if he had all the time in the world.

Rebecca felt her stomach muscles clench with desire. At the same time, a tiny thread of alarm brought her back from the edge she was fast sliding toward. She suddenly wanted to connect with him on more than a physical level. To know she touched his heart—

She pulled her mouth from his to whisper, "Oh, Connor, talk to me, please," she whispered, her lips caressing his strong jaw.

"What do you want me to say?"

She knew he couldn't say what she really wanted to hear, so she settled for second best. "I want you to tell me how much you want me."

"You can feel that for yourself."

And she could. He was pressing against her stomach, throbbing, and it gave her a little thrill to know she'd done that to him.

"Tell me anyway," she urged.

She felt his chest shake with amusement. "I've brought you here. Three thousand miles across the Pacific. If that's not proof—"

"I bet you bring lots of women here." She eyed the opening of his robe, wondering what he would taste like.

"No. Only two."

"Hmm." She supposed that pinprick in her heart was jealousy, and then she stopped wondering and pressed her lips to his breastbone. "What were their names?"

"Rebecca—" He groaned, then captured her talkative mouth with his own. She forgot about speech for a moment, but as soon as his mouth left hers to trail down her neck she tried again.

"Your bed—it's beautiful."

"It's a Chinese wedding bed. Made for the last emperor."

"You mean we're doing this in a bed made for Chinese royalty?"

His finger explored her shoulder blade as he answered. "Yes. The carvings are to ward off evil spirits and ensure fertility."

"Oh no!" She glanced worriedly at the bed, but he reached into a drawer beside the bed, pulled out a foil packet, and set it on the pillow.

"Trust me, Rebecca. There's nothing to worry about."

There wasn't, she realized, and with a little sigh, closed her eyes and jumped.

Connor's mind urged caution. This was her first time, and she deserved more than a quick toss between the sheets.

He tamped down his own needs and devoted himself to hers. He was in control, he reminded himself, with one purpose: her pleasure.

Concentration. Focus. Dedication. His guiding principles, in business and in pleasure.

Concentration. Slowly he pulled the strap of her nightgown over the curve of her shoulder, his gaze upon the smooth skin he wanted to touch, to kiss.

Focus. He lowered his mouth to her breast, making her gasp with pleasure as he touched her, caressed her with his tongue.

Dedication. He turned to the other one, circling the tender nipple with his tongue, until he heard her moan and her hands clutched at his robe.

He slipped the nightgown over her head, gathered her in his arms and lowered her to the bed. He'd never seen a more beautiful sight than her naked on his sheets in his Chinese wedding bed.

Rebecca reached out for him, pulling him toward her with more than a hint of impatience in the gesture, and he smiled. "We've got all night," he told her, but he leaned forward obligingly.

She nuzzled his neck, tasting him, stripping him of another layer of reserve.

He slid out of his robe, and as he turned to join her on the bed, she gazed at him in wide-eyed wickedness. "I want to see you, Connor. All of you."

He stripped off his pajama bottoms, and with a smile of welcome, she reached out for him, tentatively touching him.

Leaning on his arms above her, he lowered his head and kissed her. Her leg stroked him sensuously, as if she'd been studying manuals on the fine art of seduction.

She'd mastered the material, Connor decided, his muscles tensing in response.

With his mouth, he found all her erogenous zones, gave them his full attention. He ignored his own needs, putting aside his own growing impatience as he worked to make sure she enjoyed this.

He'd never been so careful with a woman before, never wanted — needed — her to crave his touch. He told himself it was because she was a virgin, and he wanted her to experience all the pleasure and none of the pain. This would be a moment she'd remember all her life, and he was determined she would never regret giving herself to him.

He would hurt her, eventually, inevitably, but for now he would make her scream with pleasure.

She stopped breathing as he traced his tongue down between her breasts, over her smooth stomach muscles, and further. A gasp left her throat when he reached his destination.

"Oh, Connor…that…ahhh…" She shivered, like a butterfly shaking its wings.

"Are you cold?"

"No, it's…it's delicious. Don't stop, please, don't stop."

"I wouldn't dream of it."

With the expertise of a master in the art of seduction, he built up the anticipation until slowly, gently, he led her over the precipice.

Joy pierced her in a thousand places: At the top of her head, where her scalp tingled and neurons sparked with satisfaction. At her throat, where a lump that felt suspiciously like tears lodged dead center. At her stomach, where muscles had clenched and quivered with release. At the hot throbbing place between her legs, where heat still pooled and swirled in little eddies of satisfaction. At the back of her knees, tension had suddenly dissolved, the tops of her feet relaxed in relief, even her toes tingled with joy.

Beside her, Connor stretched full length, covering her breasts with his arm. She could feel him against her, still throbbing with heat, his own pleasure postponed.

"Are you always so considerate?" she asked.

"Not always."

"It's because I'm a virgin." She didn't know whether to be touched or saddened by his restraint.

"I don't want to hurt you."

"You won't—"

He caught her mouth with his, putting an end to her protests.

She wrapped her arms around him, pulling him closer. With one smooth move, he flipped her on top of him, then stroked her back, her buttocks, flicking a fire alight along the way.

She moaned. The satisfaction she'd felt before turned to anticipation. She'd waited twenty-six years, and suddenly the addition of another minute seemed like an eternity. She throbbed here, burned there, and ached for release all over, in every starved pore of her body.

"Rebecca," he murmured against her skin, a sound of caution in his voice.

In response, she pressed her mouth to his, feeding her growing hunger, begging him for more between tiny moans. Soon, she found herself underneath him again.

His hands worked magic all over her body. Pleasure, pain, an abundance of feeling she'd never known existed. The glorious ache started again between her legs, tense, tight, and moist, and when he touched her, he made it worse and better, all at the same time.

Time kept stopping in tiny increments while she collected each moment to add to her memories of paradise. Above her, his body curved against hers in an arc of sculpted masculinity, graceful and sure and taking her further toward something she knew instinctively she wanted, needed, craved...

A stray breeze fluttered the candle flame, throwing shadows against the wall. Outside the open window, the surf exploded against the rocky shore. Inside Connor, an explosion began from somewhere near his heart, and it raced outward through his arteries, his veins, his lungs. He wanted nothing more, needed nothing more, at this moment but to be inside her, breathing with her, melting with her, becoming one with the energy source that was Rebecca.

"Oh, Connor," she breathed, begging him silently with her eyes, her hands. Connor reached for the condom, then sheathed himself before she drew him to her once more, as if she'd done this hundreds of times, and suddenly he was grateful for her lack of virginal reticence.

Taut muscle contracted around him, pulling him closer. He held himself back, stretched over her for what seemed an eternity of longing, until she pulled him forward, with a tiny gasp of pleasure or pain, he wasn't sure which.

He fought desperately to hold himself back, to control the raging desire that urged him to take her now, but his focus fled, his concentration shattered.

He plunged inside her, over and over until he felt her shudder beneath him.

Release came suddenly, a plutonium-fueled detonation that started somewhere deep inside and raced along the tripwires of his nerves, through his heart, his mind, and quite possibly his soul.

CHAPTER FOURTEEN

The next morning Rebecca was awakened by the sound of voices and splashing. The twins were in the pool with Mona. She lay in bed for a minute, enjoying the fact that for the first time in three months she didn't have to get up and give them their breakfast. Then she felt guilty. Here she was, basking in the aftermath of a passion-filled night, when her kids were with a virtual stranger, enjoying a swim.

She took a quick shower, then pulled on her swimsuit and a thick terry robe. Her hair still damp, she went downstairs, following the smell of fresh-baked bread into the kitchen where a loaf of bread was sliced and lying on a plate.

It was warm and tasted of the tropics: bananas and coconut and something else — limes, she guessed, seeing the squeezed rinds on the counter.

She went out back to find the twins, and they rushed up to her, eager to show her the latest trick Mona had taught them.

"Watch what I can do! I can dive!" Alex then proceeded to dive off the edge of the pool, holding his nose as he slid into the water. Aubrey sat huddled on the side, admiring her brother's bravery.

"You want to do that?" Rebecca asked, but Aubrey shook her head.

"I used to be afraid to dive too. But watch this." She pulled off her wrap, jumped up to the diving board to execute a perfect dive into the deep end, until she caught a glimpse of Connor coming up the walk from the beach. Her dive turned into a modified belly flop, but when she rose to the surface the twins were laughing with delight.

Connor stopped at the edge of the pool, not seeming to care that his trousers were getting splattered from the water Alex was kicking as he held on to the side.

"How would you all like to go see a volcano?"

When Rebecca came closer, he explained. "It's about an hour's drive to the crater of Haleakala. If you'd like, we can hike down while the kids and Mona drive back with Kimo. He'll pick us up at Kaupo near the base."

"That sounds like fun. What do you say, guys?"

Aubrey looked doubtful, and Connor explained that the volcano was dormant and didn't pose any threat. She seemed to believe him, and an hour later they climbed into the Land Rover. Connor provided tour guide services as they drove through the entrance of Haleakala National Park, continuing until they cleared the tree line and arrived at the park station at the crater's edge.

They paid a quick visit to the visitor center, where Rebecca was grateful to Connor for taking Alex to the men's room after he complained about accompanying her and Aubrey to the ladies' room — a complaint she was beginning to hear frequently. Then they embarked on the trail that led toward the center of the crater.

"Haleakala means House of the Sun," Connor told them as they walked down the steep path and into the crater of the volcano. At ten thousand feet, the air was thin, without the scented murkiness of the coastal regions. Indeed, it seemed as if nothing lived here, just a vast alien nothingness, once alive with fire and steam and hot boiling lava. Now only cool clouds followed the path the hot lava had tracked, through Kaupo Gap, disappearing over the edge of the crater, replaced by the sun's sharp rays.

Rebecca shivered. She wasn't sure if she liked the emptiness, the eerie silence of the mountain rooftop. She tightened her hand on Aubrey's. After they'd walked a few hundred yards along the path, Alex grew tired, and Connor swung him up on his shoulder.

Connor continued to point out geographic features, using child-sized language. He explained how the lava had boiled from deep in the earth, then flowed down the mountain, consuming everything in its path.

When Aubrey shivered as well, Rebecca swung her into her arms. "It's time for a nap, don't you think, guys?"

After the twins and Mona departed with Kimo, Connor and Rebecca followed Kaupo Trail down the mountain side. Both had worn hiking boots and brought water bottles. After a half hour, they hit the shade of the forest, where dense trees and lush tropical vegetation slowed the steep descent.

"Whew! I didn't realize I've gotten out of shape!" Rebecca said, stopping at a wide point on the path to catch her breath. "Where do you get the energy? Five hours of sleep and you still have enough stamina to hike through four miles of jungle."

"It's downhill, plus the path is well worn. I would have suggested we hike up, but I figured you'd be worn out yourself."

She shot him a playful glance. "Why? Because of our strenuous activity last night?"

"That, plus the fact you aren't used to the altitude."

"Neither are you," she pointed out.

"I adjust pretty quickly. I take a ski vacation every year."

She poured water down her throat, her gaze locking with his. "You ski, you play tennis like a pro, and let's see...oh, right, you work twelve-hour days, making more money than Midas. What's your limit, Connor? What can't you do?"

He watched as she wiped a drop of water from her chin. "I can't program computers. The logic totally escapes me."

"Oh, that's simple. Computers make perfect sense. Not like people. I have yet to figure them out."

"What's so difficult? Once you figure out what motivates them, you know how they'll act."

"What motivates you, then?"

"I suppose the same basic needs as everyone else. Food. Shelter. Self-actualization."

"And sex?"

"At times. Particularly lately," he said wryly, ignoring the need he felt to take her far off the trail and make love to her against a tree. Or to toss her down on a soft carpet of grass and trace his tongue over her body until she moaned and screamed and added another talent to his list of accomplishments.

His thoughts shocked him. He'd never particularly cared whether a woman considered him accomplished in bed, or even what she thought of him outside of the bedroom. Rebecca's opinion mattered to him, more than he cared to admit.

In fact, he was enjoying himself very much this weekend. Rebecca's company, as well as the sex, was as stimulating as the business deals he'd been reluctant to leave. Their conversations kept him on his toes. The sex made his toes tingle.

She was everything he'd wanted her to be, and suddenly he realized why he'd resisted the idea of taking her to bed. He had been afraid she'd fall short of his expectations, that underneath that enticing exterior, he'd find her just like any other woman. When the first flush of anticipation wore off, he'd been all but certain he'd find her sexy but ordinary. Like a work of art fascinating to look at until it hung on his wall, when it became as alluring as wallpaper.

He closed the cap on his own water bottle, tucked it back in his belt, and tried to keep his eyes off her legs as he followed her down the trail.

That night, after making love, Rebecca lay in Connor's arms, tracing a finger across his chest lazily.

Earlier they had attended a luau at one of the local hotels, where they were served a specially-prepared vegetarian feast he'd ordered in advance. They'd danced to the sound of Hawaiian song-chants accompanied by soft ukulele music. Then they'd come home and made love, the strains of the music still echoing in their embrace. Connor had explained they dealt with the subject of sex, the life force, the energy source for the creation of life.

Connor was a thoughtful lover…all she could ask for, but Rebecca couldn't rid herself of a nagging impression that he was holding back a part of himself—especially during those earthshaking moments while they made love. She totally lost herself in his arms, but Connor, she suspected, was in complete control, over his emotions as well as his body. His heart was in no danger of betraying him. She swallowed a little sigh of regret.

Just once she wanted him to lose control, to cry out with the pleasure of it, to release that energy he was holding back, the same as she did every time she died "a little death" in his arms.

"What are you afraid of, Connor?" She hadn't realized she was planning to speak until she heard the echo of her words in the silence of his moonlit room.

"What makes you think I'm afraid?" he asked, his breathing slow and even beneath her hands.

She glanced up. "I had a dream once. There were leprechauns chasing you. And you were terrified."

He chuckled. "Leprechauns don't exist."

"All the more reason to be afraid."

"Is this conversation supposed to make sense?"

She ignored his sarcasm and traced her initials over his heart. "You're afraid of what you can't understand. Leprechauns, magic, love…yourself."

He was quiet, staring at the beams that bisected the ceiling. Rebecca had the feeling she'd struck a nerve. "Connor?"

He glanced down and, with a mocking lift of his eyebrows, replied, "According to the Greek philosophers, life is an odyssey of self-discovery, an endless, lifelong search for the answer to the question 'Why are we here?'"

She frowned. "Why does there have to be an answer? Why can't we just exist? For the sheer bliss of it?"

"They have a name for that one, too. Existentialism. Existence for the sake of existence."

She gave him a skeptical look. "You quote philosophers in the middle of the night, but you don't buy any of it, do you?"

He laughed, turning to face her. "You see through me so damn easily. Tell me, what am I thinking now?"

An unmistakable heat pressed against her stomach. She smiled, and in a mystical voice, she intoned, "The philosophy of Eros appeals to you now…Make love, not war."

"I think you've got Eros mixed up with Abbie Hoffman," he said, but he seemed to agree, and made love to her with a tenderness that almost made her cry.

Saturday morning, Rebecca and the twins were busy building a sand castle on the beach when Connor strolled down to join them.

He sat next to her and watched Aubrey and Alex shovel sand into a bucket. When it was full, they lugged it over to the castle-in-progress and dumped it dead center.

"Can I help?" he asked.

Rebecca handed him a shovel. "We're stuccoing the sides." For the next few minutes he packed sand, then helped Alex lug more water from the shallow pool formed by the outgoing tide, until finally the castle began to resemble something from the Middle Ages. As soon as it did, though, the twins lost interest and went to gather shells with Mona.

Connor stuffed a shovel in the sand. "I phoned Peggy earlier this morning. She's made arrangements for a car to meet us at the airport tomorrow."

Rebecca sighed. "I hate to think about leaving. This place is so special."

"We can always come back."

She glanced at him. She wondered if he remembered his earlier statement—that his relationships lasted a few weeks, months at the most. "There won't be time for another vacation. For me at least. I have a full time job, remember?"

A lock of hair fell across her face. She blew on it, but it stayed where it was. Connor reached out and tucked it behind her ear. "Your job has flexible hours, remember?"

She leaned back. "You're my boss, remember? I can't take advantage of that just because we're having an affair. Besides—" She glanced down at the sand castle, where one turret seemed to be crumbling. "This relationship is short term. Your idea."

"Some people wouldn't consider six months short term."

"Oh, so you've decided it's to be six months? Is that an arbitrary number, or is there a formula you use?"

He sighed impatiently. "I don't know how long it will last. There's no need to discuss that now."

"You brought it up."

"I merely suggested we might return here. I see no reason why we can't."

Rebecca turned away and stared at the ocean waves breaking against the rocks. "You could always bring someone else."

"Sure. I'll invite Peggy along next time. Or Adrian. Or maybe Aunt Helen. She enjoyed it last time she was here."

"You brought your aunt here?"

"Helen's not really an aunt. She's my mother's former employer and friend. They both came here a few years ago. Those were the two women I told you'd I'd invited here. The only two."

"You mean you've never brought anyone here? Romantically, I mean?"

"No. I haven't." He looked at her steadily.

"Am I supposed to read something into that?"

"There's always a first time. For everything."

"I see. Your idea of 'parity.' I give up my virginity; you give up your private retreat."

His gaze narrowed. "If you want to look at it that way."

"Oh, Connor, I don't expect you to match my investment here. I know you can't."

He looked toward the ocean pounding the rocks, an uncomfortable look settling on his face. "I'm doing the best I can."

She took pity on him. "Yes. You are. And that's all I want."

"That's all?"

She nodded. "Your best isn't too shabby." A slow grin spread over her face. "I really liked the way you kissed my…earlobe last night."

His gaze dropped to her navel, exposed by the bikini she wore. "You liked that? What about when I —"

She covered his mouth with her hand before he could continue. The twins—and Mona—were only a few yards away.

He kissed her hand lightly, then said, "I'll take you into town this afternoon. I thought you might want to shop for souvenirs or something."

"I have a better idea," she whispered. "The twins will take a nap this afternoon. Why don't we do the same?"

Sunday came all too soon, and they prepared to go back to the real world. As Rebecca was packing, she opened a drawer and found a pile of photos: two older women, smiling, sitting on the beach beside an incredibly huge sand castle. She smiled. Connor had probably hired dirt movers to come build his mother a castle on the beach he'd built for her. The depth of his love was amazing. She sighed. He didn't feel that for her — not yet — but Rebecca was sure he felt something. Maybe, just maybe, it was enough to grow a relationship from. A permanent relationship.

If not? If not, well, she would just have to unravel her heartstrings from the hopeless knot they'd been tied in this weekend.

He'd warned her, after all, not to expect more than he could give.

CHAPTER FIFTEEN

"How was your weekend?" Peggy asked when she brought Connor his cup of lapsang souchong, a black tea he ordered from Hong Kong.

"Fine," he replied, his attention on the financial reports Adrian had left on his desk. "The babysitter worked out well. Why don't you contact a nanny service here and find someone available on evenings and weekends? Also, could you call the Land Rover dealer? I'll need a bigger car; I want to drive Rebecca and the kids up north this weekend. I'm due to visit Rodney." Connor took a sip of tea, then continued, "If you could call the Millers and let them know I'll be arriving on Saturday…and bringing guests, I'd appreciate it."

"Anything else?"

"Yes, can you get Rebecca on the phone? I haven't asked her if she wants to go yet."

"Sure you don't want me to handle that too?" Peggy asked, her pen poised midair.

"No, I…" Then he glanced up and caught the twinkle in her eye. He wasn't used to seeing his secretary's eye twinkle over his morning tea. "I think I can handle that," he said, wondering for a brief moment if his own eyes had ever twinkled.

Peggy left, humming a tune Connor didn't recognize, although he thought he might have heard the words "splendored thing" mumbled under her breath.

A few minutes later, he heard Rebecca's voice on the phone, and suddenly he decided the reports Adrian had sent could wait. "Why don't you come up here?" he asked, realizing it had been almost twenty-four hours since he'd last seen her. Besides, he'd prefer to explain their weekend plans in person.

He wasn't sure why he wanted to introduce her to his brother when few people even knew he existed. But he couldn't resist the urge to share a part of his life with her. Some part of him wanted her approval, even though their relationship wouldn't last. It couldn't, he told himself; their expectations were simply too different. But, then, he'd never had a relationship with someone he considered a friend as well as a bed partner. Maybe they could remain friends when the attraction waned.

For now it certainly showed no signs of waning, he thought minutes later when Rebecca poked her head around the door and walked in his office. She wore a short black skirt, a silk blouse, and sexy black stockings that hid her legs — legs he wanted wrapped around him as soon as possible. She leaned over the desk for a quick kiss, then claimed a spot in the center of one of the sofas.

"I'd like you to come up to Ukiah with me this weekend," he told her when his pulse had settled down. "You and the twins. There's an extra bedroom with twin beds. The ocean's not far. We could stop and see Rodney, and I promised Aunt Helen I'd drop by and say hello."

Rebecca smiled, crossing her legs. Connor found he couldn't lift his gaze from her knees.

"I'd love to meet your brother. And your Aunt Helen."

"Good. We'll leave Saturday morning." He opened his drawer and stuffed the reports inside. "Now, what are you doing for lunch?"

"Nothing. The twins are taking a field trip to the aquarium today."

"Then let's go." He rose from his chair and walked around his desk, meeting her in the center of the room.

"But it's not even twelve!"

He grabbed his jacket from the hook on the wall, then stood waiting by the door. "It will be when we get there."

"Where?"

"My apartment. Come on."

Rebecca stifled a smile at Connor's eagerness. "Okay, but I have a meeting after lunch with Bob. I'm getting a new project," she told him as he led her into the outer office, where Peggy glanced up from a busy-looking phone.

"Call Bob in Technical and tell him Rebecca will be late for the meeting this afternoon," Connor instructed her as they passed.

Rebecca came to a dead halt. "Don't you dare!" she said to Peggy, her eyes locked on Connor.

She had decided to draw a firm line between their working relationship and their personal relationship, and lingering over lunch—and whatever else—wasn't part of the plan. She didn't want to be known as the Fourth Floor Mistress, even though she probably—technically, at least—already was.

Connor made what Aubrey called his "frowny face" but didn't issue a counter order.

Satisfied, Rebecca followed him out to the hall. She wasn't sure who'd won the skirmish, but the thought of finishing the round in bed made her hormones flutter in anticipation. A tingle of excitement raced up her spine, then wreaked havoc in her midsection, accompanied by visions of what she'd do to him. Just the thought of unknotting that silk tie...unbuttoning his white shirt...undressing her very own Corporate Raider Ken doll.

"Rebecca." Connor's voice interrupted her thoughts a moment later.

"Hmm?" She turned a dreamy gaze on him.

"That was Martin Grainger."

"Oh. Yes, it was, wasn't it?"

"Do you always smile at him like he's the next item on the menu?"

"Like he's wha—? Oh. Oh, dear." She turned and looked behind her, to where Martin was talking to Adrian. "You don't suppose Martin's a mind reader, do you?"

Connor shook his head, only slightly bemused. "He didn't list membership in the Planetary Psychic Society on his resume."

"Good. Otherwise, he'd know all about that cute little mole on your—"

Sometime later, Rebecca turned her head and saw the clock beside Connor's bed. "I need to get back to work, Connor. It's already been over an hour."

He picked up a lock of her hair that had fallen on his chest and curled it around his finger, saying lazily, "As I recall, company policy encourages physical activity during work hours."

She giggled. "I don't think what we just did comes under the heading of physical fitness."

"Sure it does."

She opened her mouth to reply, but he cut her short.

"I wrote the policy. I'll decide how to interpret it."

"Ahh, I see. The same way you interpret the company policy that dictates employee relationships."

"Exactly."

She propped herself up on an elbow and looked down at him. "I don't see how you can expect your employees not to date within the company when you yourself—"

"The policy prohibits relationships between two people working in a direct chain of command."

"Exactly!" Her eyes widened as she mimicked his words. "You're directly in my chain of command. Right at the top, actually."

He shook his head. "No, there're too many links between you and me to constitute 'directly.'"

She saw the perfect opportunity to pry. "And Claire Porter? Wasn't she directly in your chain of command?"

"Yes. But I never dated her."

Her gaze narrowed. "That's not what the rumors imply."

"Rumors have been wrong on occasion."

"You mean you really didn't have a relationship with her?"

"Sure I did. We've been friends for a long time. But nothing more. She's never even been here to the penthouse."

"Never?" Rebecca said, not sure she should dump the small load of jealously she'd been carrying around.

He laughed. "You seem to find this hard to believe. You've never even met her. What makes you think she's even my type?"

"She's beautiful. Intelligent…"

"So are you."

"But she also knows the difference between a 401k and a Roth."

"You're right. When I'm ready to retire, I'll call her."

She gave an exasperated sigh, which he caught with his mouth in a light kiss. "Why don't you let me decide who I'm compatible with?" Then his expression grew more serious. "Claire and I were too alike to ever have been successful as lovers. In personality, in goals, in…background. Though I'm sure there're facets of her that I could never understand, the simple truth is that we were, well, *too* compatible. Too boring."

"You mean you *have* thought about it?"

"Of course. She *is* a beautiful woman, as you said. But she was much too valuable an employee to screw up our professional relationship with what would have amounted to a few months of mediocre sex."

"Are you saying I'm not a valuable employee?"

"No. I'm saying the sex isn't mediocre."

"How'd you know that? Before we had it, I mean?"

"I had a hunch."

"And were you right?"

"I'm always right." He turned to her, kissed her more deeply, and a few minutes later, proved it again. By the time they came up for air, it was almost time for her meeting with Bob. "Oh, Connor, what am I going to say when they ask me where I had lunch?" she moaned, as she gathered her stockings over her thumbs.

"I don't particularly care what you say."

She glanced up, surprised. "You mean you wouldn't mind if everyone knew we were having an affair?"

He watched her in the mirror as he knotted his tie. "I'd mind for your sake."

She smiled and pulled her stockings over her knees. "That's sweet."

He frowned. "If Bob gives you any trouble for being late…"

"Oh, he wouldn't. He thinks I'm a ditz anyway, ever since I 'forgot' I was taking a vacation. He asked me how my 'friend' was this morning, and I gave him a blank look." With her gaze fastened innocently on her feet as she slid them into her shoes, she added, "I think he may have noticed that love bite you gave me, though."

Connor turned and glanced at her neck. "I never gave you a—"

"Gotcha!" She laughed and kissed his own neck above the crisp white shirt collar. "Good thing he didn't see that 'I heart Connor' tattoo on my arm."

On Saturday, the drive north took a little over an hour, once they'd crossed the Golden Gate Bridge and escaped the Saturday morning traffic of Marin County. Connor drove them straight to his ultra-sleek home, hidden not far from the coast.

That afternoon, they drove into Ukiah. On the way, Connor tried to prepare Rebecca for Rodney. "Don't expect much in the way of a warm welcome," he warned her. "He often acts as if he couldn't care less that I've come. Though the Millers swear he can tell you the date of every visit I've made for the last ten years, sometimes I think Rodney would be just as happy if I sent my holographic image instead."

"Maybe that's a sign he cares, Connor."

"Or a sign he remembers the jigsaw puzzle I brought him," he replied cynically.

Connor had told her he kept Rodney supplied with puzzles from all over the world, and Rodney usually had them completed within hours after he left. Rebecca's heart quivered, but before she could think of a response, they reached the frame house where Rodney lived.

At the door, Mrs. Miller let them in and called Rodney from his room. They heard the sound of a television being turned off, then Rodney shuffled into the room. He was an inch or two shorter than Connor, with the same handsome features, though his hair was not as dark. He stood with his shoulders slumped, avoiding eye contact. "Rodney, this is Rebecca," Connor told him. "And her children, Alex and Aubrey."

"Rebecca," he said, nodding his head, then he muttered, "R-E-B-E-C-C-A. Two e's. Two c's." He slanted a look at Alex and Aubrey as if convinced they had something to do with it.

She gave him a warm smile. "Connor tells me you like puzzles."

"Yes," he answered, staring at the carpet as if her voice had come from the fibers.

"My sister and I once did a jigsaw puzzle with a thousand pieces. Except there were only nine-hundred and ninety-nine. One was missing, but we didn't know that, of course, until we'd almost finished it."

"That must have been disappointing," Connor said.

"I suppose. But we still enjoyed the puzzle—at least until we discovered there weren't enough pieces to fill the empty spaces."

Rodney nodded, his gaze still on the floor. "Nine-hundred ninety-nine. Three nines. Three nines are twenty-seven. Seven and two are nine."

Rebecca nodded. "Yes, and nine sevens and nine twos are eighty-one. So are three twenty-sevens."

Connor shook his head and said dryly, "Why do I get the feeling I'm surrounded by co-processors cleverly disguised as mortals?"

Rebecca laughed. "Nine's a magic number, Connor. I thought everyone knew that!"

"It's math, not magic," he corrected her. "Now if you and Rodney are finished discussing the peculiarities of higher mathematics, the twins, I think, might be hungry. Mrs. Miller mentioned something about lemonade and cookies."

They went into the kitchen, where Mrs. Miller had set out snacks for the twins and made a pot of tea for Connor and Rebecca. Rodney joined them at the scarred pine table, and several times Rebecca caught him glancing sideways at Connor, almost as if he were afraid he would disappear.

Connor might think his brother didn't notice whether he visited or not; Rebecca, however, was sure Rodney was very much aware of Connor's presence.

Later, as they were leaving, Rodney returned, his gaze still fastened on the floor. "Tell Rebecca and the twins goodbye, Rodney," Connor instructed him gently.

"Connor's thinking of asking her out," Rodney told them.

Rebecca looked at him quizzically. "Who?"

"Rebecca Adams."

She looked at Connor, bemused. "You are?"

"It's a long story," he replied dryly.

"Rebecca Arrowsmith," Rodney continued, his gaze riveted on her shoes. "Rebecca of Sunnybrook Farm. Rebecca with two e's and two c's and twins Aubrey and Alex."

Rebecca Evans smiled, while Rodney added, "Connor brings Rebecca to the Millers'."

Connor gave him a thoughtful look. "Do you want me to bring Rebecca back to the Millers'? Rebecca, Aubrey, and Alex?"

"Yes," was all Rodney said, shifting his gaze to the door behind them.

Rebecca reached out and touched the sleeve of Rodney's gray sweater. "Goodbye, Rodney. I enjoyed meeting you. And I'd love to come back and see you sometime."

For an instant Rodney's eyes met hers, then he dropped his lids and nodded his head. "Connor's thinking of asking her out. Rebecca of Sunnybrook Farm. Two e's. Two c's."

CHAPTER SIXTEEN

Rebecca gasped for breath. "Did we just have an earthquake? I felt the earth move."

Above her, Connor sucked in air slowly, calmly, as in control as ever despite an earth-shaking climax. "Nine point nine on the Richter scale, I'd estimate."

"Really? Mine was an eleven."

"That's theoretically impossible, you know," he said as he rolled to her side.

"Well then, tell me, why is it every time we make love, my insides feel like they're ripping through my skin...and my heart is pumping lava hot enough to ignite popsicles?" She stretched languorously against him, sighing contentedly.

"That sounds serious."

She smiled. "It is. Very."

"Maybe you should consult a geologist."

"Or a gynecologist." She glanced at his face. His eyes were closed, his face relaxed. "I was thinking about getting a prescription for the Pill."

Connor didn't reply.

"Connor? What do you think?"

"I think it's your decision."

"But we're…Well, I know it's a pain to have to put on a condom every time."

"I don't mind."

"Maybe not, but I'd like to make love to you without anything in between."

"That's not a very safe practice, Rebecca. I'm sure you don't need a lecture from me on STDs."

"No, but we are in a monogamous relationship right now…aren't we?"

"I'm not seeing anyone else. But—"

"Neither am I."

"That's not the point."

"What is the point?"

He sighed. "I'm not against you using birth control. I think it's a good idea. But I don't make a practice of having sex without using protection."

"I see."

He wasn't willing to make an exception for her, she realized. That hurt. He didn't expect their relationship to last forever, obviously, and wanted to have a "clean record" for the next woman he took to bed.

She turned over and stared out the window, where a protractor-shaped moon traced a slow, precise arc across the night sky.

"Rebecca…It's inevitable we'll have other sexual partners…eventually."

"You're right. In fact, I'm already planning on shagging the rest of the FGI staff."

He sighed. "Rebecca…" he began, sounding as if he was as uncomfortable with her bitterness as she was.

"It's okay, Connor," she said in a small voice. "I know this is just sex for you."

"No, it's not just sex. I enjoy being with you. You know that."

"But you aren't planning to fall in love with me."

"I told you, I'm not planning to fall in love with anyone. I'm simply not capable of it—not now."

"Everyone's capable of it. You just won't let yourself."

"Perhaps."

"You don't know what you're missing out on," she said, hoping the superior air she injected in her voice hid the hurt.

"I suppose you're going to tell me."

"Nope." She punched the pillow into a shape she liked. "I'll just keep it to myself."

"Fine." He sounded relieved, and Rebecca decided to torment him just a little. "I won't say anything at all about that delicious little feeling I get when you smile, which isn't very often, by the way. Or the way I quiver when you touch me…anywhere. Even when you just put your hand on my back, while we're walking…" She smiled to herself. "Or the way my heart flutters every time you say my name in that calm, know-it-all way you have." She glanced at him over her shoulder.

Connor stared at the ceiling, his arms crossed behind his head. "Rebecca, I told you—"

"I know what you told me. I have it memorized." She tapped her skull. "You don't want emotional attachment. You just want sex. Period."

"That's not what I said."

"Oh, right, and you want to remain friends when it's over," she added. "Fine. I'll be your friend. Remind me to put you on my Christmas card list." She closed her eyes and pretended she was seriously thinking about sleep.

"But it's not over. Not by a long shot," he told her, sounding a little put out. "I'd appreciate it if you'd stop sounding the death knell for a relationship that I happen to be enjoying very much."

She slid her leg up and down the length of his thigh, exploring. "How much?" she asked, wondering if it was possible he could be ready again…But, oh yes, it seemed he was.

"I told you. Nine point nine." He began stroking her spine with his thumb, lingering at the base, massaging the little knot there.

"Umm. Maybe we should try for a ten," she said, stretching like a cat under his petting. "No reason we can't have perfection."

"Did I happen to mention that I'm a perfectionist?" he said, leaning over her and nibbling her throat, sending funny little tremors racing down to her belly.

She moaned, and he caught her breath in a soul stirring kiss that lodged deep in her heart, and made her pulse shimmer with longing. His mouth left hers and slid across her chin to the soft skin of her throat, where he tickled a throbbing artery with his tongue. Then his tongue slid lower, between her breasts and over them, lingering for a delicious moment, then across her belly and down to where already she was hot and wet and ready for him.

"Oh, Connor," she breathed, and loved him silently while he tried to make her forget he was missing a piece of his heart.

Later, as they lay entwined in the warm bed, Rebecca outlined a heart in the center of his chest, then traced a crack down the middle and planted a kiss in the center.

Their lovemaking had been tender this time, not rushed and frantic as it sometimes was. Connor had caressed her, stroking her until she'd come apart, and then he'd held her while she slowly came back together.

He was good at taking care of people. She remembered what Helen Tannehill had told her earlier that afternoon, when they'd stopped by her house after visiting Rodney.

Her house, a two story with white columns and acres of green grass, could have been an understudy for Tara, and Helen herself an older version of Scarlett.

Helen and Rebecca had sat on her back porch, enjoying another round of lemonade. The two of them watched Connor as he crossed the wide lawn with the twins, taking them to see the squirrel's nest Helen had pointed out among the oaks. Helen seemed delighted that Connor had brought someone by on his visit.

"His mother would have loved to see him so happy." She sighed as if remembering. "She worried about him all the time, you see. Oh, he always seemed to be perfectly able to take care of himself. Even as a little boy, he was so self-sufficient, but underneath, he needed her just as much as Rodney did.

"That's why I call him so often, you know," she confided, her eyes lighting as she leaned closer to Rebecca. "I promised his mother I'd look after him. She was afraid he'd lock himself up inside his own mind and never give anyone a chance to get inside...to get to know him, the way he really is. Sometimes I think Connor doesn't even know how much love he has to give...if he ever finds the right person."

Rebecca smiled gently. "It's good of you to look after him, Mrs. Tannehill."

"Call me Helen...Aunt Helen, if you'd prefer," she added, with a hopeful glance at Rebecca. Then she looked across the yard to where

Connor held up Alex to peek into the tree, and a worried look creased her face. "I don't know what's going to happen after I'm gone."

"Oh, but you're not going anywhere, Mrs.…Helen," Rebecca said firmly.

Helen gave her a gentle smile. "I can't live forever, and Connor needs someone his own age looking after him. A wife and children. And a home—a real home, not that glass penthouse he lives in."

Rebecca didn't point out that Connor had at least three homes she knew of. The man who had everything had no shortage of living space. She understood what Helen meant. And she agreed with her, but Connor didn't yet understand the difference.

But he was coming round, she had thought with a silent smile as she watched him walking back slowly across the lawn, holding Aubrey's hand in his.

Aubrey didn't give her trust easily, and the fact that she was willing to place her tiny hand in Connor's said a lot for the guy.

Now, as Rebecca lay beside him in the bed, his body wrapped protectively around her, she realized she didn't want to be just another person Connor took care of, like Rodney and Helen. He loved them, she knew, but not the way she wanted to be loved: passionately, whole-heartedly, recklessly.

On Monday morning, Connor made his way around the giant palms that decorated the hotel lobby. Normally he took his own elevator down to the garage where his car was kept, but this morning he had a purchase to make.

He'd invited Rebecca to play tennis during lunch. It had been easier to convince her it was a legitimate fitness activity, though she had laughingly insisted he'd mop the court with her.

He intended to spot her a few serves, though he'd probably be too distracted by the bouncing hem of her tennis skirt to bother returning half the balls she sent over the net, anyway.

At the entrance to the jewelers, he stopped. Perhaps he should call Tiffany's instead; they would have a better selection, but he had hoped to surprise her this afternoon. He knew exactly what he wanted. He'd thought about it before going to bed last night and had decided on the perfect gift.

Diamonds weren't her style, though she'd look exquisite in them. He made a note to have a selection brought by the office. He'd seen a canary diamond once, a warm shade of golden brown, that would be lovely against her throat. Inside the small shop, he quickly found what he wanted, glad to see it came in platinum—more practical, he decided. Gold tended to lose its shape when it got warm, and Rebecca's skin was remarkably warm.

"I think you've chosen the perfect gift, sir," the clerk told him, locking the glass case again. "Practical, but with a price tag that shows how much you care."

Connor doubted Rebecca would care about the price tag. She hadn't seemed the least bit impressed with his wealth so far, more concerned with his balance of "chi" than his bank balance.

"Charge it to my account," he instructed the clerk, wondering if the man wasn't partially right. He did care about Rebecca, more than he'd ever cared about any woman. He had a tender feeling for her, an emotion he hadn't felt in a long time, if ever. He wanted to take care of her—her and the twins—and make sure she never got her heart broken by anyone other than him.

This wasn't love, he told himself. It wasn't the kind of emotion that made poets out of mortal men, or made saints out of women like his mother, who had left her home in Ireland—traded security, family, and country—for the love of a man who'd eventually left her.

It didn't seem like a very good rate of exchange to him.

After declining the clerk's offer to wrap the gift, he slipped it in his pocket, liking the feel of it against his heart almost as much as he'd liked having Rebecca wrapped about him while he slept.

"Before you go, there's something I want to show you," Connor said, walking over to his jacket and pulling out a long flat box.

They'd come back to his apartment to shower and have lunch after the tennis game, which, as she'd predicted, he'd won. But only by a few points—he'd gallantly conceded the line calls to her, Rebecca had realized, laughingly accusing him of losing his edge.

"What's that?" she asked as he handed the box to her.

"Open it."

When she did, her heart sank with disappointment. "Oh, Connor, please tell me you aren't giving this to me."

He stood very still. "You don't like it?"

"It's…it's beautiful. But…it's a watch!"

"You don't want a watch?"

"No! I mean, not from you!"

He lifted an eyebrow. "You'd prefer it came from someone else?"

Tears filled her eyes as she realized what he'd done: substituted an expensive gift for what he couldn't give her: his heart. "Oh, Connor, I can't believe you'd do this!"

He turned his back to her, slipping on his jacket. "If you don't like it, you can exchange it. It came from the jeweler downstairs. I'm sure they'll have something else you'll like better."

She shook her head, blinking back the tears. "No. No. I don't want anything else."

He shoved his hands in his pockets and glanced back at her, a wary look on his face. "I'm not sure I understand. You needed a watch. The last time we went out, you didn't wear one. I assumed that was because the only one you had was the sport watch you wore while we were hiking, the same one you wear to work."

She should be touched that he'd actually noticed. Yet although he'd noticed her lack of a watch, he'd never realized that what she really wanted from him didn't come with a platinum band.

Rejection and regret mingled in her throat and made her voice husky. "You don't understand. It's not *what* it is, but why!"

"You would prefer I gave you something you didn't need?"

"No! I would prefer you didn't give me anything!"

"I see." But the expression on his face indicated the opposite.

"You can't buy me an expensive gift and make things even between us."

"You're right. This doesn't even begin to cover what I owe you."

"You don't owe me anything!" She shook her head, helpless to make him understand. "Oh, Connor, for a smart man, you're hopelessly ignorant when it comes to relationships."

"Perhaps I am. But I distinctly recall telling you up front what this one would involve. Now you seem to be objecting to the terms."

"This isn't a business arrangement. This is us—you and me. I care about you. And I want something from you besides a watch. Or a nice evening in bed."

He looked away, gazing out the window, where the skyline of San Francisco broke through the fog. "I've told you, Rebecca. Despite your claim that I'm missing the next best thing to eternal rapture, I've chosen to forego the pleasure, just as I give up dessert now and again. And a trip to the endodontist for a root canal."

She gaped at him. "A root canal! You're comparing our relationship to a root canal?"

"No. What we have is dessert. And too much dessert leads to poor dental health. An imperfect analogy, maybe, but accurate enough."

She sighed. "Then I feel sorry for you, Connor. Because a life without joy, or pain, without all the peaks and valleys and highs and lows is boring. Flat. Dull."

"Perhaps. But then I don't think I'd enjoy the emotional high wire act." An expression very much like loathing crossed his face. "I obviously don't have the same needs you do."

"Yet you want our relationship to continue. On your terms."

"Yes. Whether or not you accept the watch."

But he would just find something else to give her, some way to repay her for the investment she was making, she realized. And she didn't want that. She wanted his love, free and clear, with no worries about falling—or tooth decay. And no convenient pay-back schedule.

She wished she could just agree to his terms. Wished she could give up on her dream, her hope of love and a happily-ever-after ending.

Maybe Connor wasn't her Prince Charming after all. Maybe he was merely the Good Samaritan, capable only of offering a hand—or a Piaget watch, in this case. He didn't seem interested in what she had to give him.

The thin hope she'd held onto dashed against reality.

She'd thought if she kissed this frog, if she showed him what a relationship could be like, if he realized how much he needed her...

But people weren't computer programs. She couldn't just plug a piece of data into them and come up with the right answer. Connor was a complex man, with needs she'd probably never even heard of, much less knew how to provide.

Although, what was so complex about love? She'd always thought it worked like sourdough starter: add a little yeast at the beginning, and a few weeks later, a bubbling cauldron of possibilities. Not a platinum watch.

She stared at the watch, its impassive face showing the current time. Maybe, she thought with as much detachment as she could muster, Connor wasn't her destiny. Maybe he could live without her after all.

Maybe it was time to find out.

She placed the watch on the edge of his bed. "It's a beautiful watch. I'm sure some other woman would love to have it."

She turned and walked toward the door, her legs trembling as if she'd just climbed a mountain, only to find an empty crater inside.

"Rebecca," he began, a note of disbelief in his voice.

But she didn't stop until she reached the door.

"Rebecca!"

"Find someone else to give it to. We're all interchangeable, aren't we? If all you want is sex."

She shut the door behind her and made her way through his luxurious apartment, the tears in her eyes preventing her from seeing the kind eyes of Mrs. Pascal as she dusted the piano in the corner.

Connor stared at the closed door, scarcely believing she'd just given back a gift that cost over twenty thousand dollars. Scarcely believing that he was hurt because she had.

He was unused to the confusion he felt. He didn't know why he hadn't stopped her. He probably could have. Easily. No one knew better than he how susceptible she was to a few well-placed kisses.

He picked up the box and opened it, glad to see the price tag had been removed.

He'd been right, and too much a fool to follow his own advice. She was too young, too inexperienced, to play on his terms.

Then why was he the one feeling like he'd just had his balls slammed against the net?

CHAPTER SEVENTEEN

"Rebecca, what's wrong?" Kevin asked when she came back to the office. She gave him a bright smile and wiped away a remaining tear.

"Nothing, just got a little wind in my eye, that's all."

"Your mother called while you were gone. She wanted you to call her back."

"Oh. Thanks for the message." Somehow, she wasn't entirely surprised at that news. She and Kim had always joked that their mother seemed to have an amazing ability to sense when they were in trouble. Rebecca had often picked up the phone and heard her mother's voice, just when she was about to indulge in a bout of child-like tears.

Mother's intuition. Another thing Connor probably didn't believe in.

She hurried to her desk and picked up the phone to call her mother.

When she finally spoke to her, she found that it wasn't intuition that had made Barb phone her daughter. "I've just found out the Seversons are filing for a custody hearing. Your cousin Penny called me this morning. Her sister-in-law is in Jo's next door neighbor's bridge club," Barb told her, and Rebecca marveled once again at how, beyond the Edens Expressway, Chicago suddenly became a small town. "They want to contest the guardianship Kim and Randy specified in their will."

"But they can't do that!"

"It looks like they can. Randy's father is the executor of the estate. He can demand the will be held in probate until the issue is decided. At least that's what Penny's husband says, and he's worked in the clerk of court's office for years."

"But I'm a good parent to the twins. There's no way a judge would take them from me."

"From what Penny's sister-in-law says, they're claiming your lifestyle is not conducive to raising two children."

Rebecca laughed. "It's not like I'm a stripper, Mom!"

"But you are single, and working full time."

"There are lots of single mothers who work!"

"You don't have to tell me that, hon. I raised you and your sister after your dad left, and I did a darn good job of it. The difference here is, you're not their mother. And the wills did mention a second choice…Randy's brother."

Rebecca frowned. "Oh, right. Not only is he single, but he has about as much maternal instinct as a lizard."

"Apparently his fiancée doesn't think so."

"What fiancée?"

"You remember, that girl he was dating last spring? The schoolteacher? They've decided to get married. And from what I hear, the wedding will be soon."

Rebecca chewed her lip, trying to ignore the clanging alarm going off in her heart. She refused to believe that she could lose the twins. "This is ridiculous! No judge in his right mind would take the twins from me. They're just starting to adjust to living here, just starting to accept their parents' deaths. The worst thing anyone could do would be to remove them from their home—again."

"I agree, but you know the Seversons haven't been happy about the arrangement. Aubrey and Alex are their only grandchildren, and they've been hinting since the funeral they wanted them raised here."

"I've told them I'll bring the twins for vacations, and they're welcome here whenever they want."

"Yes, but I did warn you there'd be fallout when you wrote that letter to Judge Walker."

Rebecca groaned. "Yes, you did." But she'd ignored her mother's advice—and, she realized, probably angered the Seversons in the process.

"The sentencing was last week," her mother added. "The judge must have taken your letter into account. After a year in prison, Melvin Dailey will perform community service."

"Well, at least he's learned his lesson. There wouldn't have been any good to come from locking him up for life. The prosecutor told me his daughter is handicapped."

"But the Seversons are spitting mad about it. They're telling anyone who'll listen they don't think you're fit to raise the twins."

Rebecca sighed, staring at the photo of Alex and Aubrey she'd made a few weeks before. They were dressed up as their favorite characters, Peter Pan and Tinkerbell. Aubrey wore a trace of the bright smile that used to appear on her face more often when her parents were alive. Alex, with a smudge of chocolate pudding on his jaw and a devil-may-care grin, looked endearingly fierce as Peter Pan.

Just the thought of losing them made her heart crumble.

"So, just because I happen to have a heart, I'm not fit to be a parent? Why is it that compassion isn't a popular concept these days?"

"One person's compassion is another's leniency. Or lunacy, as the Seversons seem to feel."

"Kim and Randy didn't seem to think any of that mattered. They asked me not long after the twins were born if I would raise them if anything ever happened. Of course, none of us ever dreamed..." The tears that had fallen earlier suddenly returned, and she wished her mother wasn't two thousand miles away.

"Let's hope the judge sees it that way. They expect to get an answer tomorrow on their request to have a guardianship hearing. And from what Penny's husband says, the judges in Lake County are inclined to be cautious on issues of child welfare. I know you're a good parent, but the judge might want to find out for himself."

Rebecca swallowed her fear. She knew the twins needed to be with her. There was absolutely no question in her mind. If she for one minute had thought anyone else could provide a better home for them, she'd have given them up in a second.

An awful ache started in her heart, joining the ache she'd felt ever since she'd seen Connor's gift earlier. She couldn't lose the twins. She couldn't face them and tell them they couldn't live here, in the house they'd decorated together, where she'd assured them over and over there were no scary monsters lurking in the closets.

They were counting on her, and Kim and Randy were counting on her to convince anyone who needed convincing that she was the best choice to raise them.

"I think you need an attorney, Rebecca. Penny says she knows one. He handled her son's divorce."

"Maybe you're right…" She hated the thought of hiring an attorney, though. Maybe she should call the Seversons, try to work something out.

Her last conversation with Jo hadn't gone well. The woman had complained about the twins' diets—Alex had told her they were having tofu pups instead of hot dogs at their birthday party, and she insisted the entire idea was flaky.

"I suppose they eat weird stuff like that out in California. I don't know why you can't raise them closer to home, anyway," Jo had said with a huff of annoyance.

Rebecca should have seen it coming, she supposed, but she'd been so focused on her relationship with Connor, she'd neglected the warning signs. She'd forgotten her first responsibility was to the twins, not to a man who thought an expensive piece of jewelry was a good substitute for love.

After hanging up with her mother, she phoned the lawyer her mother had recommended and left a message.

She didn't want to believe that a judge would take the children away from her, but she remembered a woman she'd known in college who had a three-year-old child. A judge had awarded full custody to the father, simply because she was a full-time student and the father had a stay-at-home wife.

Marriage was out of the question, but would she quit her job to stay with the twins? Move back to Illinois?

She could live with her mother, maybe get part-time consulting work. Connor would give her a good recommendation. But the thought of leaving San Francisco, her home, the job she loved, and Connor…

Her emotions had been tumbling over each other ever since Connor had handed her the gift. Had she been too hasty to ascribe ulterior motives to the gesture? Was she just naïve? Or was he the one who needed a crash course in human relationships?

The phone interrupted her musing. It was the attorney in Chicago, Tony Markham. He listened as she relayed the information her mother had given her, then promised to check out the situation and get back to her.

Before hanging up, he did caution her that because she wasn't the natural parent, a judge would be more stringent in determining that she was the best possible choice to raise the twins. That meant her background and lifestyle were likely to come under scrutiny.

"Custody cases are never predictable," he told her. "Believe me, I've been surprised more times than I can count by judges who claim to be acting in the best interests of the child."

That didn't bode well, Rebecca thought, hanging up the phone. For the first time since talking to her mother, she wondered if there really was a chance she could lose the twins.

She gave a longing look at the tissues on her desk. A good cry would be better than chocolate right now. Her love life was resembling an episode of *The Price Is Right*, a judge wanted her in court to prove her worthiness as a parent, and she had an endless list of errands before their birthday party on Saturday.

When she finally got home, she had a message from Connor: he'd be in New York for a few days and would call her when he returned to discuss "the situation."

The situation. Somehow she'd been downgraded from a lover to a situation. It was probably a good thing, she tried to convince herself. The last thing she needed now was a distraction. Although she would have loved some advice — and a shoulder, just in case she decided to cry.

"Gold." Adrian uttered the word as if it were dirt. "Trading at all-time highs. And we're short." He tossed his folder on the desk in disgust.

Connor's gaze remained fastened on his laptop. "Patience. The market's due for a correction any day. Europe's getting ready to open the vaults."

Adrian perked up. "Is that right? Have you talked to the Chairman?"

Connor glanced at him. "No. But I've read his mind. Hold on; your short position will make you a fortune."

"I'll take your advice, but if that crystal ball of yours is cracked—"

"Don't worry. It's a momentary fluctuation. Gold will be in its usual nadirs by the end of the month." He nodded toward the screen in front of him. "If I'm wrong, I'll eat this monitor."

Adrian laughed. "If you're wrong, we'll *have* to start eating our hardware." He left the room, his worried look eased somewhat, and Connor quit pretending to be absorbed by his computer screen.

They were at the Forrest Group offices in Manhattan, just blocks away from Wall Street and any number of financial institutions, one or two of which he owned. He thought briefly about paying a visit to one of them—anything to ease the restless boredom that had been plaguing him ever since Monday afternoon when Rebecca had walked out of his apartment.

Things had gone wrong. How, he still wasn't quite sure, though he'd racked his brain, trying to figure out why she'd reacted the way she had. He'd known she wasn't like all the other women he'd dated, but he'd never seen such stark disappointment on a woman's face when he handed her a gift. Instead of a watch, she seemed to want something he simply couldn't give her. Unfortunately, happily-ever-after endings just didn't exist, outside of Disney.

Connor smiled to himself. There was an idea. Maybe he'd offer to take her and the twins to Disneyland. It wasn't exactly his milieu, but if it made Rebecca happy, he'd put on a set of Mickey ears and hum show tunes.

He suddenly remembered the hand-drawn invitation still in his desk drawer. Wasn't it the twins' birthday this weekend?

He picked up his jacket, shut down his laptop, and told his secretary to page his driver. He'd been meaning to go by FAO Schwartz and find Rodney another puzzle. He'd pick up something for the twins while he was there.

Before the elevator reached the ground floor, the door opened, and Jane Prentice got on.

"Hello, Connor. What a surprise! I didn't know you were in town."

Connor usually phoned her whenever he was in New York. He'd take her to dinner and a play, and often his apartment later. It was an arrangement that worked for both of them. She knew the city well and could always recommend a great new restaurant, while he always provided her with a timely stock tip.

"It was a sudden trip," he told her. "I'm only here for a couple of days."

"Oh. That's too bad." Her smile held regret, and speculation. "I'll tell you what, I can cancel my date and meet you for dinner. Around eight?"

"Thanks, but I have plans tonight." None he couldn't change, but he didn't want to spend the evening with Jane. Not in bed, not at the theater, not at the best restaurant in the city.

Jane's green eyes hardened briefly before she glanced at her watch—a Piaget, similar to the one he'd bought Rebecca.

Suddenly, all he wanted was to fly back to San Francisco and convince Rebecca he wasn't trying to buy her off when he'd given her the watch. Hell, he should know; he'd bought off plenty of women.

Including this one, once or twice, though she preferred dinner in Tribeca and first rate seats at Schubert Theater.

Connor was relieved when she murmured a farewell and got off the elevator before it reached the ground floor. As he walked out into the shaded crevices of lower Manhattan and stepped into the waiting limo, he debated canceling his meeting tomorrow and heading back to San Francisco tonight.

There must be some way to convince Rebecca that he'd meant her no disrespect. An apology had worked the first time, but he had the feeling this went beyond apologies.

CHAPTER EIGHTEEN

The back yard of Rebecca's Victorian house looked like a kinder-garten schoolyard at recess. Five-year-olds were everywhere: in the small plastic wading pool, on the swing set, in the bushes…Rebecca was pretty certain there'd been one hiding under the picnic table for the last fifteen minutes, shooting sporadically at anyone who came near with a contraband water pistol. Next time, she'd be sure to put "no guns" on the invitation.

If there was a next time. Even with homicidal preschoolers aiming for her ankles, that possibility wasn't one she wanted to contemplate, so she fixed a smile on her face and pulled Jared down from the fence where he'd apparently been staging a break out.

"The pirates are attacking!" he yelled as she hauled his squirming body back to the mothership.

"Then you'd better stick with your comrades, mate. They need you now."

"Hey, Rebecca!" Alex yelled as she reached the swing set. "Can we have more grape juice?"

"No, you may not. Someone dumped the last pitcher all over Michael."

"But it's blood!" Alex protested. "Captain Hook chopped his arm off!"

"Violence is not the answer," she muttered under her breath, raking her gaze around the yard. Signs of destruction were everywhere. The new lawn chairs she'd bought had been tossed "overboard" into the neighbor's yard. The pool was filled with what looked like industrial sludge. The Scooby Doo piñata hung in ragged tatters near the back porch, emptied of its booty by a platoon of Lost Boys wielding a T-ball bat.

She'd known better than to invite so many. There was even a specific formula for determining the number of guests: All the books said to invite as many guests as the age of the child, plus one.

So, she'd invited five for each twin, and then two more, but she didn't want to exclude the other three members of their daycare class. Now she had seventeen party animals in her back yard—and one adult. If she were running a daycare, she'd no doubt be busted and charged with violation of the adult-child ratio.

Maybe she shouldn't have told the other parents not to stay when they RSVP'd, but she'd assumed Connor would be there, and he would be uncomfortable with their relationship being on display. Now the kids were all racing about the yard like screaming fire ants, hosing each other down with a garden hose. No one was crying, though, not since she'd patched up Heather's knee and admonished Brian to stop calling Madison a crybaby.

Even Aubrey seemed to be having a good time, though as usual, she stood apart from the action, surveying the scene, thumb in mouth, but with a smile in her blue eyes. Her pink bathing suit and rubber sandals were dry. None of the other kids had had the nerve to spray Aubrey with the hose. Her daycare teacher had told Rebecca the other children seemed to watch out for Aubrey, sensing that she wasn't as emotionally sturdy as the rest of them.

Maybe, thought Rebecca, Aubrey was tired of being treated differently. Maybe she wanted to get wet, just like the other kids. Maybe she wanted to forget her fears and run screaming around the yard...

But before she could finish her thoughts, the gate next to the garage opened, and Connor walked straight into Never Never Land.

She'd never been so glad to see anyone in her life.

Of course, at that moment, she'd have welcomed any adult, but the fact it was Connor, whom she hadn't seen since last Monday, had her heart turning a funny little flip.

He wore carefully creased khakis, a short-sleeve white polo, and dark glasses that hid his eyes. Suddenly, she imagined the water hose aimed in his direction.

She dashed to the bushes where the spigot was located and put an end to the game.

"I just saved you from a dousing by a band of pirates. Or maybe they're the Lost Boys. Are those for the twins?" she said, glancing at the gaily wrapped packages in his arms. "You didn't have to—"

Behind his shades, an eyebrow lifted. "I thought presents were required at birthday parties."

She smiled, taking the smaller package from him. "You're right. The twins will be thrilled. I'm glad you came. I need reinforcements."

The sudden lack of firepower had caused a lull in the chaos as the pirates regrouped. Connor glanced around him, taking in the soggy devastation that was once a back yard. "I've seen superfund sites that looked better than this. No one's notified the EPA, have they?"

She laughed. "No, but I think the neighbors might be getting ready to complain about the noise."

"What noise?" he asked, just as Alex let out an earsplitting whoop and pounced on little Angelica Freeman, who promptly began to wail and hit back.

With one hand, Connor scooped him up, propping the wet wriggling mass of kid on his shoulder. Rebecca cringed as water seeped onto his spotless shirt.

"Hey, look, everybody! Connor's here! Can you be Captain Hook?" Alex asked.

Rebecca started to object, but Connor replied calmly, "Sure, but Captain Hook is going to have to insist that this ship get cleaned up. Any sailor who objects gets drawn and quartered."

"What's drawn and quartered mean?" Alex asked as he scrambled down from his perch.

"It means no birthday presents. You're in charge, Alex. See that those plates are cleared out of the pool, and gather up those wet towels…and you—what's your name, mate?"

"Jared."

"Put that hose down and start picking up the lawn chairs. We can't sail this boat until things are ship shape around here."

"Aye, aye, sir!" Jared gave him a sloppy salute and raced to obey the Voice of Authority.

"Whew!" Rebecca shook her head, exhaustion pouring out of her now that a grown-up was on the job. "How'd you do that? I've been trembling in terror here for the last fifteen minutes."

"When you're outnumbered, there's only one thing to do: delegate."

She acknowledged his wisdom with a solemn nod, admiring the way the sun kindled his black hair with brilliance. "You're probably right. Thanks for coming, by the way."

Fortunately, the guests had each brought a change of clothes to the party. Before long, the pirates, all of whom were apparently issued a reprieve by the Captain after doing their share of clean-up, had changed out of their wet swimsuits. Alex and Aubrey made short work of the presents, and then, thankfully, parents began trickling in.

No one questioned the presence of the head of FGI, though most of the parents worked for him. Either they already knew about their relationship, or he was a regular on the birthday party circuit. Rebecca suspected it was the former. She'd noticed more than one speculative glance in her direction from the lead gossip mongers.

She wished she could tell them that their relationship was over, but she was having a hard time remembering why she'd ended it anyway. A guy who handled the birthday party cleanup the way he just had deserved another chance.

After the last child had left, Rebecca fell into one of the lawn chairs the kids had retrieved from the neighbors' yard. There was hardly any evidence now that a band of pirates had recently been marauding the yard.

When Connor appeared beside her, holding a glass of lemonade, she finally had a chance to offer her thanks. He brushed off her gratitude. "You had your hands full. If I'd known, I would have come sooner. And brought tranquilizers."

She laughed. "Well, the twins don't need any. They're exhausted. Alex was drooping when I took him upstairs for a nap. Aubrey looked ready to keel over too. We spent the whole morning getting ready for the party."

"I'm sure they had fun."

"Yes, they did. That's the important part. Not how many gallons of grape juice were dumped in the pool."

His gaze narrowed as he looked at the abandoned pirate ship, a green and blue striped jungle gym. It had taken her two days to assemble it, soon after the twins had moved here.

"You've done a lot with this place. I have to admit, when I first saw it, I didn't think it would last through another storm, much less an invasion of pirates."

"The landlord's been really great about fixing things up. They fixed the gate, installed a new roof, even opened an account at the nursery so I could plant shrubs."

"I'm sure you've improved the value of the property." He paused, plucked a dead blossom from the nearby rose bush, and began distractedly shredding the petals. "I was talking to Bob Steele. Apparently Adrian's trying to talk him into developing a product for home investors."

Rebecca groaned. "He hasn't given up on that?"

"You aren't interested?"

"Are you kidding? I've got a full time job, remember? Plus two kids who keep me busy."

A fleeting look — was it relief? — crossed his face, then he shrugged. "If you want to go work for Adrian's side project…"

Rebecca laughed and said firmly, "I have no interest in developing commercial software, at least not for Adrian. Although maybe for his kids…" she mused.

"What do you mean?"

"Well, I wrote this simple program for the twins, based on voice recognition technology. They write their own scripts, then have computer generated characters act them out. They really enjoy it. And it seems to have encouraged Aubrey to talk more, at least around the house."

Connor tossed the remains of the rose to the ground. "It sounds like a marketable idea. Why don't you write up a proposal, and I'll have one of the software development firms I own look at it."

"It would need a lot of work. The user interface is pretty primitive, and the VR is still buggy…"

"I'm sure you could fix that."

"Maybe if I linked…hmm, that might work…" Her voice trailed off as she considered the possibilities.

"You could easily finance the twins' education. Or buy this house, if your landlord ever decides to sell."

"Well…I'll give it some thought," she said, still in nerd mode. "I read about a new program from Cal Tech—"

He interrupted her before she could go into detail. "What are you doing for dinner?"

She laughed. "Are you asking me for a date?"

"I think so." She couldn't see his expression behind his dark glasses, and his voice, as usual, gave nothing away.

"Why don't you just stay for dinner? We can have leftover cake and whatever's in the fridge."

"Or I could order out. I noticed a Chinese place a few blocks away."

"That sounds good," she agreed, wondering what was on his mind. She'd almost decided to issue a reprieve for his attempt to buy her off, but she wasn't sure she wanted to continue the relationship—at least, not on his terms.

As they waited for the food he ordered, picking up the last of the party debris, he refused to speak of anything more personal than the weather. It was unseasonably cool in New York, he told her. In a few weeks, the leaves would begin to turn. Shares of NeurCo were trading at a high volume, which lead him to think the peak in pharmaceuticals was nearing.

When they sat in her living room, surrounded by birthday presents and balloons, Rebecca asked about Rodney.

"He finished the last puzzle I gave him. I found a new one at FAO Schwartz that's supposed to be a real challenge; it doesn't have a picture on it. But I have a feeling that won't make a difference," he said with amused pride in his voice. Then he added, "Aunt Helen asked about you. She wants me to bring you for a visit Labor Day weekend."

"I can't. I'll be going to Chicago."

"Oh? To visit family?"

Rebecca studied her sandals. "Among other things." Then the urge to confide was too great. "They're trying to take the twins away. I have a hearing with a judge the Tuesday after Labor Day."

"What are you talking about?"

Rebecca had opened a bottle of wine, and as she told him what had happened this week, she gazed at the glass leaning crookedly in her hand. "The twins' grandparents—they've filed for a custody hearing. George Severson is the executor of Kim and Randy's estate."

"I thought you were named as guardian in their wills."

"Yes, but the Seversons seem to think I'm not fit to raise the twins. Unfortunately, a judge has decided to hold a hearing to determine whether that's true."

"You've got to be kidding. You're the most responsible, morally upstanding parent I know."

"But I'm not their real mother. And I'm not raising them in Illinois, in a two-parent home, with a half-acre yard and honest-to-God hot dogs on their plates. Plus…" She sighed. "I seem to have an unnaturally forgiving nature."

"Yes, you do—I should know—but why should that bother the twins' grandparents?"

"I wrote a letter to the sentencing judge, requesting a light sentence and community service for Melvin Dailey, the drunk driver who killed Kim and Randy. It really angered the Seversons. In fact, I think that's why they're doing this."

"Have you hired an attorney?"

She nodded. "My cousin Penny gave me a name."

"Who is it?"

"His name's Tony Markham. He's represented clients in custody cases before."

"Is he any good?"

"Well, yes, I think so. My Aunt Jean's stepson used him in his divorce."

He frowned. "I'll contact my attorney, have him recommend someone."

"Connor! I don't need another attorney!" Rebecca set her wine glass on the coffee table and gave him a look of exasperation.

"Let me find you a good attorney—one who's won a high percentage of these cases before. Trust me, this isn't a time for family loyalty or scruples about accepting help from friends. You need an attack dog in your corner. The alternative," he added, a concerned look in his eyes, "might mean losing the twins."

"I'm not going to lose them," she insisted. Then she grinned shakily. "But if the judge rules against me…well, I was thinking. Maybe we could use your jet. I could hide them on some deserted island. You don't happen to own one, do you?"

"No, but I'll buy one. Pacific or Atlantic?"

Her face softened in a grateful smile. "Anywhere. Oh, Connor! What am I going to do? What if the judge really does...?" But she couldn't voice her biggest fear; losing the twins was unthinkable, for her sake as well as theirs.

"First, you let me find you a good attorney, the best money can buy. If you want to pay me back later, fine. But this is too important, Rebecca, for you to let your stubborn pride and principles get in the way."

She looked at him askance. "Pride? Is that why you think I didn't accept the watch?"

He arched a brow. "Wasn't it?"

She sighed. "Never mind. You wouldn't understand."

"I might, but that's a discussion we can have another time."

The doorbell rang, announcing the arrival of dinner. Rebecca let Connor pay for it—just to show him she really didn't have any pride—and then woke the twins so they'd at least be well fed and sleepy when bedtime rolled around.

Later, after the food had been eaten and dishes put away, Connor glanced at his watch. "I need to get back to my apartment. I'm expecting a call from Singapore. I also want to contact my attorney and find out the name of a custody expert who can handle your case."

"I'm not sure that's necessary," she began, but he ignored her protests, which was the best way, he'd learned, to get her to do what was good for her.

"I should have a name for you by tomorrow. I'll let you know. Meanwhile, don't worry. And we'll continue our discussion...when you don't have so much on your mind," he added, as Alex sent the new remote control truck Connor had brought him careening down the stairs.

"Okay, but..."

She glanced up at him, her eyes full of worry, and something else. She nibbled her lip nervously, and suddenly he wanted to take her in his arms and kiss her until she agreed to everything he wanted. He just wasn't quite sure yet what it was he wanted.

Instead, he gave her a confident smile. "Trust me, Rebecca. We'll win this one, one way or another. And if all else fails, we'll set sail for Bora Bora."

Connor put a call through to his attorney, Charles Macon, as soon as he reached his penthouse. Within ten minutes, Charles had returned the call. Connor explained the situation, and Macon provided him with the names of several prominent attorneys who specialized in custody cases, including one based in California.

Connor recognized the name. Jerry Wiley had won cases all over the country and was a regular on several network legal analysis programs. His fees were enough to outfit a small army—a very elite fighting force, with the legal firepower to scare anyone else off the field.

Charles, who had collaborated with Wiley on a case before, agreed to contact him.

Connor hung up the phone. There were times when he appreciated the power he wielded, and this was one of them. If there was any way he could arrange for Rebecca to keep the twins—and that included spiriting them away on his private plane—he'd see that it was done.

Rebecca's scruples might preclude her accepting expensive gifts, but surely she wouldn't draw the line at his helping her keep the twins. He knew how much Aubrey and Alex meant to her. And there was no doubt that she was a good parent to them, despite what the grandparents believed. The very qualities he admired about her—her generous spirit and undaunted capacity for acceptance and love, despite the return—were the very qualities that were threatening her with heartbreak if the twins' grandparents succeeded in removing them from her home.

He remembered a time when the authorities had threatened to put Rodney in a state-run home. They'd claimed it was "for the benefit of the child," undoubtedly convinced that his mother, with her meager income and long hours, couldn't provide the care he needed. Helen had helped them out then, providing Maggie with a job that allowed her more time at home with Rodney.

Maybe he was making up for past wrongs, both the wrong inflicted by the state and the one he'd inflicted on Rebecca. Giving her the watch had been a bad idea. She wasn't interested in expensive gifts, or revenge. He smiled, remembering her performance on the tennis court. She was about as competitive as a moth. She'd never be able to muster up the killer instinct needed to annihilate her opponents in a courtroom.

He, on the other hand, had no scruples when it came to annihilation.

He'd see that she won the case, and then see that she returned to his bed.

Before he left his office, Connor stared at the photo of his mother and Helen that he kept on his desk, and imagined he saw approval on Maggie's face.

Jerry Wiley had agreed to cut short his vacation and return to San Francisco the next day, Charles informed him when he phoned later. Connor called Rebecca and told her the news.

"How much will this cost, Connor?"

"Don't worry about it—"

"How much?"

"About what you make in three months." The total would probably be considerably more than that, but he didn't think she was ready for that news yet.

"Before or after taxes?"

"Before."

"Ouch! I can't afford that!"

"I can. And it's worth it to me."

"Why?"

"To see justice done. It would be criminal to take those kids away from you. No one could possibly do as good a job as you in raising them."

"Connor, you don't have to take on my battles."

"I'm more experienced in legal wrangling than you. The very qualities that make you such a good parent make you ill-equipped to battle the forces of evil in a courtroom."

She laughed. "You make it sound like I'm taking on the Death Star. It's just a hearing."

"In front of a judge who has the power to take the twins from you. I don't intend to let that happen, not if I have to call up every legal X-wing fighter in the Rebel Alliance."

His cell phone picked up the sound of her sigh.

"I don't like to be in your debt."

"Is that why you didn't take the watch?"

"Umm…" She hesitated. "I think that might have had something to do with it."

"Remind me to show you my tax return some time. The price of a watch, or a good legal team, is hardly a factor."

She laughed. "Well, I suppose I could pay you back…in thirty years or so."

"Sounds good," he said, though he had no intention of accepting her money. "We can meet with Wiley Monday, in my office. I'll have Peggy set up a time."

"All right," she agreed, and Connor decided to ignore the note of reluctance in her voice.

"Can mice be ballerinas?" Aubrey asked, when Rebecca finished reading her the Angelina Ballerina book that Connor had given her for her birthday. It had come with a doll, an adorable mouse in a tutu, that made Rebecca smile when she thought of Connor picking it out.

"Sure. If they take lessons," she answered. "Would you like to take ballet lessons?"

"Is that what ballerinas do?"

"Yes. They usually start taking lessons, oh, when they're five."

"I'm five!"

"That's right, Mouse." Rebecca dropped a kiss on her nose. "I can find out about lessons on Monday. Maybe there's a class on Saturdays." She set the book on the nightstand. "Do you think we should invite Madison over one day? The two of you could play ballerinas."

Rebecca thought the two would get along. Madison's mother was also a single mom, an analyst who never seemed to have time to have lunch with her daughter at daycare.

"Maybe after I take ballerina lessons," Aubrey said, fastening Angelina's tutu.

"I'll call about that, first thing Monday."

She kissed Aubrey good night, wondering if she was just whistling on her way through the graveyard. The hearing was two weeks away. The twins might not live with her long enough to take ballet lessons or have friends over again. She could pretend it wouldn't happen, but that was no guarantee the boogeyman wouldn't jump out and bite her on the butt.

Maybe Connor was right. Maybe hiring the best custody attorney in the country—with Connor's money—was the right thing to do. If it meant keeping the twins, what was a little indebtedness, after all?

But she hated being in his debt. Other women might not find it so awkward, but she wanted more from him than a loan or expensive gifts.

She wanted his heart. And that didn't come attached with a maturity date.

CHAPTER NINETEEN

When Connor talked to Jerry Wiley the next day, the news wasn't good. After meeting with Rebecca on Monday, Wiley had spent the last two days investigating the custody situation. Connor had no doubt he'd been thorough. He'd checked into Wiley's reputation, and the guy was known as a meticulous bulldog in the courtroom.

Wiley had argued many custody cases before, including a famous case involving two celebrities in a bitter divorce. His client, the wife, had ended up with the disputed poodle. In another, he'd represented a father who had taken his children out of the country when he suspected his wife's boyfriend was abusing them.

Connor had no doubt Wiley would do his best to ensure Rebecca retained custody of the twins. Unfortunately, it would be the judge who would make the final decision — in a little more than a week.

Connor had asked to be kept apprised of the situation, and with Rebecca's consent, Wiley had phoned him and done so. He had outlined the facts logically, in the blunt manner that had no doubt impressed the television anchors who'd solicited his on-air opinion.

"The case seems to consist of the grandparents' objections to the twins being raised in California, number one. We can easily bat that one away by offering the Seversons visitation once a year, bringing the twins to Chicago for holidays, that sort of thing."

"I'm sure Rebecca would be agreeable to that. What else?"

"Well, it seems they're objecting to certain lifestyle practices of Ms. Evans. The fact she's raising the twins vegetarian—"

"There's nothing wrong with that."

"No," Wiley agreed. "We can have a pediatrician offer evidence it's a healthy dietary practice. Plus there are several studies suggesting no adverse impact on growth, intelligence, et cetera. We'll throw that at them, too. The main concern a judge might have is the fact that she's single, and presumably dating."

"And that's a problem?"

"She's raising two impressionable kids. Judges don't like to see parents having sleepovers on a regular basis."

"She doesn't have sleepovers on a regular basis. Trust me on that," Connor added dryly.

There was a brief pause, then the attorney said, "I assumed your interest in this case was due to the fact that you and Ms. Evans were involved romantically."

"We've been seeing each other—exclusively—but there've been no regularly scheduled sleepovers. We've taken a trip to my estate in Maui, another up north to my home there—hardly an indication of immoral behavior," Connor said. "And since when is a judge in the business of deciding what constitutes moral behavior?"

"I know it sounds old fashioned, but we give lots of leeway to judges in these situations, I'm afraid. The best thing she has going for her is the fact that she was the parents' first choice for guardian, but the judge may decide they would have preferred the brother if they'd known of his impending marriage."

"What difference does it make if the guy's married?"

"I spoke with several attorneys involved in cases this judge has heard. He's particularly partial to two-parent homes, especially when one is a stay-at-home mom. One colleague told me he's even given custody to the father and a new wife over the recommendation of a psychologist. It turned out the stepmother was willing to stay home with the kids."

Connor frowned. "That sort of thinking was outdated two decades ago."

"Sure, but he's the one wearing the black robe. He can pretty much do what he wants, as long as he feels it's in the best interest of the child." Then Jerry switched tracks. "The report from the social worker should tip the scales in our favor, plus the psychologist's recommendation. Of course, they've hired their own psychologist to report on the twins' adjustment. It'll likely be less favorable—you get what you pay for in these situations."

"Anything we can do to tip the scales even further?"

"Make sure that social worker's visit goes well. She's hired by the court and is presumed to be non-biased."

"I wouldn't anticipate any problems there."

"Believe me, anything can go wrong. There's no such thing as an open-and-shut case when it comes to custody."

"I've hired you to make sure this one stays shut."

There was a pause, and Connor thought he'd cowed the feisty attorney, then Wiley cleared his throat and said, "I have to ask. You seem to have quite a personal interest in this case."

"Yes, I do."

"May I ask why?"

"She's a personal friend of mine."

"And?"

Glad to see the attorney didn't back down from tough questioning, Connor answered him. "I've seen first-hand she's a good parent to those kids. She'd be devastated if she lost them. Not to mention Aubrey and Alex would be unnecessarily traumatized if they were separated from the aunt they've begun to think of as a mother, so soon after losing their parents. I simply want to ensure that doesn't happen."

"Then I'm working for you as well as Ms. Evans."

"That's right," Connor said. "And as my attorney, it's in your best interest to see that we win this case." He paused before adding, "Otherwise, it's quite possible you'll be representing me on charges of abduction."

"I'll pretend I didn't hear that," Wiley said, before promising to phone again with any updates.

Connor couldn't deny there was a possibility Rebecca could lose the twins. And he didn't like losing.

His influence should guarantee that didn't happen—that and a high-priced legal team—but Connor always made sure he was prepared for the worst-case scenario.

"We can't find Sam anywhere! I think he's dead!" Alex moaned Saturday morning as Rebecca was trying to clean up the house in preparation for the social worker's visit. Alex had spilled a bottle of shampoo on the bathroom floor, and there was a pile of laundry at the top of the stairs.

"I'm sure he's somewhere. Have you checked under the bed? You know he likes to hide under there sometimes and chase the dust bunnies."

"He's not there! He's not anywhere! I think he's in heaven with Mommy and Daddy!" Tears filled his blue eyes, and Rebecca immediately put the mop down. "Oh, honey, he's not dead! He's just missing. We'll find him. Did you look behind the sofa?"

Together, they looked in all the usual places—behind the furniture, under beds, in the window sills—without finding so much as a hairball.

"I'm sure he's just hiding somewhere hard." Rebecca hoped her voice sounded more cheerful than she felt. Aubrey was staring at her silently. Her thumb—which Rebecca had noticed was more and more often nowhere near her mouth—was now firmly stuck between her teeth, and her eyes were big with worry.

"We'll find him," Rebecca vowed, but thirty minutes later, even she had to admit the situation was ominous.

By this time, both children were in tears, and the house was an even bigger mess from having been turned upside down in the all-out search. And just when she'd decided matters couldn't get worse, the doorbell rang.

Rebecca's heart sank. The social worker wasn't due to arrive for another half hour! When she opened the door, Mrs. Chapman didn't seem pleased with the wails of unhappiness that greeted her. Aubrey, her head tucked in Rebecca's skirt, refused to look at the stranger. Alex glared at her, seeming to suspect her of somehow being involved in the cat's disappearance. Rebecca had told them they would be having a visitor, but she hadn't gotten around to explaining exactly who, or why. She didn't have the heart to tell them there was a chance they might not be allowed to live with her. She was betting on the fact the judge would see that the twins were happy, healthy, and as well-adjusted as could be expected.

Yet as she followed Mrs. Chapman from room to room as the woman peered into every dusty corner, even Rebecca began to doubt her house on Carroll Street was a safe haven for five-year-olds.

The woman opened the cabinet under the sink—Rebecca wished she'd cleaned it out after she'd unstopped the drain the other day. She pulled out a bottle of drain cleaner. "There are no latches on the kitchen cabinets."

"Should there be?"

Disapproval leaked from the edges of her frown. "Do you know how many children die each year from poisoning after ingesting common household cleaners?"

"But the twins are five years old! They would never—"

"Never assume a child is too old to be curious about household chemicals." Mrs. Chapman sounded as if she'd recited the words dozens of times before. "And I see the electrical outlets have no safety plugs. Were you aware that it's recommended in homes with young children that all unused outlets be covered up?"

"No...I mean, yes. When they were younger, their mom and dad—"

"It only takes a hundred volts of electricity to shock a child, Ms. Evans. You're their guardian now. It's up to you to ensure their safety."

"Of course."

Then the woman looked down at Aubrey. Her gaze riveted on the thin arms poking from the sleeves of her lace-edged T-shirt.

"Now. About the tattoo..."

When she finally shut the door behind the social worker, Rebecca sank into the old-fashioned armchair with the hand-crocheted antimacassars. The visit had been a disaster. She'd be lucky if the social worker didn't immediately retrieve the twins from "the unsafe environment" she'd thoughtlessly put them in. It hadn't helped that Sam had finally made an appearance, just as the woman was leaving—by jumping on her purse and attacking it as if it were a hound from hell.

Rebecca wanted to call her mother. She wanted to call Connor. She decided, instead, to finish scrubbing the bathroom floor. Then she'd take the twins to the park and try to forget that it might be their last trip together.

Aubrey, with an armful of very satisfied cat, came and curled up in her lap. As Rebecca stroked her hair, she said, in a dejected little voice that matched Rebecca's mood, "Sam didn't like that lady."

"No? What made you think that?"

"He told me."

"Really? Sam talks to you?"

"Sometimes. But sometimes he doesn't feel like talking."

"I see. Did he tell you why he disappeared this morning?"

Aubrey chewed at her thumb. "He was looking for his mommy."

"He said that?"

"Yes. But his mommy's in heaven with his daddy. They can't come back, but he doesn't understand that."

Rebecca wondered if Aubrey had been reading the psychology textbooks in her therapist's office. "Well, we'll just have to help Sam. What do you think we could do?"

Aubrey stroked Sam's head. "He said he likes ice cream."

Rebecca smiled. "He does? What kind is his favorite?"

"Chocolate. With rainbow sprinkles."

"The kind they sell at the park?"

Aubrey nodded.

"Hmm. That's funny. I was just thinking we'd go to the park this afternoon."

Aubrey wiggled around to face her. "Can Sam go with us?"

"I don't think that would be a very good idea, sweetie. There are lots of dogs at the park, and cats don't like dogs."

Sam licked his paws, seeming to agree. Aubrey looked disappointed, then brightened. "Then, can we call Connor and see if he wants to come to the park? He might be lonely."

Rebecca lifted a brow in surprise. "You think so?"

"He gets a lonely face sometimes."

Rebecca nodded thoughtfully, but didn't tell Aubrey that Connor probably had a database full of available women who'd be eager to keep him company. Instead, she smiled at Aubrey, pleased she had formed a bond with Connor. "Then we'll call and invite him." Before she could change her mind, she scooped Aubrey and Sam off her lap and found the phone.

Her horoscope today had said she'd be lucky in love; his had said today was a day for unexpected company. If horoscopes and Asian philosophy could be trusted, they were a perfect match. He as a Pisces; she was a Leo. He was a Metal; she was a Wood. A perfect combination.

Maybe, she thought as she located his home number in her phone contacts. Mostly, she just liked to be with him. She enjoyed his strength, his maturity, his premeditated way of going through life. He was the ideal companion for a woman with the spontaneous nature of a butterfly. She loved his wry humor, his calm exterior. The cool, collected businessman, with a tender, hot blooded lover hidden under the tailored suit.

No other man had ever thrilled her senses the way he did—his body, finely muscled and graceful as a yoga master, his good looks courtesy of his Irish ancestors, sharpened by intelligence that probably registered in the wee end of the bell shaped curve.

A man like that shouldn't be lonely, but for now she had her own problems to look after. Fixing Connor would have to wait. Today, all she was offering was ice cream and friendship.

Connor answered the phone on the second ring.

It was Rebecca, inviting him for an afternoon in the park. He glanced at the electronic calendar he'd pulled from his pocket. He didn't need to turn it on to know what it contained: a meeting in an hour with a reporter from *Barron's,* a phone conference later—

"Sure. I've got some free time. Shall I meet you there?"

"How about at the ice cream stand outside the de Young? We'll be the ones wearing chocolate and sprinkles."

He canceled his appointments and met them a half hour later. Subtle signs of fall had invaded the park, but Rebecca looked fresh as the dawn of spring in an old-fashioned flower-strewn sundress. She wore purple sandals and a pair of dark sunglasses that hid her normally revealing eyes. The summer sun had lightened her gold-streaked hair, and her skin still bore traces of the tan she'd acquired in Maui.

He smiled at the vision. Modern sandals and a vintage dress. Ancient wisdom combined with youthful spirit. The incongruity defined Rebecca: completely unexpected, and utterly delightful.

As he got closer, he could smell the warmth of her skin, and the same attraction he'd felt the first time he'd seen her—in this very park—instantly resurfaced. His mind mentally logged the time since he'd last been with her: six days, nineteen hours, and approximately twenty-three minutes. An eternity.

"Hey, Connor!" Alex ran toward him, a new target, it turned out, for the latest joke making the preschool rounds. "Knock knock," he said, breathless with excitement.

"Who's there?" Connor duly replied.

"Cowsgo."

"Cowsgo who?"

Alex dissolved into giggles. "No they don't! Cows go moo!"

Connor laughed. "I'll remember that one. Let's go see what they're charging for ice cream these days."

Aubrey tucked her hand in his, and with Alex leading the way, they headed toward the ice cream stand where a ragged line of children and parents stood waiting.

They joined the families enjoying the warm September afternoon. Connor usually avoided the park during crowded weekends, but today he looked forward to being a part of Rebecca's impromptu family outing. If anyone had told him a few weeks ago that he'd enjoy spending the day in the park, dodging strollers and skateboarders and tourists, he'd have laughed.

But here he was, with Alex tugging on one hand and Aubrey glancing at him shyly, her hands linking his and Rebecca's—a perfectly matched family unit. Nearby, a clown dressed like Charlie Chaplin twisted balloons into cartoon animals and gallantly bestowed them to the younger children. Connor gave him a twenty dollar bill, and he knotted several balloons into a pair of giraffes for the twins. Then with a bow, he presented a balloon flower to Rebecca.

"Thank you, kind sir," she said with a little curtsey, then sniffed the *flower*. "My favorite. Tulips," she said as they walked toward a shady knoll nearby. She kicked off her shoes and curled red-polished toes into the grass. From beneath the sunglasses now propped on her head, her eyes slanted at Connor. Suddenly, he felt a swelling of heat to his groin, and he wondered if Mrs. Pascal could babysit the twins tonight while he took Rebecca to bed.

"How did the social worker's visit go?" he asked as Alex and Aubrey moved out of earshot, frolicking with their giraffes on the make-shift Serengeti.

Rebecca grimaced. "Don't ask."

He propped his own sunglasses atop his head and frowned. "What happened?"

Rebecca sighed and lowered herself onto the grass, her legs disappearing under her dress. "I think I'm probably in violation of about a dozen child welfare laws, including possession of hazardous substances and keeping a dangerous animal."

"Sam?" Connor lowered himself beside her.

Rebecca nodded. "He attacked her purse as she was leaving. I think he sensed her intent."

His frown deepened. "Just what did she say, Rebecca? She can't be intending to recommend the children be removed simply because you've got an overprotective cat."

Rebecca's gaze locked on the twins, and she shrugged. "Maybe not. But everything added together—the cat, Fred's body on the windowsill—"

He raised an eyebrow. "Fred?"

"A fly. He was bugging Aubrey one day, and I told her he was our pet. You should have seen them trying to teach him to fetch a crumb." She smiled, then a look of despair fell over her face. "Oh, Connor! What am I going to do? If the judge rules against me—"

It took him only a moment to answer.

"Marry me." As soon as the words were out of his mouth, Connor felt his breath lodge in his throat, as if he'd been playing a challenging game of tennis or facing a tough competitor across the negotiating table.

Rebecca just smiled and said lightly, "Thanks for the offer, but—"

"I'm serious," he heard himself saying, the bucket of air in his throat not preventing his voice from working just fine. "Marry me. The judge couldn't care less about flies and cats and potentially dangerous substances if you're my wife. It would resolve the entire situation." It would, he realized—particularly the problem of finding a babysitter every time he wanted to take Rebecca to bed.

But from the way she was looking at him with a stunned—no, appalled—look on her face, he didn't think she saw the logic. "I can't marry you. You don't love me."

"That's beside the point. You need a husband to convince the judge you're qualified to parent the twins—"

"I don't *need* a husband! I need someone who loves me, Connor! And unless you've had a change of heart in the last two weeks..." The sentence dangled treacherously.

He looked away. "The status of my heart is hardly the issue. In a little more than a week, you're going to be in a hearing to determine if you're a fit guardian to raise those kids you love so much. The way I see it, you can guarantee you'll keep them if you can provide a two-parent home, free from any financial obligation for you to work full time."

She gaped at him. "Connor, I can't marry you just to fool the judge into thinking...into thinking I've suddenly become Mrs. Betty Crocker, with muffins in the oven and safety latches on all my cabinets! It would be a lie."

"You said yourself you thought the brother-in-law was marrying in order to do the same, for reasons that were less 'pure.'"

She frowned stubbornly. "He may be, but that doesn't mean I have to fight just as dirty."

Connor shook his head. "It isn't fighting dirty. Marriage to you would serve more than the obvious purpose."

"Oh?"

He looked at her steadily. "It would suit me very much to have you as my wife."

Her face dissolved into puzzlement. "Is this your idea of a romantic proposal?"

"If you want it to be." His voice was surprisingly steady. He still wasn't sure what had prompted the idea, but now that he'd thought it over, at least on the surface, he knew it was a good one.

"It would be more romantic if you told me you loved me. If you told me you can't live without me. If you told me you'd walk through hell and back just to be with me..."

"Or perhaps I could just buy you some flowers," he suggested, slightly horrified at the picture she'd painted.

"I'd rather have the words."

He didn't say anything. He couldn't. His voice suddenly was dry as the Serengeti Plain, and just as far away.

"I'd rather have the words, Connor, more than anything — more than an expensive watch, more than a trip to Hawaii, more than all your expensive lawyers. All I really want from you is your love. It's that simple. And you've known it all along. But it scares you to death to think you might ever feel something for me other than friendship. Or lust. Isn't that right?"

"Rebecca," he began, "all I want is marriage. It's something that would benefit us both, for the moment."

She turned away, staring at the columns of the de Young museum. "Don't offer me a marriage of convenience, Connor. I'll keep the twins, even if I have to agree to keep my pets chained up and install safety latches on every door in the house. The judge can't take these guys from me." She pointed to where they were still playing on the grass. "Look at them. Aubrey's laughing! Out loud! She hasn't wet the bed in weeks, and Alex is starting to control his aggression. Just the other day, he was pretending he was Gandhi."

Connor blinked. "Alex pretends he's Gandhi?"

"I read them a book about famous humanitarians. Aubrey wanted to be Mother Teresa. They were pretending Sam was a starving Indian child." She smiled at the memory. "They really have an enormous capacity for love, despite what happened to them."

"I'm glad they're doing better. But if you should lose them…"

"I won't — I can't," she said stubbornly. "But only by being myself. Not your wife, not some patched-together version of Mary Poppins. I'm just me, slightly flaky and decidedly single. I'm good enough for the twins, and good enough for Kim and Randy. That's all that matters."

The earnestness in her voice touched him. Rebecca wanted to win the battle on her own. Connor could understand that, but it also frustrated him. As ill-advised as his proposal might be, he still wanted her to agree.

For an instant, he wished he could do what she wanted, say what she wanted to hear, be who she wanted him to be. But a fist gripped his heart, clamping his emotions together too compactly for them to ever ease their way out. Fear flooded him whenever he thought of spending his life in complete devotion to another human being. Just the memory of his mother's face as she gazed at the photo of Mitchell Forrest she kept beside her bed...

If Connor could have found the man and paid him to return to the wife who loved him, he would have. But his father had disappeared, taking with him the undying love of his wife and leaving his oldest son with a responsibility that was sometimes too heavy for ten-year-old shoulders.

Another family walked past, pushing strollers and holding ice cream cones, and Connor shook off his thoughts. It was rare he even remembered his father, and now, when he should be concentrating on his own life—and on keeping Rebecca's family intact—he was daydreaming about a man who didn't deserve the love his mother had sacrificed over the years, nor the devotion of a ten-year-old boy.

Suddenly Connor had had enough of the park. He wanted to go home to his carefully managed penthouse, where Mrs. Pascal kept his shirts laundered and his shoes polished and his bathroom tidy. He didn't need a wife, or the responsibility of a family he couldn't love.

He stood, pulling his cell phone from his pocket. He checked for messages and was glad to see Adrian had called. There was a problem with the Hong Kong deal. A problem he could easily solve.

Quickly he explained the situation to Rebecca, then said his farewells, glad the sunglasses hid the look of disappointment he knew was in his eyes.

Rebecca watched him walk away, his head bent, his hands stuffed in his pockets, a lonely man who'd just offered to let her share his loneliness. Who'd just asked her to share his life.

She didn't think he'd meant it. He was just trying to help her out, a remnant of the Good Samaritan she'd first met here. Something about this park obviously brought out his selfless tendencies.

She didn't even want to think about his offer; it was far too tempting. She was afraid she'd run across the park and jump into his arms and tell him yes. Marrying him would ensure she'd keep the twins. It would guarantee Connor in her bed at night, making love with her, but it wouldn't guarantee his love. How long would it be before he found himself wishing he hadn't made her a permanent part of his life? In fact, she was pretty sure he'd regretted the offer as soon as he'd made it.

She felt like crying. She wished she could call Kim. She wished she could fix her own problems the way she could fix a glitch in the computer system at work.

That more than anything was why she'd turned down his proposal. She didn't want him solving her problems like she was some medieval wimp. Instead, *she* wanted to fix *him*. She wanted to save him from whatever he feared, from that part of himself that might have shriveled up long ago from lack of care.

Or maybe it had never existed.

She sighed and stuffed her feet back in her purple sandals. "Come on, guys, let's go home and install those new safety latches."

CHAPTER TWENTY

The day before the hearing, Rebecca and the twins flew to Chicago, where they stayed in her mother's tri-level house in Forest Park. The next morning, Rebecca sent the twins to her cousin Penny's and put on her most conservative outfit: a navy suit she'd bought on sale at Nordstrom and an off-white rayon blouse. She wound her hair into a trim little chignon and briefly regretted not having a pair of glasses to complete the librarian look.

With a regretful look at the sandals she'd worn on the plane, she slipped her feet into a pair of navy pumps and glanced at herself in the same mirror where she'd primped for the high school prom. The stakes were much higher now; instead of securing her a spot in Brian Cuello's affections, she was hoping to ensure her place as the twins' guardian.

It hadn't worked with Brian, though. When she'd refused to take off her bra while they necked in the front seat of his mother's Taurus, he'd gone out with Shelley Winningham the next weekend.

She sighed. Dating was the least of her worries nowadays. Again she questioned her decision to turn down Connor's offer. As husband material, he fit the bill perfectly.

She had only spoken to him once since that day in the park, and he hadn't mentioned his impromptu proposal. He'd offered his jet to fly her and the twins to Chicago—she'd politely refused, and then he'd offered reassurance, which she gladly accepted. "Don't worry, Rebecca, I'm sure it will take little to convince the judge you're the perfect person to raise the twins."

He'd ended the conversation without mentioning whether or not he intended to be at the hearing. She knew he was busy; he'd mentioned something about an upcoming trip to Taiwan. Still, she couldn't help wishing he would be there.

Refusing to feel sorry for herself, Rebecca found her purse, then joined her mother downstairs.

Barbara Evans was a slightly plumper version of her daughters, with blond-gray hair cut in a short style that complemented her no-nonsense features. In temperament, she was more like Kim: practical, frugal, with Midwestern hardiness baked into her genes.

"Are you ready? It's a thirty-minute drive to the courthouse. We'd better leave now if I'm going to find a parking space."

"Ready as possible," Rebecca replied with an uncharacteristically glum expression.

"Now, don't you worry, hon. Everything's going to be just fine. You'll see."

"I hope so." Then, as Barb turned toward the garage door, Rebecca asked, "Mom? Do you think Kim knows what's going on?"

"If she does, I imagine she's turning flips in her grave right now. She never did get along with Jo Severson."

"I was just hoping she'd put in a good word with whichever angels patrol the court system," Rebecca said wryly.

"That would be Lady Justice. There's a statue outside the court-room; I remember seeing it when I went for my divorce hearing. Frankly, I'd put more faith in your attorney," her mother added with a bitter look that always accompanied mention of her divorce.

They got in Barb's ancient Honda and drove to the courthouse. Barb dropped her off in front and went to park. Rebecca found the hearing room on the second floor. Tony Markham and Jerry Wiley were waiting outside. Jerry, sporting a bolo tie and cowboy boots that had probably never seen dirt, looked ready to take on Injustice with both barrels smoking. Beside him, Tony, in a black double-breasted suit, could have passed for a mob lawyer. His services had been retained as local counsel, though clearly Jerry was running the show.

The doors opened to the hearing room where the case would be heard. Rebecca's attorneys had explained to her that it wasn't a trial, since no criminal conduct had been alleged. It was simply a probate hearing to determine guardianship. The judge would listen to each side of the issue, take the testimony of the expert witnesses — the psychologists hired by both sides, and the social worker who had been hired by the state. Since she was in California, her deposition would be read into the record by one of the court clerks.

The Seversons were already there, in the small crowd milling just inside the hearing room, along with Eric, Randy's brother, and his brand new wife, Felicia. Jo Severson, dressed in the same black suit she'd worn to the funeral, gave Rebecca a swift glance and then ignored her altogether. Eric craned his neck to stare at her as she entered, then turned to his father in the seat next to him.

Felicia came over and introduced herself, apparently misreading her new family's barely concealed hostility toward Rebecca.

"I can't wait to get to know the twins better. I've got their picture on my desk at school. Plus I've already talked to the principal about taking the rest of the year off so I can stay home with them full time."

"Really? I thought you enjoyed teaching."

Felicia's smile faded. "Well, yes, I do, but you understand. When you've got little ones at home, they become your first priority." This time there was no mistaking the superior note in her voice.

Rebecca wanted to gag, but instead she nodded her head. "Of course. I imagine Eric agrees with you completely."

Felicia looked at her husband of forty-eight hours and smiled indulgently. "Oh, yes, and he's looking forward to having home-cooked meals every night."

"I'll bet he is," Rebecca replied, gritting her teeth. "Aubrey's favorite is peanut butter and jelly, cut in triangles. Alex likes tofu nuggets and ketchup. But Sam is easy to please — dead crickets are his favorite snack, along with nylons and cashmere sweaters."

A look of uncertainty replaced the smile on Felicia's face. "Sam?"

"Their cat. I wouldn't dream of separating them."

"But Eric's allergic to cats."

"Is he?" Rebecca said innocently. "How fortunate they make really good allergy meds now. And since I've starting supplementing Sam's diet with cod liver oil, he hardly ever spits up a hairball." Jerry Wiley caught her eye, frowning. He'd already told her he didn't want her exchanging words with the opposition. She gave Felicia a wide smile. "Maybe we can talk later. I'm sure you're not bothered by that whole 'ex-boyfriend' issue, right? After all, I only went out with Eric once." Then she walked over to where Jerry and Tony sat, surrounded by stacks of briefs they'd filed in the case. Her mouth set in a determined line, and she hoped fervently the high-priced attorney Connor had hired was worth every billing hour she still intended to pay back.

They all stood as the judge entered the courtroom, and Rebecca found her legs wobbly. She was glad her mother stood next to her, along with the two attorneys and their assistant.

Because they had brought the suit, the Seversons' case was heard first. Their attorney, a stolid woman in sensible shoes, first gave an eloquent speech about how the Seversons were interested only in the welfare of the children. Even Rebecca was touched. Beside her, Barb turned a disbelieving snort into a cough.

The first witness called was the psychologist the Seversons had hired to examine the twins. According to him, they were still in denial about their parents' deaths and were calmly putting up with the temporary parent until they could return to Illinois and the safety of the Seversons' home. Rebecca was surprised to hear they'd said as much during the one hour visit—at least Alex had. Aubrey had refused to say a word, which in the doctor's view indicated a severe maladjustment.

His arguments were convincing, and Rebecca herself couldn't help but wonder if he was right. The first stirrings of despair hit her.

Then another expert witness presented findings claiming a two-parent home was preferable to a home with a working single mother. Rebecca wanted to groan.

A second expert echoed the opinion of the first: children in homes where a parent stayed home were much better off, according to several studies he cited. Rebecca watched the judge jot down notes, a vision in her mind of twin sets of blue eyes filling with tears as she explained the judge's decision.

Tears came to her own eyes at the thought.

The next few witnesses were even more damaging: Several friends of Randy's swore they'd heard him express his doubts about his sister-in-law. They all seemed to indicate he wasn't thinking clearly when he'd signed his will naming her guardian.

Rebecca couldn't even look at the Seversons during the testimony. She felt like she'd been kicked by a ghost. She'd always thought her relationship with Randy had been a good one, though there had been a time when he seemed to resent her closeness with her sister.

Beside her, Jerry Wiley listened, took notes, and when the time came, asked a few pointed questions. Rebecca knew he was saving his best arguments for later, but she was beginning to wonder if the strategy was a good one. Already the judge, who seemed bored by the proceedings, had probably formed a negative opinion of her. He leaned back in his comfortable chair, eyes closed during much of the testimony, no doubt already composing his ruling.

Then Jo Severson took the stand. Small-boned and gray-haired, Jo placed a trembling hand on the Bible and was sworn in. After proclaiming her undying love for the twins, she told the judge her suspicions regarding her daughter-in-law's flaky sister.

"I always felt Kim would have been more sensible when it came to raising the twins if she hadn't listened to her sister," Jo said with a disapproving glance at Rebecca.

Rebecca's heart sank. She'd made every attempt to be courteous to Jo Severson; the fact that the woman still bore her ill-will crushed her spirits. Jerry, however, made sure the judge was aware that her testimony consisted of little more than her opinion, which didn't count for much on the witness stand.

The most damaging testimony was yet to come and consisted of facts: An investigator hired by the Seversons took the witness stand. Apparently, he'd been asking questions about her relationship with Connor. When prompted by the Seversons' attorney, he revealed, "I obtained evidence that Ms. Evans and the twins accompanied Mr. Forrest on his private jet" —he managed to make it sound as if they'd been cavorting naked the whole flight— "to his home in Maui, where Ms. Evans and the two children were in residence from Thursday until Sunday. Since that time, Mr. Forrest has visited the home where Ms. Evans lives on several occasions."

The judge remained impassive. Rebecca glanced at Jerry, but he didn't seem alarmed. Single mothers dated every day, he'd told her, and the fact that she had a romantic relationship wouldn't be held against her. But then the investigator's next words shocked her even more. "The home occupied by Ms. Evans, located in an older section of San Francisco, is in fact owned by a subsidiary known as Forrest Properties, which is wholly owned by Mr. Forrest."

Rebecca blinked. Connor owned her house? She glanced at her attorney, expecting him to jump up and shout "Objection!" but he merely jotted a note on a legal pad in front of him. "There must be some mistake," she whispered. Without looking up, he added a question mark on the legal pad. A few minutes later, when the investigator had completed his testimony, Wiley declined to further question him. With the Seversons' case presented, Judge Bailey called a recess.

As soon as the judge had left the room, Rebecca again said to Jerry Wiley, "There must be a mistake! Connor doesn't own my house. It belongs to an old lady who had to go to a nursing home. I still have her antimacassars!"

Jerry gave his already straight tie a little tug. "Are you sure about that?"

"Of course." But even as she answered, doubts entered her mind.

She remembered the amazingly easy search for a house once Connor had discovered she needed an affordable place to live. And how the "owner" seemed eager to accommodate anything she asked for. And the look on Connor's face whenever she mentioned her house, just like the look on his face when he'd handed her the watch — wary, guarded, as if he were afraid she'd see through the casual indifference all the way to the heart hidden inside. She'd turned down the expensive watch, but had inadvertently accepted a much more valuable gift: the very roof over her head.

He'd deceived her, made her look foolish, and possibly jeopardized her chance to keep the twins. A knot of anger welled inside her, but it was tempered by the knowledge that he'd done it because he cared about her. He'd been trying to make it easier for her, the only way he knew how.

He'd held her, let her cry on his starched shirt, then bought her a house.

He'd made love to her, treated her like his best friend, then given her a watch.

He'd asked her to marry him, looked at her as if he wanted to swallow her whole, then paid her legal fees.

Was this how he showed his love? By offering expensive gifts, as if she needed inducement to care for him. It was too bad, really, that Connor wasn't poor.

Yet even without his billions, he would still be the most powerful man she knew. He seemed to naturally dominate any room he walked into—including this one, she noticed with surprise as Connor himself strode into the room.

He paused beside her, taking in the government grandeur like he was considering auctioning it off, then he let his gaze settle on her.

She returned his look with a slightly accusatory one of her own. "I didn't know you were coming. You never mentioned it."

"Didn't I? I intended to. I think I proposed instead."

She ignored the wry look in his eyes, and instead pounced on his statement. "Just like you intended to tell me you owned my house?"

He lifted an eyebrow. "How did you find out about that?"

"An investigator hired by the Seversons. Why didn't you tell me?"

"I think perhaps we should discuss this—"

Just then, Jerry Wiley, who'd been speaking with his assistant, hurried over and began relating the day's events to Connor. Rebecca stood listening.

Apparently, the hearing wasn't going nearly as badly as she feared. Her attorneys seemed to think they could easily make up any lost ground.

Rebecca hoped so.

The judge returned, and the proceedings continued, this time with Rebecca's team at bat. Jerry first called the twins' psychologist, Dr. Lang, who refuted the testimony of the earlier expert psychologist. He strongly recommended the twins not be uprooted from the home they'd had for the last four months. He went over the progress each had made during his care, and answered the attorney's questions, some of which Rebecca thought were a little redundant. How many ways could you say, after all, that the twins had "successfully recreated the parental bond with their aunt"?

She was interested to learn, however, that Aubrey's stick figures she drew of her mother matched those she drew of Rebecca, though no one pointed out that she and Kim had been remarkably similar in appearance. Alex, on the other hand, still drew pictures of monster cars (which bore an amazing resemblance to Hook's pirate ship) tearing off after little boys with huge eyes, which demonstrated his "ability to deal with his fear in a safe environment."

Then Jerry Wiley called Rebecca to the stand. Still reeling from the accusations the other side had made—she'd never really thought of herself as a slut—she placed her hand on the Bible and took the oath.

Briefly meeting Connor's gaze, she settled in to the witness chair, crossing her legs, and then uncrossing them when she noticed her skirt ride up her thigh. Flashing the judge probably wasn't a good idea.

From his seat in the courtroom, Connor watched with a narrowed gaze. He'd known the opposing side would try to paint her in unflattering terms, but still a dry white fury had him clenching his fists over the armrests. A steely determination settled in his gut—to win this battle for her sake, for the twins' sake.

The thought came with mild surprise. He *had* come to care for her children. Aubrey, timid and cautious, full of shy giggles. Alex, bold and boisterous, a pirate who cried at the sight of blood. And Rebecca, the Tinkerbell who'd taught them to be kind to fairies as well as houseflies.

She was the perfect parent. The perfect wife.

He jerked his attention back to the witness stand. Jerry was questioning her about their visit to Maui.

"You had separate bedrooms?"

"Yes. But—"

He went on, before she could admit that she and Connor had indeed slept together in his bed.

"Where did the twins sleep?"

"In a room across from mine. Next to Mona's."

"Mona?"

"The nanny Connor hired to help with them while we were there. She was a college student majoring in early childhood education. She was wonderful with the Alex and Aubrey."

"And how often did Mona care for them during the visit?"

"Only while we went to dinner each night, but that was usually around their bedtimes. During the day, the twins and Mona were with us. We went hiking, swimming—"

"Of course. I'm sure you enjoyed your vacation. Can you tell us, Ms. Evans, do you habitually leave the twins in the care of babysitters while you go out with your friends?"

"No. I've only left them once, other than in Hawaii."

"Once? In four months?"

"That's right. Connor invited me to a play, and we left them with his housekeeper. She has five grandchildren and is used to four-year-olds. But she came early to get acquainted with them before we left."

"And has Mr. Forrest ever visited you at your home?"

"A few times."

"And did he sleep over on those occasions?"

"No! We didn't even…I mean…" Her cheeks turned pink.

"I think we understand. You haven't had sexual relations with Mr. Forrest while in the same residence as the twins, except during the few days you were in Hawaii?"

"And when we were at his home in northern California. But the twins had their own room then, too."

"All right, let's talk about their day-to-day care. Their diet, for instance…"

By the time she was finished testifying, Rebecca felt her credentials as a parent had been analyzed in minute detail. She'd been stripped of all her secrets, not that she'd ever had many. Her values, which she'd always considered pretty innocuous, had been questioned by the opposing attorney. Her brief affair with Connor was painted as a promiscuous, gold-digging romp, and despite the attempts of Jerry to blot the stain, she felt her reputation had been permanently tarnished.

As she stepped down from the stand, she was surprised to hear Jerry call Connor to the stand. She hadn't known he would testify, but then Jerry was known for keeping his cards close to his chest.

"Can you tell me the nature of your relationship with Ms. Evans?" Jerry asked him, after he'd been sworn in.

"I'm her employer. I'm also her friend."

"Are you currently in a romantic relationship with Ms. Evans?"

Connor crossed his legs, carefully arranged the crease in his trousers, then leveled his gaze at Rebecca. "I've asked her to marry me."

Rebecca swallowed. Beside her, Barb gasped. The judge perked up from his somnolent position behind the bench, but Jerry Wiley, having known the answer in advance, was unfazed.

"And her answer?"

"She turned me down."

Jerry feigned surprise. "She refused to marry you?"

"That's right." Connor glanced at Jerry, and a nerve in his cheek twitched. "However, I'd like to take the opportunity to ask her again now. Perhaps she's changed her mind."

At this, scattered laughter broke out in the courtroom, from everyone except the Seversons, and Rebecca, who sat woodenly, staring at the county seal in front of the judge's bench.

Judge Bailey cleared his throat. "I think this may be the first time anyone's proposed in my courtroom. However, I'll admonish the witness to stick to the facts. We're talking about the character of Ms. Evans and whether or not she's qualified to raise the children in question, not whether you're looking for a wife, Mr. Forrest."

"Actually, character is something I value highly in a potential spouse, Your Honor, in addition to an ability to nurture children. Rebecca Evans has both. She's got more integrity than anyone I've ever met, plus she cares deeply for the twins. She'd do anything for them."

"Including accept your charity when it comes to paying for her house?" Jerry asked smoothly.

"She didn't know about that — until today," he added, irony coloring his voice. "I bought the home without her knowledge and arranged for her to pay rent to a third party."

"And why did you do this?"

"I'd like to say it was because I was afraid of losing a valuable employee. I'm fairly certain, however, I was more afraid of losing the companionship of Miss Evans, were she to move back to Chicago."

"So, you bought her a house to ensure that didn't happen."

"Yes. I've done whatever I could to make things go smoothly for her, but the truth is she's doing an excellent job all on her own.

I've often passed by and seen her spending her lunch hour with the twins. Although it's encouraged, not many parents can find time during the day to visit their children. She's remarkably patient with them. When they ask questions—and believe me, you attorneys have nothing on a pair of four-year-olds when it comes to mounting an inquisition—she answers every one of them, or provides resources so they can find the answer on their own."

"And their reactions to their aunt?"

"They obviously adore her. Aubrey lights up when she comes into a room, and Alex seems to trust her to take as good care of his sister as he tries to."

"You've spent a considerable amount of time with the three of them?"

"As much as anyone."

"And your observations?"

"Rebecca Evans fits the definition of 'good parent' better than anyone I've ever met. Except perhaps my own mother," he added. "If I could choose a mother for my children simply on the basis of mothering skills, I could think of no one more qualified. I would want my own children to have what the twins have: security, love, joy. An appreciation for little things, like a line of ants crossing a sidewalk or the crumbling turrets of a sand castle. Compassion for those less fortunate." He glanced at the Seversons, then, with a little smile, added, "A sense of the absurd. But most of all, endless amounts of love. A somewhat rare commodity, I've discovered."

For all the expression he gave to the words, he could have been talking about soybean futures, Rebecca thought, gaping at him. She knew she should be flattered. He wanted her to be the mother of his children, but she felt more like carefully-chosen breeding stock than a woman.

She had to tighten her fists on the chair to keep from jumping up and pelting him with a few questions of her own: *How long have you been looking for a substitute for your mother, Mr. Forrest? How long have you wanted children of your own? And how many women have you interviewed for the position of "nanny"?*

Jerry continued to question him, but the rest of their exchange faded into the background as she considered the affront. Then suddenly she heard Connor mention the name George Severson.

In response to a question from Jerry, Connor answered, "According to publicly filed claims, the insurance agency George Severson co-owned with his sons suffered significant financial losses last year and owed over half a million dollars to various creditors. On the same date the insurance policy was paid out to him as the estate's executor, a number of creditors were paid off."

He'd apparently had his own investigators look into the finances of George Severson. Connor, who had a reputation for playing hardball in the boardroom, wasn't above throwing a few curves on her behalf, it turned out.

Around the courtroom, the atmosphere had changed. The judge was wide awake and listening to the voice of authority, the man whose comments could create panic or peace on Wall Street, the man who'd just proposed in his courtroom. Connor had succeeded in making the Seversons look as greedy as they'd portrayed her, yet Rebecca couldn't celebrate.

Connor stepped down from the witness stand, and Jerry continued to call witnesses, all of whom Rebecca had known would testify on her behalf: the twins' daycare teacher; their pediatrician; and an expert on childhood nutrition, who explained that children raised on a vegetarian diet suffered no ill health effects. Plus a child psychologist, who provided evidence that children with mothers who worked were just as well adjusted as children whose mothers stayed at home.

Eventually, after several hours of testimony, Jerry decided the earth was scorched enough. In his closing remarks, he proved eloquent as ever. Even Rebecca was awed when he referred to her as "a shining beacon for motherhood." Apparently, the judge agreed. Though Rebecca's attorneys had warned her he would probably take another day to make his decision, he announced that he was ready to issue a decision from the bench.

Rebecca hardly had time to wipe her sweaty palms before the judge made his announcement. "It seems to me that in this case, the children's interests would be best served by remaining right where they are, with their aunt, Rebecca Evans. Proper provisions must be made, however, for visitation with their paternal grandparents, George and Josephine Severson, as well as the rest of their deceased father's family.

"Further, I'm ordering the insurance proceeds rightfully owed the two children be remanded to the oversight of Ms. Evans, in order for her to adequately provide for their needs during the time they're in her care, as per their parents' wishes.

"And last —" he turned a stern gaze toward the Seversons "—I must say, seeing a young woman with the nerve to stand on her own, without the aid of a hastily-arranged marriage conducted for the sole purpose of influencing the court's decision, was a deciding factor in this decision." He paused for a moment before adding, "Court is now adjourned."

And with a bang of his gavel, Judge Bailey reaffirmed that Lady Justice was alive and well and living in suburban Chicago.

CHAPTER TWENTY-ONE

Driving home from the courthouse, Rebecca knew there was one person she had to share the news with. She dropped her mother off at her home, then went to visit someone she missed dearly.

As she drove down the quiet paths of the cemetery, past row after row of tranquil headstones, the feeling of relief she'd had since the judge's decision was announced subsided into peaceful sorrow, an echo of the raging grief she'd felt the last time she was here.

This was her first visit back to the gravesite since Kim and Randy had been buried on a cool afternoon in April. She parked along the road under a yellowing maple. Her heels digging into the well-trimmed grass, she walked toward a double monument adorned with plastic lilies. A cool September breeze chased her, tugging at her skirt, teasing a tendril of hair from the clasp at her nape.

She slowed as she reached the grave. Grass had begun to grow on the hard-packed dirt, sparsely, like the new memories that had gradually scarred over the raw ache of loss. But the sight of Kim's name carved into the granite ripped a fresh hole in her heart. She reached out and traced the letters, blinking back tears.

"Oh, Kim!" The words seemed to pierce the quiet air. Rebecca had a strange sensation that her words had been heard by some residue of Kim's soul, through six feet of earth and a lovely teak casket.

Comforted by the thought, she continued, "Oh, Kim. I wish you were still here. You'd have loved it in the courtroom today. Remember how I was always telling you to try to get on better with Jo? It turns out she thought I was the bad influence on you. Me, the flake."

She smiled bitterly. "Ha! When all I wanted was to settle down, have my own kids. I really didn't want your kids, Kim—not this way!" In Rebecca's mind, Kim smiled sympathetically, forgiving her for loving her children. She swallowed a lump in her throat. "But since you and Randy couldn't stick around, I intend to do the best I can. I love them so much, you know. As much as I could my own. But I'll never be their mom. I'll never replace you."

She wiped the tears that had fallen on her cheeks. Kim wouldn't want her to cry.

"You want to know how they're doing? Alex can read his Peter Pan book now. I think he's memorized it, but when he forgets a word, Aubrey helps him out. She's going to be taking ballet lessons. Can't you just see her in a little pink tutu? She's not sucking her thumb so much these days, and her teacher said she actually spoke during the field trip the other day."

Then she remembered something else Kim would want to know. "I didn't send them to kindergarten. Their therapist said it would be best to wait a year, when they're more emotionally secure. And besides, when I went to the school and checked it out, they said we'd have to separate them. I couldn't see Aubrey being in a classroom without Alex. She needs him too much right now."

Just like I need you, she wanted to say, but she knew that would make Kim feel bad.

She crouched in front of the gravestone, staring at the inscription. *Beloved wife, mother, daughter, and sister.*

"Hey, guess who I saw yesterday at the airport? Jason Harper. Remember when he told me there was an ice cream truck on the next block? And you eventually found me, ten blocks away, clutching my piggy bank…" The memory of her big sister making a beeline for her across the convenience store parking lot only sweetened the ache that was crushing her heart. "Oh, Kim! I miss you so much! There are so many things I want to talk to you about."

She tucked her head on top of her knees and let the memories come like a videotaped memoir: giggling under the covers late at night, with a stash of gummi bears and teen novels; crying with their arms around each other the day their father had moved out; learning to diaper the twins the morning they'd brought them home from the hospital.

Suddenly, a warm current of air touched her shoulder, and she smelled the faintest scent of perfume—Kim's favorite Gap scent, Heaven. She could almost feel her sister's presence beside her on the hard ground—comforting, calm, reassuring, ready with advice and admonishment.

"*Go ahead, get it off your chest. I know you want to talk about him,*" Rebecca heard Kim say, her voice distant yet strong. It didn't occur to her not to answer.

"You mean Connor?"

"*Of course. Mr. Tall, Dark and Handsome.*"

"Don't forget he's also Mr. Emotionally Deficient."

Rebecca felt Kim smile.

"*You're still looking for Mr. Perfect, aren't you? You think you can get it all in one package. But it doesn't work that way, sis. People have faults. Even you.*"

Rebecca laughed. "Well, yeah, you should have heard the Seversons' attorney. I'm just one fault after another."

"*Oh, that was just legal bullshit. You're doing a great job.*"

"You think so?"

"*Sure. Aubrey told me about the computer game you made for them. It sounds really cool.*"

"It was easy. I just interfaced the AVR technology I studied in grad school—"

"*Hey! No nerd talk, okay? But you ought to think about marketing it.*"

Rebecca's gaze narrowed. "You haven't been talking to—no, never mind." Then she confided, "Connor asked me to marry him again. On the witness stand."

"*So I heard.*"

"You did?" Rebecca wondered if she should ask for an explanation…but, then, she was having a conversation with her own imagination, wasn't she?

"*You're going to tell him no, aren't you?*"

"I can't marry him, Kim. He doesn't love me."

"*Do you love him?*"

"Of course."

"*Then, what's the problem? You love him; he's asked you to marry him—twice.*"

"The problem isn't me, it's him!"

"*So, he's got a flaw or two. What'd you expect? One kiss from you, and voila, the Frog turns into a Prince? That always was your favorite fairy tale.*"

Rebecca sighed. "Are you telling me Connor's not a prince?"

"*His family were potato farmers in County Cork. I've met his mother.*"

"You have?"

"*Nice woman. Reminds me of you—when you're older.*"

The less one knew about the afterlife, Rebecca decided, the better.

But Kim was on a roll. "*Face it; the man's not perfect. But neither are you, sister dear. So, the question is, can you live with his faults? Can you accept him the way he is, warts and all?*"

"But he doesn't love me! That's the problem."

"*The guy wants to marry you.*"

"He wants to put a ring on my finger and take care of me and possibly make some babies with me. He's never said one word about love, except to point out that it doesn't exist."

"*I remember Dad telling Mom he loved her—just before he went off to meet his secretary at the Holiday Inn.*" Kim was still bitter, Rebecca realized, despite four months of eternal bliss. "*Sometimes you have to look beyond the words. It's a person's actions that speak for his heart. You think Randy whispered sweet nothings in my ear all the time? It was all the other things…the way he cleaned the grill after a barbecue and made sure the oil was changed in the car. And when he stood up to his parents and told them we'd decided to get married rather than wait until we had saved enough for a down payment on a house—that was love. Not the hearts and flowers and Hallmark cards.*"

"You think I should marry Connor—even though he doesn't love me?"

"*The man obviously cares about you.*"

"That's not enough!"

"*Maybe he's right—that's all he can feel.*"

"I think he's capable of more than that." Rebecca heard the stubborn note in her voice and realized she was arguing with her sister—atop her grave.

"*Then, you have to show him that.*"

"But what if I'm not the one? What if he really doesn't love me?"

"*Life's full of risks. I took one when I married Randy. After all, after Daddy left us, I thought men were scum. I was counting pretty heavily on the fact Randy wasn't.*"

Rebecca sighed. "Well, Connor's not scum either. Far from it. He's very gentle, and funny, and sweet, and he laughs at Alex's knock-knock jokes." Then she grinned. "He's also great in bed."

Rebecca imagined Kim rolling her eyes. "*Spare me the details.*"

"I guess you're above all that now, huh?"

"*Not entirely. I can't help but notice he's got a great bod under those three thousand dollar suits.*"

Rebecca narrowed her eyes. "Just what *can* you see these days?"

"*I see that you're lonely out there in California, despite the fact you've got the Demon Duo for company.*"

"You think *I'm* lonely; you should see Connor," Rebecca scoffed. "He lives by himself in this huge penthouse. But, then, he's one of those people who are lonely even when they're surrounded by people."

Rebecca could sense Kim's sigh. "*I can relate. You have any idea how many billions of people there are where I am?*"

Rebecca nodded thoughtfully. "I guess you're right." And most of them were older than Kim and Randy, who hadn't even made it to thirty.

She couldn't think about that, or she'd start bawling. Not to mention waste a perfect opportunity to get advice from her sister. Kim seemed to know Connor almost as well as she did.

"I think he thinks he's having a midlife crisis or something," Rebecca told her.

"*Has he bought himself a Harley?*"

Rebecca laughed. "Connor? You've got to be kidding."

"*Then don't worry about it. He'll realize what he has, sooner or later.*"

"You really think so?"

"*It's amazing what your big sister knows these days.*"

Rebecca felt Kim's gaze looking down at her confidently, wiser than she'd been in life. Or maybe, Rebecca realized, this was her own subconscious talking, trying to rationalize her own feelings regarding Connor. Maybe she had set her expectations too high…or maybe Connor just wasn't the one to fill them.

But he understood her the way no one else ever had. He supported her and respected her, no matter how "flaky" her ideas were.

There was something else she needed to get off her conscience, though. "Kim, one more question, okay?"

"*Sure. I've got all day, you know.*"

"Melvin Dailey…the man who —"

Kim interrupted. "*I know all about that.*"

"You do?"

Rebecca pictured Kim nodding. "*I've become good friends with Lady Justice.*"

"You aren't mad?"

Rebecca felt Kim's arms around her, and she really did want to cry.

"*Mad? I expected it of you,*" Kim said. "*Remember that time I borrowed your charm bracelet and broke it? You forgave me, even before I apologized. You've always had empathy for your fellow man — and beast, I might add. But why is it you could always see into everyone's heart, yet when it comes to your lover, you're blind?*"

Rebecca smiled wryly. "Because if I make a mistake, it hurts too much."

"*Ahh. Pain. Been there, done that. There are worse things than a broken heart, you know.*"

Rebecca immediately felt remorse. "You're right. I shouldn't have said that."

"*I meant lost opportunity. The fact is, Rebecca, you have to snatch happiness when you can. It doesn't last. Grab the ring and hang on tight. What have you got to lose?*"

"My heart. Losing you almost did me in. I can't face losing him too!"

"*You can't lose what you've never had,*" Kim pointed out, as logical as ever.

"Exactly! I'm afraid I'll never have what *I* need — a guy who loves me with all his heart and soul and isn't afraid to tell me."

"*Maybe you have to reverse the equation. You know, divide both sides by the same denominator.*"

Rebecca raised an eyebrow.

"*I did listen in math class occasionally,*" Kim said, a grin in her voice. "*You already know he's got what you need—strength, kindness, a good heart beneath that stiff reserve. A sense of humor. And don't forget he's great in bed.*"

Rebecca laughed and Kim went on.

"*And you have what he needs. He just hasn't figured it out yet. You have to keep on giving it to him, in whichever form he'll accept it. And eventually, the two sides of the equation will equal. Trust me.*" Her voice was wise, knowing, and becoming fainter with each word. "*Give him your heart, Rebecca. He needs it. More than you need to protect it.*"

"Oh, Kim," Rebecca said, wanting to protest, but Kim was gone, vanished with the breeze, though the ground was still warm beside her, and a lingering trace of heaven clung to the evening air.

CHAPTER TWENTY-TWO

Rebecca left the cemetery and turned the Honda in the direction of downtown. A phone call to Peggy informed her Connor was staying at the Drake, in the Presidential Suite. Traffic into the city was light this time of the evening, and within a half hour, she was at the entrance of the hotel on East Walton Place. Peggy had told her he was meeting with the directors of a company he was considering buying. Of course, Rebecca thought, he'd combined the trip with business, efficiently killing two birds with one flight: buying a new company for his portfolio, and testifying in her custody hearing. Proposing was probably just an ancillary thought.

A doorman directed her to the elevator which would take her to the fifth-floor suite, and within minutes she was knocking on the door, hoping Peggy was right and the door wouldn't be opened by some visiting dignitary.

Connor answered the door in his shirtsleeves, his hair slightly disheveled as if he'd been running his hands through it. Rebecca noticed a few more gray strands scattered among the black, but they only made him look more distinguished, more delectable.

"Peggy told me you'd called," he told her.

"So much for surprise. Can I come in?"

"Of course. I was just getting ready to order from room service."

"I won't stay long."

"I'm sure I could get reservations if you'd like to go to dinner."

"I'm sure you could. Maître d's probably drop their pants when your secretary calls. Just like judges and high-powered law firms and real estate agents—"

"Unfortunately, computer programmers take a little more work."

She frowned. "I thought I was pretty easy. I did fall at your feet—literally, remember?"

"I remember. But I'm the one who's been off balance ever since," he said with a wry smile.

She tried to feel satisfaction at his words, but dizzy spells weren't what she wanted to inspire in him. She followed him into the room, glancing around curiously. She'd never been in a presidential suite before. In addition to the obvious luxury of the furnishings, there was subtle attention to detail everywhere: a towering arrangement of fresh fruit, a bowl of color-coordinated potpourri, a selection of books and magazines she was sure Connor hadn't brought with him, a telephone that looked capable of handling the direst world crisis. Only the best for billionaire financiers who had the ear of the current President and the heart of the ones on Mount Rushmore.

"So, shall I arrange for reservations?" He nodded toward the phone. "The concierge can no doubt do as good a job as Peggy in making some poor maître d' drop his pants."

She laughed. There was an edge of tiredness in his voice, one she didn't normally hear, and on the table were signs of his work she'd interrupted. His shoes had been kicked off, as if he'd been prepared to settle in for a work-filled evening. She felt a tiny bit guilty for disturbing him, but they still had issues to discuss.

"Actually, I'm not that hungry." Then her gaze slid to the silver platter of flawless fruit, and her hand realized she was hungry despite what her mouth had just said. As Connor adjusted the stereo speaker, she selected a banana and peeled it, contemplating her strategy between bites. She'd survived one confrontation today; the pacifist in her wanted to duck this one, but the inquiring mind in her wanted answers.

She swallowed the last bite of banana and tossed the peel in a wastebasket. "Why did you buy my house?" she demanded. "And then charge me a ridiculously low rent?"

"Isn't that obvious? I wanted you to stay in San Francisco. You were having trouble finding a place to live."

"I would have found something."

He shrugged. "Eventually, perhaps. But the easiest solution seemed to be buying the house."

"That's all it was to you, a solution to a problem."

"Yes."

"And what about your marriage proposal? Another solution?"

He glanced away, suddenly fascinated by the arrangement of anthuriums on the coffee table. "If you want to call it that."

"Connor! People don't get married because it's a solution to a problem. They marry because they love each other. Plain and simple."

He pushed a button on his computer, shutting it down. "Unlike you, I'm not an idealist. Yet it occurred to me that marriage would be convenient, for both of us. Perhaps I was wrong."

"*Convenient?* A smartphone is convenient. Marriage is hard work, even when two people love each other. How on earth would you expect it to last without even that?"

"I do care about you. More than I've cared about anyone in a long time. That, as well as our mutual interests, would be an excellent foundation for marriage."

Rebecca remembered her sister's words. By Kim's definition, Connor had already proven he "cared." Buying her a house was probably the equivalent of cleaning the barbecue grill.

But Rebecca wanted more. She wanted the hearts and flowers — and the words, at least occasionally. She wanted to know he couldn't live without her. She wanted to know he'd drop everything and be there for her when she needed him, when the twins needed him, when their children were born...

She wanted to know it was her name carved on his heart, her name that was last on his breath at night. Her soul entwined with his, throughout eternity.

She wanted his love and all the emotions that came with it — joy, sorrow, contentment, passion.

Unless Connor was capable of that, she didn't want marriage.

Sex, though, was definitely a possibility. After all, why shouldn't she enjoy him for his body? At least this once. She let her gaze travel down the length of him, all the way to his socks.

"Well, I don't need a husband anymore. The judge awarded me custody, despite my unmarried status."

He shrugged. "Then, it's a moot point, isn't it?" Then he added, "However, if dinner is still an option, there's an excellent room service menu."

She shook her head, perversely refusing any more handouts from him disguised as *solutions*. "I'm fine. But you go ahead." While he phoned in an order, she explored the kitchenette and spied a plate of cheese and crackers. "Were you expecting someone?" she asked when he finished the phone call.

"No. I have an early meeting tomorrow, then I'm leaving for New York."

"Oh." She picked up a thin cracker, ignoring the hunks of rich cheese, and popped it into her mouth.

"Help yourself," he said with a smile. "There's Dom Pérignon in the ice bucket."

Champagne. The drink of choice for seduction.

"That sounds nice."

"We should celebrate your win in court today." He opened the bottle, expertly removing the stopper and containing it in his palm. No out-of-control stoppers—or emotions—for Connor.

She accepted the glass he poured, then wandered over to the wide window, peering down through the night at Lake Michigan. It was dark now, and all she could see were the lights of a boat far out. On the other side of the hotel was a city of three million people, but on this side, they were all alone.

She sipped her drink, remembering the last time they'd been alone—with no twins, no secretaries outside the door, no scruples tangled up in the sheets.

She took another drink and plunged into her own explanation. "That day you gave me the watch. You know why I didn't accept it?"

"Something to do with pride, wasn't it?" He came and joined her at the window, holding his own glass of champagne.

She shook her head. "I just didn't want to be another possession you'd bought and paid for. Like some Western version of a geisha girl."

"It *was* an expensive watch," he agreed, gazing thoughtfully at the black lake. "Top quality geishas, however, are considerably more expensive."

She swallowed the sip she'd been savoring. "Really? You haven't…"

He smiled. "No. The concept's a bit old fashioned for my tastes." But then his gaze filled with honesty. "I will admit there's been a time or two…when women were 'available'…at an undisclosed price. Maybe it was an unwritten part of a deal I'd signed…a sort of bonus, so to speak, a courtesy extended to a guest in a foreign city. Or women who knew up front there'd be a financial incentive. It just seemed easier that way. More cut and dried. When everyone knew the score ahead of time. No disappointments later—on either side."

Rebecca tried to feel disgusted by such behavior, but all she felt was sorrow for a man who couldn't afford human emotion. Disillusionment was too great a price to pay for success, in her opinion.

But, then, dollars didn't break one's heart. Dollars didn't walk out after fifteen years of marriage. She remembered the bitterness she'd felt when her dad left home. Connor's father had done the same thing, but she'd had Kim and a mother who had promptly decided she didn't need Donald Evans, or any man, for that matter. Connor's mother had never given up hope her true love would come back—a different example entirely. One that had obviously left its mark on the man standing in front of her.

She'd just have to show him her love was forever—and worth the risk.

"That's sad, Connor," she said, turning from the dark lake below.

He shrugged off her pity. "Both parties got what they wanted. Me, a bed partner in a strange city, one who's reasonably attractive and free of disease."

"And for her? What did she get?"

"A financial reward of some type."

"You think that's all? What about the pleasure of your company?" she argued. "What do you think that's worth?"

He gave a humorless smile. "My 'company' is worth six point two billion dollars. At yesterday's closing, anyway."

She sighed. "Oh, Connor, you've got no idea what your true worth is—as a man. As a lover." She shook her head. "Dollar values—and expensive watches, I might add—don't measure a person's worth. Just like insurance doesn't replace a person you've lost."

A look of compassion replaced the hard cynicism on his face, and Rebecca thought how much Kim would have liked him.

"You're right, of course. I'm sorry."

But Rebecca had mourned already today. She crossed the room to the sofa, setting her glass on the coffee table next to an *Architectural Digest* magazine. She slid off her jacket, draping it over the back of the brocade sofa.

"If you're hot I can adjust the thermostat."

"Oh, no, I'm okay." She ran a hand over her nape, lifting a strand of hair that had fallen loose from the chignon, then unfastened the clasp, letting her hair fall over her shoulders.

"The twins—they're with your mother?" Connor asked, refilling his glass from the bar.

"No. My Aunt Penny kept them today. She's driving them over to the Seversons to spend the night."

He gave her a sharp look as he joined her on the sofa. "You're letting them stay with their grandparents? After what they pulled in court today?"

She shrugged. "Bygones are bygones and all that. The judge did give them visitation rights."

"And you have a remarkably short memory when it comes to insults. I should know," he added wryly.

"Oh, don't think I've forgotten what you did. You lied to me about my house." She turned an accusing gaze on him. "Why?"

"I told you—"

"You told me why you bought it, but not why you never told me the truth. I even asked you to be honest with me before we left for Hawaii. Yet all these months, you've never said a word about the fact you own my house—*your* house!" Her voice rose with indignation as she remembered. "You even asked me what color I was painting it!"

"I didn't give a damn about the house. I didn't care where you lived as long as it was near me. Near my company. You were a valuable employee."

"You wouldn't have bought Kevin a house. He's a valuable employee."

"He doesn't need one."

"Connor," she said, leaning closer, invading his space. "You didn't do what you did because you were afraid of losing a valuable employee. You did it because you cared. You just couldn't tell me that."

"I believe I have told you that. On numerous occasions."

"When you make love to me?"

His gaze shifted to his glass, now empty. "Perhaps."

"No. You haven't told me when you make love to me." She slid closer. "Although you're very…thoughtful…" She laid her palm on his knee. "And considerate."

He smiled mockingly. "'Considerate and thoughtful.' You forgot 'kind.'"

"You're not very kind. Generous, yes, in bed and out."

He raised an eyebrow but she continued, with a tender, teasing smile.

"You're awfully sweet, too. Especially when you compare my eyes to champagne," she said, swallowing the last of the liquid in her glass. "Any girl would have given you her virginity."

He looked slightly embarrassed. "All right, now that you've extolled my virtues—"

"You don't believe a word of it, do you?"

"Neither would the *Wall Street Journal.* I think the adjective they prefer is 'ruthless.'"

She laughed. "You're that too. Especially when you defend someone you care about."

He picked up her hand that had been wandering up his thigh, absently caressing her fingers. "You don't know me as well as you think you do. Trust me, I've spent almost forty years becoming acquainted with my Inner Louse. I know who I am, what I'm capable of."

"What color are your eyes?"

"My eyes?"

"You don't know what color your eyes really are. You've only seen them reflected in the mirror. I bet you don't know they darken to cobalt when you're aroused. I bet you don't know they crinkle when you're amused. I bet you don't know they look scared…lonely, sometimes, when you think no one's watching."

"Scared?" He laughed. "What on earth would I be afraid of?"

"Yourself. And what's inside of you."

He raised an eyebrow. "Had a peek inside, have you?" His thumb pressed into her palm, massaging the flesh and sending tingles of desire racing up her arm.

She shook her head. "Just observant of a man I happen to care about very much." Her voice grew husky with emotion. Oh, how she wanted to tell him, again, she loved him, but he wouldn't appreciate it, wouldn't even believe love existed. "You're afraid to let your heart go on its own journey, discover its own path. Even when you're at your most vulnerable—in the middle of a climax—you have such a tight grip on your emotions, like they might get out of line and admit you care, admit you might love me."

He frowned. Dropping her hand, he said, "I think your imagination is taking a journey of its own. If I truly felt such a thing, I'd readily admit it. To you, to myself."

"Oh, Connor! You really believe that?" Her heart cracked, but she'd asked for honesty. She knew if he thought for one minute he truly loved her, he'd tell her so. He was too kind, too ruthless to do anything else.

He looked at her steadily. "I don't want to love you, Rebecca. I don't want that kind of emotional commitment. I don't take those kinds of risks. They just aren't...cost effective."

She returned his gaze regretfully, torn by pity for him and sorrow for her own lonely heart. The equation was certainly balanced now. They were both miserable without each other. Only one of them hadn't realized it yet.

She sighed, her fingers absently circling his kneecap, and said, "I don't even want commitment, yet you offered marriage. I don't want your life, Connor, just your heart."

"It's not available."

She smiled a sad, resigned smile. "Okay, fine. How about your body?"

His eyes darkened, his nostrils flared slightly. She moved her hand upward along his thigh. Again he intercepted it, placing his palm against hers in warning. "Don't settle for this if you're going to resent me in the morning."

"Who said anything about the morning? I was only planning to stay an hour," she said lightly, hiding the hurt very well, she thought.

Then she leaned over and kissed him full on the mouth. He returned her kiss, his mouth taking and tasting, a man strictly in control of his passion.

For now.

A Chopin nocturne floated through the room from a speaker hidden in the wall, a throbbing tempo that matched her pulse. She undid the buttons of his shirt, one by one, pressing her lips to the opening she made as each button slipped free from its mooring. She could feel his heart beating beneath her palms.

A wild urge to cover him with her body, with her love, grew within her, and she pushed him back, unprotesting, until he was flat on the couch, hard and solid beneath her. Her skirt slid up, exposing the tops of her thigh-high stockings. He slipped a finger beneath the elastic, stroking her skin until she burned for him to touch her all over.

She was settling for second best, but his body, warm and familiar against hers, felt awfully like her first choice right now. "Oh, God, I've missed this…being with you…being a part of you…" She kissed his neck, his shoulder, the little tuft of hair that grew at his collarbone, just above the undershirt she was planning to rip off.

"Marry me," he said. "We'll have this every night."

"No…"

He stroked her thigh, easing her stocking down the length of her leg. "Why not?"

His hands were sending waves of desire straight to her belly, little piercing arrows of pleasure. He kissed her shoulder, nibbled the flesh above her silk blouse.

"Because you don't…love…me."

"But I love making love to you."

"It's not…the same…" She breathed in the scent of him — starch, soap, and hard male, so familiar and so unlike her own softness.

He caressed the back of her knee. "But it's better than nothing."

He was right. It was better than not having him at all, and she could settle for this feeling that slid over her like warm honey on toast. She tasted his mouth, in tiny nibbles, dipping her tongue against his sensuously, then melding, until wild frenzy pounded in her veins and made her dance against him, grinding against his hardness, his heat.

Within minutes he was naked, and she was wearing only her bra and a pair of lace panties that would have confirmed the plaintiffs' opinion of her as a fallen woman. Connor seemed to love them. He couldn't keep his mouth off the lace. He teased, pulling at the edges, dipping into paradise, until she ached to have his mouth on her, pressing into her tender flesh.

She arched beneath him, her breasts on fire, aching for his touch, and he gave it to her, considerate, as always, but she wanted, needed, more.

With a few well-placed tugs, he removed her panties, then her bra. His mouth lowered to the triangle of golden curls, and she felt sunlight swell inside her. Glorious, sweet release only a moment away, but he kept it just out of her reach, teasing the aching place inside her until she grabbed his head, held him still, and moaned.

"Oh, Connor, oh, Connor, oh, now. Pleasepleaseplease!" and then the world crashed around her.

Connor felt her tremble, and it wasn't enough. He wanted more. He wanted to give her every delight known to man, and then invent new ones. He wanted to take her to the Orient, to Antarctica, to the moon. He wanted to give her silver stars, golden sunsets, platinum days. Diamonds the color of her eyes. Rubies the color of her heart. Pearls the color of her skin.

He wanted to dress her in cashmere and silk and warm, woolen maternity clothes.

He wanted her in his bed, in his car, in his house.

In his life.

More than anything, he wanted to be inside her. Warmed by her, caressed by her, loved by her…

He lowered his mouth again, and feasted on her breasts like a starved man. She moaned and sighed, her breath fanning his over-heated skin until he could think of nothing but sinking into the desire. Around him, world trade crises loomed, stocks climbed, and interest rates bottomed out, but all he wanted was this.

She twisted until she was straddling him, her legs gripping him. He took in the vision above him, her skin glowing like the hereafter, her breasts twin points of perfection, her hair a blond halo, tousled and beautiful.

"Payback time," his angel said with a teasing smile that promised earthly rewards.

Limbs tangled, there on the brocade sofa of his suite, a sofa that had seated presidents and rock stars. Now it was cushioning their love, a heated writhing embrace that threatened the security of Connor's world as surely as the discovery of plutonium threatened world peace.

Rebecca stroked him, her hands soft and firm, her mouth wet and greedy, each pull of her lips and tongue increasing his pleasure until he thought he'd explode from wanting to be inside her.

He needed her, needed this, and the realization shocked him. He'd never needed another soul, not since he'd been old enough to walk. Now her hands touching him, caressing him, were his lifeline to heaven.

He rolled her over, pinning her to the couch, hot and tense and breathless with desire. He was determined to make her come again and again, until he'd given her all he could.

She moaned beneath him, rocking her hips to urge him to take his place inside her. "Oh, Connor, hurry, please!" she begged, her voice husky with longing, her legs grasping his.

He complied, for the first time in his life with no thought for protection. Rebecca guided him, with her hand then with her body, accepting his entrance as if she'd been made for him. Never had sex felt so good, so right, so complete. He lost himself utterly in passion, his previously contained emotions stripped bare.

He filled her, over and over, with every particle of himself—his lonely heart, his mind, his soul, until finally he let himself fall into her.

Ecstasy engulfed him. He dissolved into a hundred, a thousand, then a million particles of raw, sweaty, energy.

A last shuddering gasp, and from somewhere he found strength enough to raise himself off and over her, unpinning her from his weight. He was surprised, moments later, to hear Chopin still on the stereo, surprised to see their clothes, scattered on the floor in an impatient heap.

Surprised even more to hear a knock on the door, stirring him from a haze of sexual satisfaction he wanted to sink into.

Room service. Or else the hotel bomb squad, responding to reports of an explosion.

He got up, pulled on his pants and shirt, still half-buttoned. Fortunately, the door was in an alcove, the scene of seduction hidden from view.

His legs shook, his hands trembled as he accepted the tray. He'd stocked his pockets with tip money, and the guy seemed satisfied with a twenty.

The bill could have had Ben Franklin's face on it for all he cared. He just hoped his own face didn't wear a silly grin.

He deposited the tray on the breakfast table. Forget the sandwich; he wanted to feast on Rebecca for the next decade or two. She was still on the sofa, her feet propped on the armrest, her hands crossed behind her head, naked and satisfied, and sexy as hell.

"I ordered another sandwich. They had vegetarian. No mayo, right?"

"Um-hmm. Have I mentioned what a thoughtful person you are?" Her voice was lazy, satisfied. Tender.

"I believe you did."

"Easygoing, too," she added, picking up her panties with her toe.

"Of course," he agreed, wondering where this was leading.

"Good. Then you won't mind if we get crumbs in your bed?"

And just like that, the silly grin he'd hoped to avoid appeared.

Rebecca stayed the night after all. They made love until she was limp, then she fell asleep with Connor's arms around her.

Several times during the night, he repeated his proposal—between kisses and again just before she dozed off. It was sweet, really, she thought the next morning, as she prepared to slip away while he was in the shower. He'd invited her to join him, teasing her about her sudden onset of modesty.

But she had a plane to catch and the twins to pick up—and she was wearing the same outfit she'd worn to the hearing. She'd have to go to her mother's house and change.

She groaned. She'd told Barb she was going to Connor's hotel, but she hadn't planned on staying the night.

Despite being almost twenty-seven, Rebecca blushed at the thought of facing her mother, even though the woman had surely figured out her daughter had spent the night with the man. Even though that man had asked her to marry him.

Marriage to Connor would be bliss, just as he'd promised. But it would be a bliss tempered with the knowledge that he didn't love her. She couldn't live with that.

She sighed as she found a stocking under the sofa cushion. She'd leave him a note, she decided, where he'd be sure to find it.

She opened his notebook, tore out a sheet of paper, and wrote out what had been too hard to say in person.

In the other room, the shower cut off. Rebecca grabbed her purse, took a muffin from the breakfast tray that had been delivered earlier, and left the suite.

When Connor came out of the bathroom, the emptiness hit him like a lonely echo. Rebecca had left, and he was alone again, except for the low hum of his laptop.

He crossed the room to the desk, where next to his glowing laptop was a note. Her handwriting scrawled across the notepaper:

Connor,

I had a lovely time last night, but I can't do this again. I want the hearts and flowers. I can't be the heavy end of the equation anymore. Maybe I'm asking too much—Kim seems to think so—but then, you can't divide an equation by zero.

Unless you believe in imaginary numbers.

Or love.

Rebecca

The most richly appointed suite in Chicago was bare without her presence. His life just as empty and meaningless, despite dozens of charities depending on his generosity. Even the thought of finalizing his business deal later today held no appeal.

He'd offered her anything, but what she wanted was, of course, more than he could give.

She wanted him to rip out his heart and offer it up, bleeding and raw.

She wanted the same thing she'd offered him.

220

He remembered the times at night when she thought he was asleep, when she'd whispered "I love you." He'd preferred not to hear it, avoiding the embarrassment. Instead, he'd pitied her, mocked the idea.

Sure, he cared for her. More than he'd ever cared for another woman. But he couldn't let himself feel more for her than that. There was too much risk, too many potential heartaches.

He flipped the laptop shut. She wanted to end it. That was fair. He couldn't pay her price. There was probably someone else, somewhere, who could. He swallowed what felt suspiciously like jealousy—another reason to keep his heart in his pocket.

He went into the bedroom and started packing, carefully placing his disappointment right alongside his shirts.

CHAPTER TWENTY-THREE

Three days later, Connor jogged along the beach, listening to the sea crash against the rocks. The Pacific was restless today, a moody Poseidon flaunting his power in one wave, tamed into submission by the next.

It matched his own mood. He'd been restless, off center ever since Rebecca had left his hotel suite. Optimistic that she'd change her mind one minute, determined to change it for her the next, and equally determined to avoid her and the complications she represented after that. He wanted to work out a compromise, but she'd left no room for negotiation.

Still, he intended to try.

He'd bought a ring in New York—a rare canary diamond in a platinum setting. Flawless and unique, six carets of depthless facets. Iridescent gold, almost brown, earthy and immaculate. As beautiful, and as fascinating, as the woman he'd bought it for.

Now he just needed a strategy to get her to accept it. He'd negotiated his way through financial thickets; surely he'd manage to convince one clever computer programmer to become his wife.

He hadn't been able to think of anything else the whole time he was in New York, and then in Philadelphia, where he had a quick meeting with Claire Porter. She'd noticed his distraction.

"Something on your mind?" she'd asked after he'd had to ask again what the retail forecasts were for the upcoming year.

He'd started to deny it automatically, then realized she'd have some insight; she was a woman, after all. And an old friend. Plus the best negotiator he'd ever met.

"I bought a ring—an engagement ring."

She had appeared startled. "Oh. I didn't realize you were...I guess congratulations are in order."

"Not yet. She hasn't accepted my proposal."

"Ahh." She'd laid her pen down on the reports they were discussing, giving the matter her full attention.

"Any advice?"

She'd studied him thoughtfully. "She loves you?"

"She claims to. I haven't signed on to the theory myself, but—"

"The theory? You mean love? The 'happily-ever-after' theory of human relationships?" She adjusted her silver-framed glasses, the ones she used for reading as well as self-protection.

He nodded, saying, "The notion that two people's lives happen to coincide with destiny. Then they forsake all others and, through sickness and health, good times and bad, through whatever misfortune fate throws at them, stick with the plan."

"Oh dear. Aren't we cynical," she'd said mildly.

He shrugged. "Or just unwilling to accept our fate."

Claire nodded, understanding. "I could insert a few choice words about fate myself." Then she smiled. "But I won't. We're old friends now, fortune and I. I've made my peace. Forgiven the old bat for intervening in what I thought was a perfectly good life."

"No regrets?"

"For marrying Matt?" She shook her head. "None. I'm totally happy, Connor. It's as if I'd been missing a piece of myself all along. Sure, I could have lived without it, but it's a lot nicer having it around. Having him around."

"You honestly believe we're meant to be with another person—and that person only? That defies logic."

She gave a helpless shrug. "I know. It certainly isn't practical. What if we happen to miss the street corner where we're to meet out intended mate?"

"Exactly my point. There's too much room for error."

"I think fate sends us up the right path. And sometimes logic is overrated, especially when it comes to love. We do things for our children, for those we love, that the logic of self-preservation would rather we not."

"Of course. We don't have a choice about loving our children. But when it comes to choosing a mate, that's another matter."

"We don't have much choice about that, either. There's one person, out of millions, who fits the requirements perfectly. Some kind of emotional synchronicity. You can fight it—God knows I did—but if it's right, it will happen. Regardless of all the logic we throw in the way."

Was she right? he asked himself as he continued to jog along the beach. Or had marriage given her a different perspective? Made her sentimental?

The concomitance of it all—the idea of two people, perfectly matched, destined by fate to find each other—just wasn't possible. Life didn't work like that. You made your own bed, engineered your own solutions.

Fate didn't come popping up like a jack-in-the-box, ready to trip you up and offer you a partner for life.

Logic—and hormones—determined your choice of mate. The problem was, logically and hormonally, Rebecca was right for him. She was everything he'd ever wanted, though, admittedly, he hadn't known he wanted it before she came jogging into his life. Ever since that day in the park, he'd been tugged by hormones, by brain synapses beyond his control, until he wanted her, needed her, couldn't imagine life without her.

He just had to make her agree that marriage was the answer. The only logical result of this attraction between them.

His feet carried him farther than he normally ran, as if determined to ensure he had adequate time to ponder the situation. He passed the point where he'd scattered his mother's ashes. He'd taken a boat, just himself and Rodney, and gone a few miles out to sea, where there were no other boats, nothing but the distant sight of the shore. He felt her presence every time he passed this spot. He'd never told anyone, but he'd often suspected her spirit hung around, watching over Rodney, keeping an eye on Helen, even observing his own success with a shake of her head and a baffled look. His mother had never understood what drove him, the need he had to show his missing father they hadn't needed his support.

"*He knew you didn't need him, Connor.*" The lilting Irish voice spoke to him from nowhere, and he almost answered it, but stopped at the last minute. It was merely his subconscious.

His subconscious, however, had a point to make.

"*Mitchell left knowing you didn't need him. And the man was pretty sure I'd be okay — I was a nurse, after all. Used to taking care of others. It was your brother he was afraid needed something he couldn't provide. He was scared, Connor. Scared of the commitment he'd made when he was just a twenty-year-old boy with a lonely heart in a strange country. He stuck it out, you have to admit, longer than I ever thought he would.*"

Connor couldn't resist a reply, although he knew his words were only heard by the wind. "You mean you knew going into the marriage it wouldn't last?"

"*Nothing ever lasts — for certain. There's no guarantee the sun will rise tomorrow, now is there? Yet we go on, day to day, doing for others and ourselves…loving each other, despite what your logic tells you about human nature. Giving ourselves. It's the giving, Connor, that makes life worthwhile. Deep inside, you know that.*"

"Some would think so," he said, annoyed that first Rebecca, then this voice of his mother, could read him so well, and had no qualms telling him what was on the inside of his heart, his soul.

"*You've saved your heart from hurt. Now you're like a wild animal that's chewed off its leg to avoid the trap. Open your heart; let yourself know what's there.*"

"What if there's nothing there?"

"*Ahh, that's just not true, love. You're generous, kind, all the things she thinks you are. You're just so used to being the strong one, taking care of Rodney, of me, hating your father for leaving…I didn't hate him. I never could. Love doesn't work like that, dear boy.*"

"Love means never having to say you're sorry? That's not only a cliché, but also a false sentiment."

He could swear he heard her click her tongue. "*But 'tis true, to my way of thinking. Love accepts all, even a person's need to leave. Your father couldn't handle what he had. Two lovely sons — one who needed too much help, one who didn't need anyone.*"

"And what about his wife?"

He heard her sigh in the ocean breeze. "*A wife who expected too much of him.*"

"A wife who wanted a knight in shining armor and got a soldier with a drinking problem instead."

"*Aye, that's true enough,*" she agreed. "*But Mitchell Forrest was still a prince among men. For me, at least. The only man I could ever love.*"

"Rebecca thinks I'm a prince."

"*You* are *a prince. You're everything she needs. You're everything you need to be, everything you've ever wanted to be: a good brother, a fine son, a wonderful lover...*"

He couldn't help chuckling. "Who told you that?"

Blithe laughter rang out in the salty air. "*A mother hears things.*"

He didn't say anything, not wanting to disagree with a spirit he wasn't even sure existed. He was trying hard to remember it was his subconscious he was dealing with.

A subconscious he'd never had any problem suppressing.

Maybe that was the problem. Maybe he hadn't spent enough time on self-examination, thinking it indulgent, a sure sign that midlife crisis he feared was a birthday away.

That brought up another good point. "I'm too old for her."

"*Aye, that you are. But maybe it's maturity she's looking for.*"

"It's raw emotion she's looking for. She wants me to give her something I can't."

"*She wants your heart, dearest. Your love. That's easy enough to dig up from the rock you put it under. Why don't you just give it to her?*"

He had a perfectly logical answer to that one; he knew he did.

But his mother had never been one for logic. "*Love's not worth anything unless you give it away, you know. It's like a vein of gold, hidden away in a mountain. Not worth a penny until you take it out.*"

"It's not that easy," he replied, and was answered by a disbelieving snort.

"*And since when has a little difficulty stopped you?*"

"She'll marry me," he predicted confidently. "It's what she wants. It's just a question of convincing her."

"*Not without your love*," the voice in his subconscious replied. "*Give her your heart, and you'll be the richest man alive.*" It wasn't material wealth she meant, Connor knew.

"You don't recall where I put the damn thing, do you?" he asked, but he realized, with a sharp sense of loss, that he was talking to the wind. His mother, if that's what—who—it had been, was gone, having said her piece. He was getting no more help from that quarter.

The whole thing had been an illusion, a dream. A sign his solitary life was wearing on him.

He'd wrapped himself in work, in solitude, in the company of women he didn't care for, as a protective device. A shield, just like the FGI logo. Too much solitude was hazardous, a trap he'd built for himself.

A top-notch security team, the latest in electronic alarms—none of it had warned him of his own emotions intruding.

He advised his fund managers of the dangers of too much risk aversion. No risk, no gain, he'd always preached, yet he'd been blind to the insulating effects in his personal life. He'd miscalculated, misjudged his own capacity for emotional involvement.

Connor hated mistakes. Whether they were made by him, or others. He'd fix this one as soon as he got back to San Francisco.

He'd take his heart out of hiding and offer it to her, along with a ring. That should do the trick.

He walked the last mile to his house, steeped in thought. Was it possible to uncover his heart at this late date? Was he capable of the all-consuming love she wanted?

He didn't think so. All the same, he intended to try.

It just might be possible he loved her; stranger things had happened, he realized.

Like a conversation with his dead mother on a deserted stretch of California coast.

CHAPTER TWENTY-FOUR

"What's this, an air freshener testing facility?" Kevin poked his nose around the corner of Rebecca's cubicle, sniffing loudly. The sight that greeted him stopped him cold. "Uh-oh. Did I forget your birthday?"

There were roses on the desk, tulips on the floor, and daisies perched in the hutch. Flowers everywhere, in all hues and sizes, a botanical bonanza.

"No. My birthday's next week, though, in case you want to put it on your calendar," Rebecca told him with a grin. She glanced at the paper in his hand. "Is that for me?"

Kevin handed her the note. "Bob asked me to give it to you. Looks like you're wanted upstairs."

She scanned the note: It was from Peggy. A second summons to Connor's office. The first had been delivered by email, and she hadn't replied. She crumpled up the piece of paper and tossed it into the wastebasket.

Kevin eyed her warily. "Tell me something…There's a rumor going around that your job will be open soon. If so, I have a friend…"

"Not unless you know something I don't know — like I'm being fired. Otherwise, I'm planning to stay right here. Literally," she added, with a wry look around the stuffed cubicle. "I don't think I could get out of here if the place were on fire."

"Maybe you should just tell the guy yes. Put him out of his misery."

Rebecca frowned. "He's not miserable, believe me. Besides, I kind of like the flowers. I've been taking them to a battered women's shelter around the corner from my house. The women there really get a kick out of them."

"What about the chocolates?" Kevin eyed a box of Godiva sitting next to her keyboard.

"I was going to take those, too, but…" She shoved the box closer to him. "Want one?"

"Sure." He picked out a chocolate nut cluster and popped it in his mouth. "You know, there are some who'd question your sanity. Not many women would turn down a chance to win the 'who wants to marry a billionaire?' game, hands down."

She gave him an admonishing look. "Love isn't a game, Kevin. Love is forever. And marriage without love is like…nuts without chocolate." She dug another piece of chocolate from the box and nibbled the end.

"Well, I have to admire you for sticking to your principles. If you don't love the guy…"

"It's not that. I *do* love him—with all my heart—but he doesn't love me. That's the problem."

He looked around the room, his gaze settling on an exquisite spray of delphiniums. "Doesn't seem like a problem to me. I'd think a guy who sends flowers by the truckloads has a major crush."

She dismissed his comment with a wave of her hand. "Anyone can call Teleflora. Or in this case, the corporate headquarters of Godiva Chocolate."

"True, but it's still a nice gesture."

"Exactly. All it is is a gesture, plus a ten-second phone call and another entry on the spreadsheet he keeps for 'Wooing Expenses.'"

Kevin shook his head ruefully. "Last time I tried to woo a girl, I gave her a stuffed poodle. Turned out she was allergic to dogs; the stuffing made her sneeze."

"Aw, that's too bad," Rebecca sympathized. "But it was still a nice gesture."

"You mean you'd prefer he gave you a stuffed poodle?"

"Well…" She pondered the question. "I'd prefer a little Scottie. Or maybe a cocker spaniel."

Kevin pretended to take a note of that. "Any particular color?"

She laughed. "Pink. Now, go on. I've got work to do." She waved him away, and Kevin left, a secretive smile creasing his mouth.

Later, as she was preparing to leave work, Rebecca looked up to see the now familiar sight of the delivery service guy. This time, instead of another bouquet of roses, he was holding a pink cocker spaniel with a white bow that said "Marry me."

Rebecca laughed. Her coworkers, apparently, were sidelining in corporate espionage.

No amount of cute antics, even from a guy who didn't normally engage in them, would change her mind. She only wanted one thing from Connor, and it wasn't available from Teleflora.

"Did you get the flowers?" Connor's voice on the phone greeted her just as she arrived for work the next morning. She had half-expected him to phone her house last night, but he seemed to think wooing hours were between eight and five.

"Yes, they were lovely. The ladies at the shelter loved them. The dog was a big hit with the twins, too."

"And the chocolate?"

"Kevin took them as payment. One of the perks for spying."

"Good. I was planning to give him a raise."

She laughed. "Connor, the whole building is talking about us. I feel like a contestant on *The Dating Game*."

"Well, bachelor number one has a proposal he'd like to show you. Can you come up to my office?"

She sighed. "I do have a job to do, you know."

"That's what I wanted to talk to you about."

"You want to talk about my job?"

"Among other things."

"You're firing me?"

His voice turned serious. "Rebecca, I hope you know my...pursuit of you...has absolutely nothing to do with your working here. It never has."

"I know that. Although I'm not sure exactly what your 'pursuit' does have to do with."

"Why don't you come up here and find out?"

"All right, I'll bite. I'll be there in a few minutes." She hung up the phone, chose a rose from the arrangement on her desk and, twirling it between her fingers, and went upstairs to the executive offices.

Peggy was on the phone, but she waved her into Connor's inner sanctum. Rebecca closed the door behind her, and Connor came around his desk, meeting her in the middle.

"I've missed you," he said, a slightly startled look in his eyes, and Rebecca's heart melted a tiny bit.

He took her in his arms and kissed her, a tender, poignant kiss full of promise and purpose. Rebecca responded; she couldn't help it. This man was her weakness — his joy her happiness, his passion her craving.

Oh, how she loved him, how she wanted him! But not on his lukewarm terms.

"I have something to show you," he said at last, letting her go. He walked to his desk, and picked up a set of legal-sized papers.

He handed it to her. "It's a prenuptial agreement."

She jumped back as if it were a snake. "Connor! Why on earth have you..."

"Read it. It's very short, simple, and to the point."

"I don't want to read it."

"It gives you everything. In the event of a divorce or annulment, you'll receive the entirety of my assets. Everything except my home in northern California."

Rebecca's mouth flew open in shock. "Connor! I don't want your assets! Not any of them!"

He went on as if he hadn't heard her. "That includes this company. And the company I intend to start up which you will run, a software business that will showcase your talents as a programmer."

"You're trying to buy me," she accused.

"One could look at it that way. I want you, Rebecca, as my wife, and no price is too high."

She sighed, and when she spoke, disappointment edged her voice. "You still can't afford me."

He gave a small shrug, and Rebecca wondered how often he'd been told that before.

"It's just a matter of finding the right price."

"The price is your love. Is that included in that agreement?"

He tossed the paper on his desk and crossed his arms, regarding her patiently. "It's implied. I have enough faith in this marriage — in the fact that we're right for each other — that I'm willing to risk losing everything I have."

"Everything except your heart."

He looked away. "I would have thought that was obvious."

"Obvious? Unless this agreement you want me to sign — which I have no intention of signing, by the way. Unless this agreement lays it out in black and white that you love me, with all your heart and soul, when you can't even say the words…"

Say the words, Connor! she silently pleaded, but he seemed frozen.

His jaw clenched, as if holding himself firm was the only thing saving him from falling. Finally he said, "It's obvious we share the same values, the same concerns…a love for the twins. For family."

She shook her head. "I share the same values as the Dalai Lama. That doesn't mean I want to marry him. You've got to come up with something more, Connor. Something more than all your assets and a room full of flowers."

A look of hopelessness entered his gaze. "And if there's not any more? I'd give you my name, my home, my respect…my body, on a regular basis. What you want is —"

She laid her hand on his chest, just above his crossed arms. "Your heart. Your love. If you can't offer that, I'm not interested. You can keep your agreements, your stuffed puppies. I'll take the respect, though." She smiled weakly. "It'll come in handy the next time I see that delivery guy."

His mouth curved into a reluctant smile, and he covered her hand with his. "I didn't mean to embarrass you. You mentioned something about hearts and flowers. I figured I could certainly do the flower part."

"Anyone could do the flower part. That's the point."

"I suppose it is." He gazed at their joined hands, frowning.

Rebecca wondered how such a smart man could be so be so clueless when it came to a basic human component like emotion — specifically, love — but then, she herself had shied away from committing to love until now.

She smiled at him gently. "I want more, Connor. And if you really want me, you'll figure out how to go about finding out what."

He glanced up, and then reached into his pocket. "I don't suppose this is it." He opened a jeweler's box and passed it to her.

Rebecca gasped. She stared at the ring. It was stunning, breathtaking. Another expensive gift she couldn't accept. A bittersweet sigh escaped her throat. "Oh, Connor, it's beautiful. But —"

"But it's not enough to do the trick."

She shook her head, blinking back tears.

"What if I told you I loved you?"

"That would depend…on whether you meant it, or were merely using a convenient phrase to get what you want."

"It's hardly convenient. At least until this point, it's been damned impossible to come up with it."

She looked up at him, at his dear face, his expression so serious and guarded. "Do you love me, Connor?"

He gave her a tight smile. "The signs do seem to point in that direction."

She studied him, wishing she could believe those signs. But signs had led her down the wrong road before. She was tired of trusting her heart, her instincts. This time she wanted it spelled out — and not on eleven-by-fourteen legal paper.

In her hand, the ring glowed like a nugget of clear gold. It was a dramatic gesture — she had to hand it to him there — but it wasn't enough. She wanted it all: hearts and flowers, love and honor. Till death, and perhaps even beyond. Her conversation with Kim had her reassessing her views of the afterlife these days.

With a slow shake of her head, she said, "I think you're stymied. You want something you can't have any other way, so you've decided to up the ante. It's just a business transaction to you, isn't it?"

"I don't want to disappoint you. Emotional declarations seem to be out of my realm."

As if punctuating his words, the morning sun ducked behind a cloud, and the office was suddenly bathed in gray. Rebecca set the ring on the desk, where it shone dully despite the lack of a worshiping sun.

"Emotions aren't something to fear, Connor. They won't topple you when you least expect it, like some internal tripwire. They're a part of you." She looked in his eyes, read the doubt, the fear. "You *can* fall in love. Maybe not with me, but once you acknowledge you have the ability, you'll find the perfect woman for you."

For a moment, she thought he might object, but he stayed silent.

She withdrew her hand, and without a glance at the papers on his desk promising her a fortune to marry him, or at the rare diamond that must have put a severe dent in that fortune, she said, "I have to get back to work now. I hope the ring's returnable."

She walked out of his office, hoping her instincts were right this time.

He watched her go, a woman wise beyond her years who'd just turned down an opportunity others would have snatched without a second thought.

The one who wants me more than his kingdom, she'd said once. *Or a pair of shoes...* and yet she'd just turned down everything he had to offer.

He went to the window that looked out on the streets of San Francisco, busy with people racing around on their own personal odysseys. Off in the distance, the Golden Gate Bridge reached across the bay, tripping the re-emerging sun with its orange-gold spires.

A few miles away was another bridge, one that had once collapsed.

Hazards everywhere, it seemed, yet millions of people disregarded them and plunged across a bridge—or into love.

Connor turned and picked up the ring, gazing into its depths. Rebecca saw something in him others didn't see, a nugget of gold hidden in a harsh mountainside, a diamond glinting amongst the rocks. He wanted to reward her insight, to confirm her prognosis, but the fear that she was wrong held him back.

Her heart—her emotions—floated near the surface, reminding him of a Japanese carp he'd seen once, its blood red heart transparent through its flesh, visible even at the surface of the pond.

What if what he felt wasn't love, and he ended up hurting her? Not even his wealth was compensation for that kind of damage.

He'd always thought himself incapable of emotions, incapable of feeling what he was more and more certain he now felt. This strange tightening in his chest, around the vicinity of his heart. Was this love? How did one know for certain?

CHAPTER TWENTY-FIVE

"Rebecca, do mice have feelings?" Aubrey snuggled up against Rebecca while she booted her computer. They'd just arrived home after a stop to deliver flowers to the women's shelter. Rebecca welcomed the distraction; she wasn't ready to think about the conversation she'd had with Connor. The look in his eyes as she'd walked out of his office had almost convinced her to turn around and rush into his arms. She'd hurt him; she knew that. But if he truly loved her, he'd figure out that it wasn't his worldly possessions she wanted.

She gave Aubrey a squeeze. "Of course they do, sweetie. Why do you ask?"

"Because we found a dead mouse on our field trip to the park today. I think it was a mommy mouse."

"Oh, that's sad. I bet her babies miss her."

Aubrey rarely mentioned her parents; instead, she preferred to work out her grief by transferring the feelings to others.

"We looked for them, but we couldn't find them."

"Maybe they ran off with their daddy mouse."

"Or maybe they went to live with their aunt."

"I hope they're not still sad."

Aubrey shook her head. "They still miss their mommy, but their aunt probably takes them to the park sometimes."

Rebecca smiled. "I bet she does."

Aubrey waited patiently as Rebecca clicked on the email icon. "Our computer has a mouse," she said, in an unusually chatty mood. "But it's a different kind."

"That's right…Although Sam teases it sometimes, doesn't he?"

"He thinks it's a real mouse. But real mice are furry."

"That Sam, he's so silly. I think he must be chasing one now. Look at him…"

At that moment, Sam was stalking a wayward sunbeam across the floor. He'd been acting strange ever since they arrived home. Maybe it was time to have the little guy neutered. She'd call the vet tomorrow, she decided. She didn't want to be responsible for any more unwanted kittens.

Sam gave a plaintive yowl, as if reading her thoughts. Rebecca could have sworn he had a distressed look in his green-gold eyes.

"It's okay, buddy."

She reached to pick him up, but he scooted away, heading toward the bag of groceries she'd left on the floor. She'd been in a hurry to check her email and hadn't yet put them away.

Maybe Sam was just hungry.

"Come on, Aubrey. Let's feed Sam, and then see what we can find for dinner. How about tacos?"

Just then, Alex opened the back door, and the cat slid past into the back yard. Rebecca sighed. She was definitely getting him fixed.

Connor was at home, scanning yesterday's news in the *Wall Street Journal*, when it started. A low rumble, gathering speed and strength for what seemed like minutes, but must have been only seconds as time stood still and the earth moved.

An earthquake.

Although tremors weren't that uncommon, this one was definitely more than a gentle shake. A herd of helicopters landing on the roof couldn't have been any louder.

As the walls around him shivered and the floors swayed, Connor's first thought was for Rebecca and the twins.

The Towers was earthquake retrofitted and not likely to suffer much damage. But Rebecca's house was built before construction technology had improved. It had survived large quakes before, but no two earthquakes ever released energy in the same pattern. There was no predicting where damage could occur, or how severe it would be.

Finally the shaking stopped, the grotesque rumbling receded, the walls realigned, and the floor became stable.

He found his phone and, his fingers trembling, punched in Rebecca's home number. There was no answer. Did that mean she wasn't there, or that she couldn't get to the phone? He tried her cell. Maybe she was out shopping with the twins. But this time, he got an "all circuits busy" recording.

The lights flickered and went out. There was an emergency generator in the hotel, but it would have to be turned on by hotel staff. Connor knew the staff was well trained for earthquake emergencies. His presence wasn't needed here.

The thought of Rebecca, in her charming Victorian with paper-thin walls, built during the time of gaslights. *Oh my God,* he thought. *Rebecca!*

Everyone who'd lived in California for long knew that the most danger was after a quake—when broken gas lines erupted in flames. It was imperative they be shut off immediately. Countless newcomers had inadvertently lit candles when flashlights weren't available, and they'd blown themselves to bits.

A shudder ripped through him. He had to find her, warn her of the danger, make sure she and the twins were safe.

He slipped his cell phone into his pocket and found a battery-powered radio he kept for emergencies. Sirens wailed on the streets below, and when he tuned the radio to a local all-news station, officials were already urging residents to stay put.

The roads would be congested, the street lights out, and millions of people would have already fled homes and buildings in fear of aftershocks. Connor ignored the cautions, as well as common sense. He had to get to Rebecca, to make sure she was safe and stayed that way.

His heart slammed against his breastbone as cold fear raced through his veins.

Rebecca! Even now, she could be hurt, trapped in her home, or worse—

Connor rushed from his apartment, bypassing the private elevator for the stairs. As he reached the lower floors, he found the stairwell was crowded with hotel guests hurrying from their rooms, many of them panicked out-of-towners who'd never experienced even a moderate earthquake.

Connor tried to reassure them as he passed. "The hotel has safety precautions in place. Go to the main lobby. Someone will assist you there. You'll be fine."

Meanwhile, he ignored the sheer panic that filled his brain whenever he thought of Rebecca and the twins in the house, remembering scenes he'd seen after the Loma Prieta earthquake, where entire blocks in the Marina district had been damaged, later declared unsafe for habitation.

She lived outside the Marina district, not far from the beach—another spot built on loose sandy soil that had a tendency to liquefy during large quakes. He tried to swallow his fear, but it seemed stuck somewhere in his throat.

He reached his car. He'd seen no major damage to the hotel, thank God, although there was an ominous X-crack in one of the concrete beams spanning the lower parking garage. But earthquake damage was often sporadic, depending more on the structure itself than on the magnitude of the earthquake.

He tuned his car radio to the local news station. They were reporting the quake had measured 6.5 on the Richter scale—a moderate one, yet still capable of inflicting considerable damage, depending on how near the epicenter was.

He blinked as his car left the garage, the sun too bright in the sky, painting a surreal scene of normalcy amidst the sirens and frightened faces on the people spilling from buildings, cars, and homes.

Connor wanted to pray, to any god who would listen, for Rebecca's safety—for the twins' safety—but the only word he seemed to know was "please."

Please, let them be all right!

His heartbeat skipped as he neared Rebecca's neighborhood, driving as fast as he dared across the busy thoroughfares. Street lights were out in parts of town, making the typical late afternoon congestion even worse.

Car alarms were going off, as if the cars had joined in the general panic ensuing all around. Although Rebecca's house wasn't far, the drive across the peninsula took twice as long. Connor tried to call her, but the circuits were overloaded. Everyone was trying to call their loved ones, ensure their safety. Connor was no different, he realized. His loved ones—Rebecca and the twins—meant more to him than he'd ever realized. Their safety had suddenly become his only priority.

Rebecca! His gut clenched in terror as he thought of her and the twins. God knew, he loved them as much as he would his own children. He wanted to protect them, send them to the best schools, cheer at their soccer games, watch them graduate—with Rebecca at his side, the perfect mother, the perfect wife.

He wanted her beside him now, more than he'd ever wanted anything.

The traffic eased, and Connor pressed harder on the gas pedal. There were few signs of destruction along the way, but as he neared Rebecca's neighborhood, the damage grew more severe. A few blocks from her house, he saw a tree uprooted, a brick chimney toppled, and one block away, a street was accordioned, the asphalt torn by ground waves.

Finally, he turned on to her street and saw her house intact, thank God. Her car was in the drive. They were home and hopefully safe. Connor parked on the street. He got out of the car just in time to feel the rumble of an aftershock shake the earth.

The ground in front of him seemed to disintegrate, turning into a pit of earth pudding.

Before he could find solid footing and reach the front door, he saw, as if in slow motion, the bottom floor of the house shimmer and then crumble, the top two floors sliding downward to land crookedly atop the remains. What had been a three-story house suddenly became two, the small porch left standing to welcome visitors to a flattened first floor.

The solemn echo of destruction split the air, followed by eerie silence and an awful squeezing in Connor's heart.

"Rebecca!" he shouted, his feet moving him somehow across the small lawn. "Rebecca!" Sickening fear flooded his mind. He reached the useless porch, standing before a second story window, the frame bent and cracked. He ripped away the screen, picked up a clay flower pot, and broke the glass, making an opening large enough to pass through. Shards of glass ripped at his face and clothes as he climbed through the window, but he felt nothing but fear…excruciating fear.

"Rebecca!" he called, praying she'd answer. But there was no sound except the far away sirens.

Dear God, if Rebecca and the children had been on the first floor…His mind refused to give space to that awful possibility.

They couldn't be dead. *They couldn't be!*

He looked around. He was in a bedroom, the furniture rearranged as if on a checkerboard. A mirror hung crookedly on the opposite wall. Connor didn't recognize the face that stared at him, pale, streaked with dust and fear and a thin line of blood.

On the floor was a framed photo of Rebecca and the twins. He remembered taking it in Hawaii, at the top of Haleakala. A place no more surreal than where he found himself now, in a half-toppled house that could collapse at any moment.

He weighed the danger—not to himself, but to anyone trapped below. His own movements might jar the house enough to finish the job the aftershock had started. But he had no choice. He had to determine if they were trapped below in the rubble—if they were beyond help, or if prompt rescue could save them.

"Rebecca!" he shouted, his voice hoarse with emotion. "Alex! Aubrey! Can you hear me?"

No answer. Not even a whimper. Sweat dripped into his eyes, dust and blood and tears mingled to form a trail of anguish leading straight to his heart.

The house leaned precariously, the floors tilted at an angle that made it difficult to walk, but Connor ignored that, as well as the fact that the ruin was dangerous. If he couldn't find them alive, he didn't care if the house crashed around his head.

He quickly searched, as best he could, the remains of the top floors, calling for them repeatedly, hoping to hear a sound. Debris had toppled from shelves, from bureaus, breaking his heart with the poignant reminders of the family he loved.

But he saw no sign of survivors. If they had been in the house when it collapsed, they were trapped below, in the destroyed first floor.

In Alex's room, he found a Mickey Mouse flashlight, spilled from a nightstand. Connor grabbed it; it might be handy later.

The staircase had broken in two, half demolished below the teetering second floor. There was a space just wide enough for him to fit through—a tight fit, dark, smelling of gas. The place could catch flame at any moment, Connor realized. Even more reason to stay, to try to get them out.

He slid into the crawl space and heard a sound—a mewling. He twisted sideways and came eyeball to eyeball with Sam. The cat jumped onto Connor's shoulders and began licking the dust on his neck. Absurdly grateful to see a sign of life, Connor didn't attempt to remove him.

"Sam, where are they? Dear God, where are they?" But the cat just continued licking.

There were shouts from outside and the sound of sirens coming closer, but neither were the sounds he wanted to hear.

With barely enough room to crouch on his hands and knees, he finally managed to get himself into a position to see under the dangling beams of the second floor.

The sturdiest furniture had stopped the total descent of the structure, but antique tables and overstuffed chairs couldn't bear the weight forever. Another aftershock could bring the whole structure crashing around him.

He turned on the flashlight, shining its beam in the depths of the ruin.

Then, in the dust, he saw a tiny hand trapped under a beam. He reached out and touched it: cold, lifeless—and made of plastic, he realized. A doll. *Thank God.* He swallowed what tasted like bile and tried to slow the pounding of his heart.

He had to think logically. Where would they have gone, with the house shuddering around them? Connor imagined Rebecca hurrying to grab the twins. Her desk was in the dining room; it was the sturdiest piece of furniture in the house. Perhaps they'd been able to take shelter there and were alive…

There was no way to get there from where he was; too much debris blocked the way. But on the other side of the flattened living room he saw light—what had been the dining room window, now a gaping hole. If he reentered through there, he might be able to maneuver through the rubble.

He quickly crawled back the way he'd come, up through the stairwell, Sam clutching his shoulders, his claws digging through his shirt and drawing blood. Connor pulled him off, transferring him to his arms. As fast as he dared, he crossed to the window he'd climbed through earlier.

Blinking as he emerged, Connor didn't at first see the crowd that had gathered. But he heard the voice.

"Oh, Connor! You found him! Look, guys, it's Sam...and Connor! Oh, God, you're hurt! You're bleeding!" Rebecca ran toward him, the twins on either side...unharmed.

They're alive! All three of them. Rebecca, her hair shining bright gold in the last rays of the sun; Aubrey, with her thumb tucked inside a happy smile; and Alex, his eyes small blue pools of wonder. *Alive!*

Connor couldn't move. He was frozen to the spot, a cat in his arms, a Mickey Mouse flashlight lit up like a beacon, a stunned feeling in his heart. She was alive! Walking, talking, breathing...safe.

Sam leaped from his arms, and Rebecca replaced him. Connor held her, crushed against his heart, as if she were his very life.

He could feel blood seeping down his forehead, from a gash he must have received from the window, and something else—tears. Tears of joy.

"You're bleeding, Connor! Where are you hurt?" Rebecca dabbed at his face, inspecting his clothes for indications of damage.

"Nowhere," he whispered. "Nowhere. I'm fine. You're safe. You and the twins."

"Yes, we're safe. But my house—"

"Forget the damned house. I'll buy you another."

"I don't want you to..."

Instead of answering, he kissed her. A long, deep, slow kiss, with all his heart in it this time, all the love he'd been denying for so long, devouring her mouth, her sweetness. She was *alive*—and Connor rejoiced.

With the ruins of her home for a backdrop and onlookers who'd gathered to admire the destructive power of the earthquake as witnesses, Connor finally knew the truth:

He loved this woman, and her children, more than anything, and the only thing he would ever fear again was a life without her in it.

He leaned back and, looking into her eyes, told her so. "I love you, Rebecca. I love you so much. You and the twins—I want to adopt them...I want to have more children. I want to live with you, dear God, in a house that won't crumble to the ground!"

She laughed. "I know! I know!" She kissed his filthy cheek tenderly, a poignant look in her eyes. Tears clung to her lashes, like drops of rain on a spider web. "I knew you did, Connor, deep down. You just had to convince yourself!"

He kissed her again, his face smudging hers with blood, dust, and tears.

Love. It was remarkably easy to get used to, a lovely concept to accept. There were worse things in life, Connor had learned. Worse things than having the woman you loved in your arms, a ready-made family, a testament to survival. Worse things than knowing you were loved for yourself, for who you were.

Worse things than finding your heart in the rubble left by an earthquake.

He swallowed the emotion in his throat and smiled at her. "I was so damned wrong, wasn't I? All that garbage about not being able to love you."

"Yes, you were, sweetheart." She reached up and kissed the corner of his mouth. "Totally, incredibly wrong."

"Does this mean you'll marry me?" he asked, never one to miss an opportunity to close a deal.

Rebecca leaned back and looked into his eyes.

"Please, Rebecca. I can't live without you. Not another moment." He shuddered. "To think I almost lost you..."

She nibbled her lip, questioning his commitment one last time. "It took an earthquake to convince you of that?"

He smiled. "Let's just say it cemented the idea." Then he turned serious. "Marriage, Rebecca. Now, or later, I don't care when. In a church or in a garden or by the sea, I don't care. Just please, be my wife."

She gave him a sweet smile full of promise. "I would love to be your wife."

Relief washed over him, and peace, as if he'd arrived at a destination he'd been seeking all his life. He knew at last what was in his heart—who he was. Not a prince, not a rusty knight, but a man who felt fear and hope and love.

Logic—and all its neatly tied-up reasons and excuses—be damned.

Alex tugged on his pants leg, and when he looked down, he was gazing at the house with a troubled look. "Connor, I don't think we can live here anymore."

Connor bent down until he was eye level and squeezed Alex's thin shoulder. "You're right. You and Rebecca and Aubrey are coming to live with me. In my penthouse for now, until we can find a bigger place."

Alex gazed at him. "What about Sam? Can he come live with us in your pennyhouse?"

Connor smiled. "Of course he can. And we'll get a dog…and a horse. And whatever else you want."

"Can we get a hamster?"

"Sure. A dozen hamsters." Connor grinned, giddy now with joy. "And a view of the soccer fields."

Rebecca bent down beside them and laughed, refraining from saying "I told you so."

Aubrey pulled her thumb out of her mouth, and Connor had to strain to hear her as she whispered, "Were you scared when you couldn't find us?"

"Yes, I was. But not anymore," he added, looking back at the house. He barely suppressed a shudder at the thought of what had almost happened to this family he loved. "We're all going to be safe from now on. All of us."

THE END

About the Author

Kathryn Barrett reluctantly put aside childhood dreams of becoming an author and took a more practical approach, majoring in Business Administration in college. But after marrying an Air Force officer, she realized a career in high finance didn't suit an itinerant lifestyle. She happily returned to her first love, writing stories that feature larger-than-life characters, family relationships, and of course, a happy ending.

Her award-winning novel *Temptation* was published in 2013, followed by *Redemption* in 2014.

Having lived all over the world, Kathryn and her family have recently relocated to northern Virginia. She enjoys long walks with her squirrel-obsessed dog, traveling to tiny European countries, cooking vegan feasts, and, only occasionally, she still reads the *Financial Times*.